Praise for *In Polite Company*

"Here is the captivating story of a contemporary young woman navigating the expectations of family, the traditions of Charleston's elite, and the fierce pull of her own heart. You will revel in her humor and humanness, her poignant takes on love and loss, her stunning look at power and privilege, but mostly in her brave quest to become herself. This is a beautiful debut novel."

—Sue Monk Kidd, #1 *New York Times*
bestselling author

"Reading *In Polite Company* is like visiting a college friend from downtown Charleston—the one who brings you to all the glamorous, old-fashioned events you might not otherwise get invited to. But it's not all parties. . . . Gervais Hagerty's keen insights on the quagmires of the modern South set it apart from other summer reads. I loved this book."

—Katie Crouch, *New York Times*
bestselling author of *Embassy Wife* and *Girls in Trucks*

"Gervais Hagerty's compelling debut novel allows us a fascinating glimpse into an elite Southern society trying to hold on to age-old traditions and values in a rapidly changing world. Caught in the middle is a daughter of old Charleston, a young woman struggling to find her place without rejecting all she holds dear. This is the kind of highly readable, richly populated, and beautifully written book you will be eager to recommend to others!"

—Cassandra King, award-winning author of
Tell Me a Story: My Life with Pat Conroy

IN POLITE COMPANY

IN POLITE COMPANY

a novel

GERVAIS HAGERTY

WILLIAM MORROW

An Imprint of HarperCollinsPublishers

P.S.™ is a trademark of HarperCollins Publishers.

IN POLITE COMPANY. Copyright © 2021 by Gervais Hagerty, LLC. All rights reserved. Printed in the United States of America. No part of this book may be used or reproduced in any manner whatsoever without written permission except in the case of brief quotations embodied in critical articles and reviews. For information, address HarperCollins Publishers, 195 Broadway, New York, NY 10007.

HarperCollins books may be purchased for educational, business, or sales promotional use. For information, please email the Special Markets Department at SPsales@harpercollins.com.

FIRST EDITION

Designed by Diahann Sturge

Library of Congress Cataloging-in-Publication Data has been applied for.

ISBN 978-0-06-306886-5

21 22 23 24 25   LSC   10 9 8 7 6 5 4 3 2 1

for
Momunit
Babs
Babulous
Barbarella
Glama
Barbara G. S. Hagerty
Mom

1.

The Plunge

Each year, summer seems to arrive earlier in the Lowcountry: it's only May third, and already the springtime riot of blossoms has budded, bloomed, and shriveled. Brown petals—vestiges of lavender wisteria, butterscotch jasmine, and taffy pink azaleas— litter sidewalks these days, spoiled confetti leftover from a party.

I bike through the stewing haze to visit my grandparents before my afternoon shift at the news station. Steam travels from the hot, wet asphalt up to the hot, wet clouds. Caught in the middle of this heat transfer, I might as well be pedaling a radiator.

For generations, we Charlestonians have endured the heat. This is our home, after all. My family, like the others who grew up within the historic district, will never leave. So, we do what we can to keep from dissolving into the thick humidity that weighs down this southern coastal town as much as its complicated history does. We wear linen and guzzle iced tea. We exercise early in the morning, late in the day, or not at all. We put on sun hats and slather on sunscreen. Still, the sun blasts through, emblazoning us with burns, blisters, and sweat stains.

The sun cooks our doorknobs. It toasts cars, roasting the seat belt buckles until they're lava-hot across our laps. It sears the crabgrass and gums the blacktop. The Lowcountry sun drains and wilts and simmers the flatlands below. But no matter how much the mercury soars, the zinnias stand tall, their candy-colored petals reaching high toward the sun.

My grandmother Claudia taught me to love zinnias. My gardening lessons began years ago, on an Easter Sunday after our two o'clock dinner beside her zinnia bed, which still runs out past the swimming pool, a sort of marital DMZ where my grandfather rarely ventures. He thought the flowers too tawdry and common for an English garden noted for its formal Ligustrum hedges and boxwood topiaries. "But I think they're pretty," she said, with a wary eye pointed at the back door. She told me to keep quiet about our annual planting project. We've kept quiet about many things.

A chorus of St. Michael's bells rang around us as she slowly, almost reverently, studied the seed packets labeled *Persian Carpet*, *Queen Red Lime*, and *Uproar Rose*. Some packets were open already from last season, thriftily rolled up and sealed to preserve the extra seeds. Though my grandparents own one of the most handsome houses in the city—and one of the biggest, on nearly half an acre—they were also children of the Depression. They are savers; they practice frugality. She instructed me, "Simons, plant last year's first."

Laudie—as my sisters and I call her—showed me how to

poke holes into the dirt in orderly rows, drop a seed in each, cover it with earth. When I was six, two months seemed an eternity to wait for the first blooms. Every time I came by for a swim, I would weed and water and fuss over the seedlings, hoping there was something I could do to hurry them up. "They'll come, Simons," she would say. Since that long-ago afternoon, we've planted zinnias every Easter in that same flower bed in that same garden. It's been twenty years.

I pop my bike up on a curb. The jolt reactivates the throbbing in my head. I was reckless last night, for sure, but I also fear I crossed a line. I'll have to ask Martha for advice. She'll tell it to me straight.

I round the corner from Meeting Street onto South Battery, once the neighborhood of wealthy indigo and cotton planters escaping the malarial summer heat on their plantations. The most architecturally elaborate houses in the city line these three blocks facing White Point Garden, known to us locals simply as "the Battery." The antebellum park is situated on the tip of the old peninsula, where any native will tell you, grandiosely, the Ashley and Cooper Rivers meet and join to become the Atlantic Ocean.

Live oaks with long, undulating branches canopy its walking paths and benches. At its center is an old-fashioned bandstand; scattered throughout are statues from the wars: Revolutionary, Confederate, and twentieth-century. Symbols abound here of both war and peace: old cannons aimed at Fort Sumter in the harbor; a bronze angel sculpture, which doubles as a water fountain.

The most prominent installation lunges from the corner of the park, where the two rivers intersect. Standing on an octagonal pedestal, a naked man raises a sword, his muscles rippling. He defends a woman cloaked in a robe. In one hand, she holds a garland of laurel. With the other, she points to the enemy, the Union Army, out at sea.

As a child, I climbed around the base of that statue, groping for footholds along the slick granite. I had stared at the naked figure, a fig leaf covering his penis. It wasn't until some bubba started driving his truck here every Sunday with a Confederate flag mounted on an absurdly large pole that I realized the naked man embodied the battle cry of the Confederacy. And that beautiful woman, her hair lifted by the breeze, cast frozen in time, was an allegory for my city at the time of the Civil War. Had she known better, she would have waved the Northern soldiers in, maybe offered them some tomato sandwiches.

Across the street from the old park are a seawall and a long promenade, where tourists and townspeople walk or jog or push baby strollers. The clip-clop of horse-drawn carriages, the shriek of herring gulls, and the murmur of pigeons make the Battery sound old-fashioned and out of time. Every day, the waters lick the barrier between the city and the sea. The insidious, salty tongues reach higher and higher and, some days, the water flows over the retaining wall. Drivers take detours. Runners leap over puddles. Tourists take photographs. Those some days come more often these days. Our city is sinking. Maybe the lady statue was warning us about the sea rise all along.

Laudie's imposing brick house, capped by a mansard roof, anchors the middle block. Two-story piazzas—the old-fashioned Charleston name for porches—grace the front of her house. Once almost blindingly white, the piazza columns now collect grime in their flutes, giving them permanent shadows.

I take a hard left, my wheels crunching the oyster-shell driveway, the high porticos rising to my right. I lean my bike against an old crepe myrtle and push the squeaky wrought iron gate that opens into the deep lot behind the house.

The grounds are divided into thirds. The section closest to the house is a formal garden, with symmetrical paths bordered by low-growing boxwood and accented by giant topiaries. It's a miniature version of Versailles.

Behind the garden is the pool, which is nestled into the brick patio like a gem in an antique ring. Finally, far from view of the house and obscured by a fortress of greenery—aspidistra at the walkway, sago palms at shoulder height, and ancient camellias at the top of this hidden urban canopy—is the wild land left for Laudie.

In this little outdoor room, fully open to the sun, is a garden of Eden. Fat-leafed hydrangeas grow beneath alligator-green ferns. Butterflies lazily sip from patches of hearty milkweed. A Ficus vine begins its summertime crawl up the back brick wall. Mint and rosemary hover over our prized treasures, collected through years of beachcombing and tucked into the flower beds: whelks, bull's-eyes, lettered olives, cockles, and blood ark shells. Feathery plumbago leaves shake in the breeze. Lantana petals are scattered over the brick path that leads to the potting shed in the corner.

Rimmed by the greenery, planted in the exact middle of the garden to soak in the high-noon sun, are the kaleidoscopic zinnias. Cherry, canary, margarine, bubblegum, grape. I've always known that these plucky flowers, with their intense colors and firm stalks, are hardworking, but even I am surprised by how they've grown so fast. I'll give my report to Laudie.

I head back toward the pool, through the tunnel of deep shade. I stop at an Adirondack chair, strip down to my bathing suit. With my toes gripping the warm bricks, heels hovered over the lip of the pool, I lift my face to the unrelenting sun. I close my eyes and fall backward into the pool.

The water cools my throbbing temples. It hides me from my possible indiscretions. This amniotic space cocoons me from the hot, nagging world. I wish I could stay here all day—away from work, away from Trip, away from the lingering suspicion that I did something idiotic last night. In the pool, I am cleansed. Baptized. In the water, my sins are forgiven. Eventually, though, I have to surface.

"Simons, is that you?" My grandfather's spotted, bald head peers out from behind the screen door. He shuffles to the top of the back steps, waves his cane in greeting. This little back porch has practically become the perimeter of his world.

"Hi, Tito! I'll be there in a minute."

Tito was a tax attorney and worked at his father's firm, which had been established by his great-grandfather in 1858. Tito ran it until his retirement. He has reaped the benefits of privilege all his life, including memberships in exclusive clubs and friendships with local politicians and bankers.

He worked, but as a southern white male, most of his day-to-day tasks were done for him. Maids washed his laundry and ironed his shirts. They dusted his dresser and mopped his bathroom floor. Laudie ran his errands, fixed his meals, raised their children. Though Tito hasn't been to the office in fifteen years, I've never seen him make a sandwich, set the table, or clean a dish.

"Don't let her cause you any trouble." That's what Laudie's mother warned Tito the day they got married. As family history goes, Laudie was a stubborn girl who didn't take well to authority. She snuck out of Sunday school to go crabbing. When the boy down the street tried to kiss her, she threw rocks at him; one took a chunk out of his cheek. She hid her stockings under the logs in the fireplace and tossed her dolls up in the magnolia trees. Neighbors whispered about the eerie black smoke wafting from the chimney; the baby-doll-eating trees spooked the kids down the block.

But the Laudie we know has always been serene. Although they have a cook for the midday meal, Laudie serves breakfast every morning at eight and supper every evening at seven on the dot. She always wears a dress or a skirt, never pants. (Tito doesn't like women in pants.) When I first became consciously aware of Tito's chiding her—complaining that the shrimp creole was too salty—I licked my fork to test the tomato sauce, which tasted fine to me. When he said she looked frumpy in a shift dress, I followed her up the stairs to help her pick out a belt. When he asked her for more iced tea the moment she finally got to join us at the table, I found myself digging my nails into my chair cushion.

By the time I entered high school, I spoke up. If he said the kitchen floor was a mess, I'd say it was my fault for tracking in dirt from the garden. When he complained about the room being too cold, I would say that Laudie probably didn't notice because she was running around so much. In all those years, Laudie never answered back. She just bowed her head and stared at her folded hands. But sometimes I thought I almost saw her turn inward, as if drawing on some invisible, utterly private reserve of power.

When I turned sixteen, she asked me to drive her to visit a friend in Beaufort. For the full hour-and-a-half ride, she sat with her trademark perfect posture in the passenger seat, tapping her feet to the songs on the oldies station. She was wearing her customary Capezio shoes—they're leather with a low block heel and a strap over the ankle; she never went barefoot. We had reached the exit to Adams Run; we still had another hour to go. Maybe it was then, on that boring stretch of the two-lane highway, that I began actively to wonder about Laudie's past. Why did she always wear Capezios, a noted dance-shoe brand, when a mule or a pump would have suited the occasion better? And why did she not, after all those years, ever think to hurl one of them—no matter what the style—right between Tito's critical eyes when he picked on her for the littlest of things? What happened to that truant girl with a contrarian heart and good aim? I thought I'd start with a softball question: "Laudie, what did you want to be when you grew up?"

"A dancer. A ballerina. You know that."

Of course. I knew the story. Laudie ran off to Atlanta when

she was twenty. She hitched a ride there with a friend return-ing to Agnes Scott College. For six months, Laudie lived in a boardinghouse and worked as a secretary for a Coca-Cola ex-ecutive. But her real reason for going was to audition for a spot as a ballerina with the Atlanta Civic Ballet.

I hated the story, because it was always told by Tito—never by Laudie. He didn't write it down, but he may as well have be-cause the narrative never varied. He would say he had warned her, that she was being foolish, that she'd never make the cut. She telephoned him in the spring, begged him to pick her up when she wasn't chosen for the corps de ballet. He always made sure to add "I told her so." He drove her home to Charleston, and ever since, that wild thoroughbred was tame as an old broodmare.

"I'm sorry you didn't make the company. I bet you were bet-ter than all of them." I knew it must be a source of pain for her. She still obsessively practices her ballet moves, as though the audition is next week.

"Your grandfather doesn't know the whole story. There's more to it than that. I have my secrets."

"Ooh. Was there a guy involved?" I teased.

"Yes"—she nodded—"that's part of it." I took my eyes from the road, hoping to catch a smile, but she just stared blankly at the flat road ahead. "I'll tell you when you're ready."

"I am ready! I'm sixteen."

She laughed and patted me on my thigh. "I'll skip to the end. I'll tell you the moral of the story."

"What? That's not fair."

"Life isn't fair. And you've got more than your share of good fortune, so don't complain."

"Okay, fine. What's the moral of the story?"

"To be brave."

I felt brave in that car, a decade ago. I made the varsity volleyball team, I could legally drive at night on my own, and Martha, my best friend, had taken me to my first house party. It was also that year that I first skipped school to go to the Waffle House with a boy in a band named Harry.

"Simons?"

I yell back to Tito, this time louder. "Coming!" With another wave of his cane, he retreats indoors; the screen door slams shut behind him. I push myself up and over the lip of the pool and slip my dress over my wet bikini.

Laudie and Tito are in the kitchen, seated at what was known as the "children's table." My sisters and I weren't allowed to eat in the formal dining room until we were teenagers. To be fair, the dining room is stuffed with fragile, perishable things: a rickety vitrine, stacks of old Limoges too good to use, sherry glasses on spindly stems, two Chippendale chairs no one is allowed to sit on.

The table is wedged next to the window. Tito sits at the head, as always. Laudie sits to his left, nibbling on half a pimento cheese sandwich. She does a little hop in her chair when she sees me. "Hi, Simons."

Tito rises to pull out a chair for me.

"Our zinnias are looking good. We already have some blooms." Laudie has lately become more vocal about our secret garden in Tito's presence. I think she's testing him, pushing back a bit.

Tito would never roll his eyes; that would be too tacky, but the muscle at the corner of his jaw visibly tenses.

I shimmy my chair away from my grandfather and lean across the table to make myself closer to Laudie. "I saw them; they look great. I think it's all the heat we've been having."

"We just planted them."

"So crazy."

"Well, be sure to take some home with you, dear." Laudie wears her ash-blond hair in her everyday 'do, gathered in a bun at the back of her head. A simple pendant necklace rests at her sternum. Pearl clip-on earrings illumine each side of her oval face. As always, she's wearing her Capezio shoes, this pair the palest of blush pinks, like the flesh beneath the nail. She holds a glass of iced tea in her right hand, accentuating the delicate curve of her wrist. It has been a lifelong habit of hers to rest in pretty poses.

She was born with long, willowy arms and legs. Even in her mid eighties, she's still taller than I am. She has maintained a slender silhouette all her life. Genetics played a big part, but Laudie has also been fastidious and disciplined about her body. She watches her weight, which never fluctuates more than a pound or two. For cocktail hour, she allows herself one glass of Chardonnay, no peanuts or cheese. Her idea of dessert is to eat an apple or orange. She has maintained these disciplines throughout her life.

When she and Tito bought the house on South Battery, she

instructed the movers to put her barre in the bedroom. Tito demanded she remove it. "A bedroom is for sleeping," he told her. So Laudie moved it herself to the grand hallway and had a carpenter mount it to the wall. In that big hallway at the top of the grand staircase, there is ample light and space, though there isn't any air conditioning. (Laudie and Tito use window units in their main rooms, but—characteristic of their thriftiness—leave the halls and storage rooms unair-conditioned.) If the heat bothers her, she never lets anyone know it.

Most days, Laudie wears a boatneck shirt with three-quarter-length sleeves, a long skirt, and stockings. This way, she's always two minutes away from time at the barre. She removes her day skirt, lays it on the bed, and ties a ballet wrap skirt around her waist. She swaps her Capezio heels for her performa canvas flats and exits her bedroom, closing her eyes as she settles into first position.

In the winter, she exercises midday. In the summer, she divides her routine between the early morning, before breakfast, and the evening, after supper, when the dishes are put away and Tito is glued to the news.

Of course, Laudie encouraged the three of us girls to be dancers. From childhood, Weezy preferred rough sports: basketball and soccer. Caroline danced beautifully through middle school but quit in high school when she was elected cheer captain. I simply wasn't graceful.

Laudie will turn eighty-seven this year. Three weeks ago, she felt her heart flutter—an arrhythmia. That night she stayed in the ICU. While I had noticed her normally square shoulders had started to curl inward and her arrow-straight spine had begun to bow, these diminutions grew more pronounced after that trip to the ICU and in the following days. She looks smaller now, as though Father Time himself is pressing on her from all sides, insistent on shrinking her completely until, *poof,* she vanishes.

In this room, time slows. The clock ticks forward reluctantly. The space between conversations yawns wide. Laudie and Tito don't seem to notice the static silence. Or they do notice and don't care. It's as if time freezes everything but me, as if I can observe my grandparents as elements in a still life. A painterly tableau. Man, woman, bowl of grapes, glass of water. They sit, paused at their meal, staring at nothing. For how long have they been so old?

"I have something for you." I slide a little white envelope across the kitchen table. On her left wrist, I see that she wears a removable cast. "What happened?"

"Oh, it was nothing. A little bump."

"She was on that barre again." Tito says. "I told her to stop it."

After her most recent trip to the hospital, the doctors said she should stick to chair yoga. I hate to admit it, but I think it might be a good idea.

"Oh hush, I'm fine," she says.

"I keep telling her the auditions were over sixty-five years ago."

I start to protest, but Tito screens himself behind the back page of the Local section and all I see is a large ad for dentures. Laudie ignores him and removes two tickets from the envelope. She strains her eyes to read. *"La Silly . . . La Silly—"*

"*La Sylphide*," I interrupt, not wanting to hear her struggle to read, to observe insidious reminders that she's slipping away from me a bit each day. "The ballet is coming to the Gaillard in August. Will you come with me?"

Laudie brightens. "Yes, of course."

A horn blasts. Tito's ride to Battery Hall is here right on time to take him to the weekly chess tournament he and his friends started when they retired. He stands and places his hand on the table in front of Laudie, between the two of us. "Claudia, you could fall and break the other hand. I forbid it." He shuffles across the kitchen, gets his cane, and heads out the back door.

I could follow him, loop a young arm through his skeletal one, guide him down the steps one at a time, but I stay put. Sometimes I imagine tripping him. I wouldn't ever, of course, but the thought has crossed my mind.

Laudie eventually extends a feathery arm, brushes a finger on my cheek. "How is Trip?" She fixes her wide-set eyes on mine. A lot of people say I take after her. "Do you miss him all the way up there in Columbia?"

I wish I missed him, but I don't. And it's the one thing I haven't been able to tell Laudie. In all the conversations we'd had over the years, I've never held back. She would make me a glass of her sugar-free instant iced tea and clip the day's coupons from the *Post and Courier* while I'd tell her every detail of my teenage life, and later, in my twenties, my romance with Trip. When Tito was in the kitchen, we'd wander up the stairs so she could exercise at the barre. I went to Laudie whenever I felt ostracized—as a fifth grader pocked with whiteheads,

crowned with greasy hair, my eyes spaced so far apart my class-
mates called me "praying mantis." I sought her out when I
was mortified, like the time I borrowed a skirt from the most
popular girl in the class, only to stain it with menstrual blood.
Maybe it was because of her wisdom or her age or both; she
always had a way of making sense of my world.

Perhaps because she recalls things from the past like butter
and gasoline shortages, Laudie is grateful for all she has. She
might live in a mansion, but she shops at Harris Teeter only on
Thursdays because of the 5 percent senior discount. She saves
gift wrap and string, cuts the spoiled parts off overripe fruit, and
shops the sales, especially the clearance tables. And although
she may have been a rebellious free spirit once, that was more
than six decades ago. She's been married to Tito for sixty-five
years. How could she make sense of my doubting heart?

Trip is a good guy. He's handsome. He loves me. He's kind
and ambitious in exactly the way my parents like. But as each
new day brings me closer to marching down the aisle, a voice
from inside me screams to run the other way, to run hard and
fast and not look back. I can't tell her. She's so excited about
the wedding, which will be sometime next May, or maybe June.
There's so much to celebrate in our family, with Caroline's
debut later this year and Weezy's second baby on the way.

Still, I know she keeps a secret from me; if only I could decode it from the way she wears her hair, her choice of shoes,
the tight smile her mouth forms during Tito's nitpicking. And
I know it has something to do with Atlanta, her dancing, and
maybe a lover. I asked her about it constantly after our road trip

to Beaufort and pestered her all through my college breaks. Mostly she laughed and changed the subject. A couple of times I saw her take a quick breath, like she was ready to talk, but then she'd pull her neck in and scrunch her nose, as though the idea smelled bad.

It was around my senior year, the year I met Trip, that I stopped asking at all. An aspiring lawyer, he told me once that some things are best left unsaid. Maybe that's how she felt.

"He's great, Laudie." I squeeze her bony hand. "I've got to get to work."

"Hmm." She narrows her eyes.

"What?" I instinctively fold my arms over my chest, feeling a bit like an aphid on her zinnias.

"We'll get to the bottom of this." She starts to stand. "Before you leave, I have something for you." Her body sways a bit, like she's had too many martinis. If she were to fall, she'd snap in half. If I were to help her, to guide her through the kitchen maze with my hand against her skin—thin and white as film from boiled milk—I'd be telling her that I don't trust her body, the temple that she toned, trained, and disciplined for the better part of a century. I remain seated, telling myself that she got herself downstairs to the kitchen table on her own, and she can probably still throw her leg up on the barre in the great hall upstairs.

Hands grazing the green countertops, she teeters toward the corner of the kitchen. I spin the porcelain saltshaker and pretend not to follow her every step, ready at any moment for a mad dash around Tito's chair and a leap over the linoleum to dive beneath my collapsing grandmother.

She lifts a gold watch from the counter and extends it toward me. "I want to give this to you."

I cross the room to get a better look. The slender watch has hash marks running throughout its surface, giving the band the look of golden snakeskin. "Laudie, that's your watch. You still use it." In the last year, she's had the habit of giving away her finer things: a vase to me, silver platters to Mom and Weezy. I wish she'd stop. She isn't dead yet.

"I can't wear it with this thing on my hand. It won't fit. I was going to give it to you anyway, so you might as well have it now."

"Yeah, but your wrist will get better and you can wear it again. Let me put it on your right arm."

"You're stubborn."

"*You're* stubborn!"

She laughs. "Oh, all right." She extends her arm, like a prima ballerina executing a classic port de bras. "Mother gave it to me when I left for Atlanta so that I'd call her every Sunday at exactly three o'clock." She hasn't mentioned Atlanta in years. Laudie's eyes drift. She speaks as though in a trance. "I want you to have it later, as a reminder."

"Laudie, I'll never forget you."

"Simons." She beckons me closer, her milky eyes hardening to a bright crystal blue. "It's not a reminder of me; it's a reminder to be brave."

2.

Toxins

I line the little batch of zinnias on my countertop to determine a precise stem length for my arrangement. I trim the ends and pull off the fuzzy leaves, then drop the zinnias into the porcelain vase Laudie gave me. The bouquet looks lopsided. I extract the largest flower, a peach one, and tuck it back into the center. Better.

After leaning over to place the flowers on my coffee table, I straighten to a dizzying cosmos of stars blinking and fading in my periphery. The main events of last night come into focus. I let a man buy me drinks. I gave him my phone number. I shake out a couple of ibuprofen, chase them down with a giant glass of water, and try not to remember any more.

My apartment sits on the second floor of what's called a Charleston single house. This style of house is long but narrow, just one room wide when viewed from the street. Like all Charleston singles, its porches run the length of the house. When the landowners chopped the home up into three units, they boarded up the first-floor porch to make more room for storage and the staircase that brings me to my second-floor apartment. Fortunately, there's a small second-story porch on the east side of the house, accessible only from my living room. I don't consider myself a traditionalist, but it does seem sacrilegious to live in this city and not have a piazza.

Mom says it has "character," which is her euphemism for "shabby." My walls are pale gray with eggshell trim. The paint is peeling. The windows are warped, and there's visible wood rot. It's one of the few remaining dwellings that has not been updated to house the thousands of affluent people moving here from New York and the Midwest, which means I can afford it, barely.

The apartment's best feature is the fireplace. Although the chimney was sealed up years ago, it's still beautiful. Two carved cherubs, one at each end, hold up the mantelpiece. They lean wistfully toward each other, clutching the ends of a carved laurel swag. A poster by local artist Jonathan Green hangs above the mantel. It depicts a Gullah woman, a descendant of enslaved Africans who live along the coast, wearing a billowing white dress against a backdrop of blue Lowcountry skies and cottony clouds. She holds a laundry basket in one hand and presses her sun hat to her head with the other. A warm breeze rips through the open air, sending the white sheets flapping behind her.

My first major purchase for the apartment was a mid-century couch, which I positioned to face the window that overlooks the porch. The window frames the upper stories of the nearby houses, some piazzas, a bit of red roof, a tangle of telephone wires.

It's quiet today. I have grown accustomed to the noises of Coming Street—techno blaring from a College of Charleston dorm room or the rev of a Jeep speeding down the street—but graduation was last weekend and the students are gone. Charleston has returned to its sleepy self. I miss the commotion. Martha doesn't. She welcomes the city's annual purge of "zits, tits, and Schlitz."

Buzz. Buzz. Another text from Trip. He expects me to answer immediately. I used to. Shouldn't I want to?

I leave my phone and go in the kitchen to put a little more distance between us. Everything in here is a bit wonky: the floor slants so much that I had to stack coasters under the oven's front legs, and the cupboards are tacked up to the walls like afterthoughts. The faucet on the right is for the hot water; the one on the left is for the cold. The only window is strangely off-center. Once in a while, a roach crawls to the center of my kitchen floor and dies legs-up. They're as big as hushpuppies, darker than dirt, and impossible to keep out during the warmer months. Despite these shortcomings, I love my apartment. I have it all to myself until about a year from now, when I will be married to Trip and living in Columbia.

Columbia is South Carolina's capital city, about a two-hour drive from Charleston. No beach, no mountains; it's just sprawling suburbia smack-dab in the middle of the state. Trip tells me that when I give it a chance, I'll see why people like it there. Though, of course, Columbia will not always be our home.

Trip and I met at a party our junior year at UNC–Chapel Hill. He seemed so normal, which was a relief. Finally, I thought, here's someone I can introduce to my parents. He's the corner puzzle piece—the one who can help me fit into the family jigsaw.

Before Trip, I fell for the misfit, truant boys—the ones who had skateboards and bad habits. From the start of high school, I chose to hang with the kids who smoked pot and hated their parents. I liked my parents and found that pot just made me feel confused. But that crowd—the boys with chain wallets and the girls with moody glares—was the one that accepted me. They intrigued me.

My sisters sat at lunch with the popular girls, always pretty in their pastel summer dresses and sun-kissed skin. And though I was asked to join that clique in my grade, I never felt comfortable. Those girls were always so confident, so sure of their place in the world. The closer I sat to them, the more amplified our differences became.

I stood out from my nuclear family as well. My older sister, Weezy, has curly brown hair like Dad. Caroline, the youngest, has thick, wavy blond hair like Mom. Mine alone is ashy brown, still as fine as a baby's. In family photos, because I'm the shortest, I always get shoved to the front, looking gangly and bewildered between the natural family pairs. In fourth grade, I discovered a rogue hash brown in my four-piece chicken nugget Happy Meal; I bit into it thinking, that's me.

But more than looks, my interests were different. Weezy was sporty, and that connected her to Dad. He drove her all over the state to compete in basketball and soccer tournaments.

When they got home for dinner, Dad would place her trophies in the center of the table, regaling us with details of her three-pointers and chip shots. And then Weezy married a nice boy at twenty-six and had her first baby at twenty-eight—right on time.

Caroline and Mom are a team, too. Even through high school, Caroline would tag along with Mom on her errands, dropping off dry-cleaning, picking up a prescription. In curlers, they read *People* magazine and munched on carrots and wore matching pajamas to watch the Oscars.

Without a family partner or after-school activities, I mostly hung around my room alone and bored. I would make faces in the bathroom mirror and practice French kissing on my arm. I stared out the window, hoping to catch a burglar in action or see our neighbors having sex. Nothing ever happened.

Eventually I left my room, sniffing for something productive to do around the house. After the Bug Squad arrived in hazmat suits, I hosted a family meeting in the living room to make a case for slapping the occasional mosquito instead of carpet-bombing our garden with toxins. I experimented with vegetarianism, tacking gory PETA pamphlets to the refrigerator and mooing like a dying cow on hamburger night. The summer after middle school, right before we cut into Mom's birthday cake, I suggested we forgo birthday presents because there's already too much stuff in the world.

"Right now I'd say there are too many opinions," my mother had said. "You need a hobby."

The most radical hobby I could think of at the time was surfing. I bought a used board and Mom didn't mind driving back and forth to the beach because I had finally picked up an interest that didn't involve attempts to change her lifestyle.

Shortly after I found my hobby, I found my kindred spirit: Martha. We met the first week of high school in the girls' bathroom. She wore Doc Martens and midnight purple fingernail polish. She noticed the buttons I had pinned to my bookbag. On one, a grumpy fish said, "Schools suck." On another was a picture of an angry baby in a bib. The text read, "Give peas a chance."

Weezy had bought me a simple pinback-button-making machine for my birthday (conveniently at a time when my stance on presents had softened). It was a metal contraption with two large discs on a swivel; it had a heavy-duty red handle for ramming all the parts into place. I spent many nights that summer, just before sleep, writing slogans over sketches and popping my little pieces of artwork onto the spring pins.

I gave Martha one of my favorites: a garbage can with long legs in fishnets that said, "Don't be trashy. Recycle."

"Can you make me one that says, 'I'd rather be smoking'?"

"Sure."

"Oh, and one that says 'Those who can, do. Those who can't, teach.'"

"Ha. Yeah, okay. Just don't tell anyone who made it."

"Deal."

We skipped assembly so she could show me how to put on eyeliner. She painted the inside corners of my eyes, drawing them closer together with black arcs. The trick made me look more daring, less naive. The makeup helped to quickly identify me as one of Crescent's alternative crowd, a collection of prep-school wannabe punks who wore Weedwacker haircuts, carefully chosen thrift-store shirts, and scowls.

By the time I met Trip, many of those misfit boys dropped out of college to wait tables, play in a band, or disappear altogether behind the heady gray fog of a bong hit. I stayed at UNC–Chapel Hill; I never thought not to. I loved studying journalism, but my friend crowd was thinning. It was time to look elsewhere, so I started hanging out with the Betas.

Trip's real name is William Simons Buchanan III. One of his fraternity brothers introduced us, warning that we might be cousins because we're both from the South and share the name Simons. In Charleston, it's a big deal, at least with Laudie's generation, to be a "one m" Simons. It's pronounced with a short "i," (like "shrimp"), not like Simon (as in "Simon Says"). The "y" in Smythe, however, is said with a long "i." When spammers call, they often ask for Simon Smith; I appreciate the heads-up.

While Laudie taught me about plants, it was my mother who gave the history lessons. She said the original Simons to come here was Benjamin Simons, a seventeenth-century Huguenot immigrant from La Rochelle, France. She also told me not to talk too much about our genealogy, because it's not polite to speak about our pedigree to people from "Off," the place people are from if they're not from Charleston.

Trip and I quickly determined that we were not related. In fact, I was surprised to learn that he had never heard of the Huguenots. Mom always talked about our ancestors as though they were celebrities.

After a few games of beer pong, he walked me out to an old green couch that had been dumped on the Betas' front lawn. We kissed. We have been together ever since.

I didn't feel excited when I first met Trip—a feeling I now realize I should have explored more—but I did feel comforted. He was so familiar. He was a gentleman, like Dad. He called to ask me out to dinner. When he arrived to pick me up, instead of sending a text ("here"), he turned off the engine, got out of his truck, and knocked on my door. When the server delivered the check, he reached for the bill. No equivocation. No hesitation. The roles were established.

During our early years, we went for long walks through Raven Rock State Park and around Jordan Lake. When I picked up a stray Snickers wrapper, he opened the pocket of his Barbour jacket so I didn't have to carry litter back to the truck. In a deep voice, thickened by his southern drawl, he identified different types of hardwood by studying the shapes of fallen leaves. I rarely spoke during those hikes; I liked just hearing him talk. "Did you know you have red in your hair?" he asked once. "I can see it when you're in the sun. It's not red, red. But a little bit. Like a cinnamon stick." The name stuck. After that he called me Cinnamon.

The night we discovered we both knew the Lindy Hop, we danced in his apartment while the pasta boiled. Like many pampered southern children, we had been sent to cotillion during our elementary and middle school years. Trip had suited up in loafers, coat, and tie for weekly dance lessons in North Carolina; I wore short white gloves and a dress with crinoline and a sash.

It seemed that each Wednesday during my cotillion years, I spent the afternoon frantically searching for those gloves. I pulled them on as I raced up Meeting Street to South Carolina Society Hall, a stately building with towering columns stacked high. I would hurry with the other tardy children, taking two steps at a time up the bifurcated staircase. Panting from the mad dash, I said hello and gave one compliment each, as required, to the ladies running the show.

Then I scanned the room for an open seat. Fifty girls lined up on the right of the ballroom; fifty boys lined up on the left. For many of us, our very first dance partners were picked in utero (sign-ups had to be with a girl-boy pair). Mom still plans her Wednesday walks around when cotillion ends so she can see the boys in blazers climbing on the wrought iron railings, girls hopping down the stairs. "It makes me happy," she said. Passersby who happen upon cotillion letting out—mostly strolling tourists—often pause to photograph this anachronistic scene.

The Lindy Hop was drilled into us over those years. *Step, ball, step. Step, ball, step. Shift weight. Step, two, three. Arch, two, three. Shift weight.* We found the steps worked for just about any band: Creedence, Widespread Panic, the Allman Brothers . . . We danced for hours that winter night, polishing off two bottles of André champagne. We forgot about the pasta until the smoke alarm sounded. We laughed as Trip chucked our burned dinner into the snow.

He took me for long drives out in the country, taking me to a river or a one-stoplight town. Hand in hand, we'd poke around, skipping rocks along the water or peeking into an antiques store.

On the way home, in the dark, I'd stare at his dashboard, the orange lights calculating our movement through space and time. His truck sailed smoothly over highways—no jostling, no bumps. Perhaps in the safety of that big leather seat I fell under the spell that many women find so intoxicating. He was the driver. I was the passenger. It was a relief to surrender.

I lost my virginity to Trip. More overwhelming than having sex for the first time was the intimacy of feeling his heartbeat. My ear became almost suctioned against his warm, damp skin. His heart thudded powerfully. We were young and so alive, which somehow left me feeling vulnerable. I ached, knowing that one day, like all things, his heart would stop. It was impossible to be together forever. Impossible for anyone.

"Are you crying?" he had asked.

That was when I told him I loved him. And I meant it. Then.

Around his second year of law school, my love for him began to fade. Instead of taking day-trips, he watched football on the weekends. I ran errands: Target, Costco, the farmers' market. Most Saturday mornings I went to a yoga class, leaving the afternoon free for a house cleaning project, like wiping the dirt from windowsills and baseboards. We haven't burned a meal since that first year. At some point, we stopped dancing in the kitchen. We cooked, and monitored, and tasted, but did not dance. He took up golf around that time, too. "Deals are made on the green, Cinnamon. I'm doing this for us."

When did we get so grown-up?

When he picked me up for a dinner party at the home of one of his law school friends, he asked me to change out of my black corduroys and into a floral-print dress. He said he'd like to run for public office one day, that his friend's family was very influential. On our drive over, the illuminated face of a new watch flashed inside the car's darkness. He always had his phone on him. Why would he need a fancy watch? Did it matter what I was wearing? And I never even thought about window-sills or baseboards before. Why was I cleaning them? It was on that ride that I first considered our end might come before our hearts stopped.

It was a toxic idea. That night at the dinner party, under the low light of a dimmed chandelier, I sank back in my seat. From behind Trip's shoulder, I peered at the other couples in the room. Who was all in? Which ones secretly plotted their next life?

When I reached for a second helping of potatoes au gratin, Trip pressed his hand against my thigh. His signal, invisible be-neath the table, told me not to stuff myself in polite company. So there I sat, in my demure floral dress, feeling small and hun-gry and trapped. I thought of Laudie.

That was when I decided to lock eyes with the host. He was married; his wife was attractive. But ever since I had met him, I always got the sense that he was undressing me. He gave me an extra-tight hug when we arrived, and his hand lingered against my waist a bit longer than propriety would allow. Men can be dogs.

Why do they get to be dogs? I tilted my head and smiled slyly, taking a baby step toward infidelity. He stiffened, his eyes widening. That stolen glance, that what-if, sent a surge through my body, making me feel ten feet tall.

The following Monday, tromping up the echoing stairwell to my desk at the *News & Observer,* where I landed my first job after college, I ran into Barnes Cather. I had frequently passed this spritely thirtysomething for three years, thinking nothing more than *He's cute, but short.* The end. But that Monday was the first time I thought about shoving him against the wall, thrusting my hand down his pants, and squeezing his balls.

Like most toxins, the idea was insidious. Not only did other men begin to appear more attractive, Trip became less attractive. I found my gaze settling on the parts of him I didn't like. Instead of wanting to run my arms over his bulky shoulders, I caught myself staring at his lips, noticing for the first time that they were thin. I saw that his stomach had started to hang over his belt, his shirt tugging at the buttons from both sides. Or was it always like that? Maybe, I thought spitefully, he should lay off those second helpings, too.

I used to crave his touch. When we passed each other in his tiny apartment kitchen during college, I happily anticipated a hearty butt pat. By the time he moved into a better apartment with a bigger kitchen with his solid clerkship salary, I winced when our bodies brushed. I spun away from him when he came near. It was a new kitchen dance.

In January, I moved from North Carolina back to Charleston when I got a producing job at News 14. Trip still had another five months to finish his clerkship in Raleigh, so my move meant we'd be long-distance for a while. I said that I wanted to move from print journalism into broadcast news. A braver woman would have said that she didn't want to get married.

Only once did I wonder whether he might feel the same way. He shocked me by picking a firm in Columbia, that scorching-hot concrete city in the middle of the state. This choice would extend our long-distance engagement, which privately thrilled me. He told me he needed to be with the lawmakers. He said when he moved down to Charleston, a city saturated with lawyers, his experience in the legislature would make him a top candidate at any firm in the Holy City, as well as for any elective office he might want to run for.

I didn't tell Trip marrying me would bring his career aspirations within reach much more quickly. I'm a Smythe, a member of Old Charleston—that hidden enclave within the city that the tourists don't see. Our society operates along its own distinct bloodlines, traditions, and rules. Old Charleston does a remarkable job of making sure that it's difficult to infiltrate. Membership at Battery Hall—a good-ol'-boy's club—provides a formalized tally of who is who, with new members voted on biannually.

Trip, with his law degree and southern pedigree, fits the mold. But even he—as someone from slightly Off—wouldn't have access to this private club without me, whose father is a Smythe and whose grandmother is a Middleton. Names matter. Lineage matters. I'm Trip's ticket inside.

Since we're now engaged, all Trip has to do is have lunch with Dad and some of his buddies at Battery Hall, and *bam*, he'll have a job downtown, probably at a prestigious Broad Street firm. With a few more handshakes and bourbons at the club, Trip could start his campaign for office. The circle is really that tight.

Charleston mothers have their own ways of securing their children's futures within the local aristocracy. The entry starts with cotillion, where Charleston's daughters and sons learn the rituals and dance steps of our culture and practice the art of giving compliments. Later, these same mothers will host parties for their friends' daughters who are first debutantes, then brides, and later expectant mothers in a series of teas, luncheons, and showers.

They throw other parties, too: holiday parties, cocktail parties, supper club dinners. "Why do Charleston men live so long?" the joke goes. "They pickle themselves!" At these parties, the guest lists look similar from year to year—heavy on names like Smythe, Middleton, and Rutledge—varying only as the generations evolve; it's not uncommon for a boy to be the fifth, sixth, or seventh person to bear a particular name.

Charlestonians rarely relocate. Our town is a bastion of homeostasis. So, when we go to a party, we see a friend we've known since we were babies. We know that person's parents and grandparents. It's tribal; our roots go back for years, decades, centuries. We are entwined.

Our wedding date won't be for at least another year—and maybe longer, if I don't get my act together and book a venue, a band, and a photographer. Plenty of time to fall back in love. But today I'm saved from the downward spiral of examining my love life; work starts in thirty minutes. I give my temples a few good rubs, whip myself off the couch, and head to the office.

3.

Control Room

I'm a news producer at WCCC News 14. On normal days, the job is a never-ending bug-eyed stress-fest of research, writing, and hard deadlines. Office chitchat in the break room? An occasional leisurely lunch? Ha! Never. Then there are the berserk days—the ones when our satellite truck has mechanical issues or a major story breaks. Sometimes I don't leave my desk for hours. I once got a UTI because I didn't have time to pee for six hours.

Inside the sprawling one-story building, it's frigid as usual. Rows of messy desks flank the dusky-violet walls. A bank of boxy TVs runs the broadcasts of our local competitors. The clickety-clack of fingers on keyboards is muffled by the never-ending buzz of police and fire scanners. Over the airwaves, operators speak to each other in staccato shorthand. I've learned quite a few codes over the years: 10–56 is "intoxicated pedestrian," 10–45 means "dead animal."

In the time it takes my computer to boot up, my left pinkie toe has gone numb in the newsroom's polar air. I swap my flip-flops for the wool socks I keep on top of a wool blanket in my drawer.

My phone buzzes. A new text. **"Hey there. It's Paul."**

Paul, from last night. Paul had a testosterone-saturated confidence, a sexual bullishness that scared and excited me. He's not my type, but the thrill of his attention deepened that growing chasm between me and my impending marriage. I let him buy me that second glass after I gave him my phone number. *As a friend*, I told myself. That's all I can remember.

I put my phone into my drawer, push it shut. It's about time for the morning meeting. Every workday at 9:28 a.m., I leave my computer to join the news team in a circle of chairs at the base of the Desk. Our lead reporter, Justin, looks up from his iPhone and flashes me a TV-ready smile. He wears a silver ring on his right thumb; his fingers are slender and tanned.

At 9:32, Angela lumbers toward us. She wrestles with a couple of empty wheeled chairs to make room in our circle. Her medium-length brown hair is always clean but never styled; she wears it loose around her shoulders. A pronounced wrinkle rises from the space between her eyebrows. She's middle-aged, average height. She wears baggy clothes and constantly dusts pale strands of dog hair from her chest.

Like so many transplants to the Lowcountry, she named her dog after the river on the peninsula's east side: Cooper. (Some people name their dog after the river on the west side: Ashley.)

She keeps framed photos of him on her desk: Cooper in a bandana at the beach, Cooper dressed in a Santa hat, Cooper obligingly raising a paw.

"We're starting at the top with Judge Boykin's little trip to the pokey. We've got some decent footage of his car backed into a utility pole. Gonna tease the hell out of it," she says.

Sonny Boykin? His daughter was on my volleyball team at Crescent Academy. He lives somewhere on South Battery, up by the Coast Guard station. He must be nearly seven feet tall, his shoulders as wide as a refrigerator. Sonny is personable like all the men of Battery Hall, but I've always felt he stands a little too close. He went to jail?

I don't ask because I don't want to draw even the slightest connection between him and me. If Angela understood the deep-rooted, entangled connections of the locals here, she'd know that of course I know him. And because even the loosest of acquaintances has a better chance of catching a sound bite than a stranger, she'd make me knock on his door to get the scoop myself.

I see Sonny at holiday parties, and I'm pretty sure he goes to the same church as Mom and Dad. Even if it was an innocent wreck involving a utility pole, questioning him assumes some sort of guilt. Like it or not, Sonny is part of my tribe. I don't care to protect him, but I know on some level Dad and Mom would be embarrassed if I were to question him. Someone else can do it. I hide my face, pretending to take notes.

Angela shakes her chocolate drink. "What have you got, Justin?"

Justin wiggles his pen between his long fingers. "A homeless man's body was found on Nassau Street. I'll interview his neighbors—"

"He's homeless, Justin. He doesn't have any neighbors."

"Yeah, well, I mean I'll interview the people who live near where his body was found."

"What else?" I can't see her feet, but I know she has crossed her legs and is bouncing her top foot. It's the same at every meeting. Her body vibrates with wild, nervous energy fueled by caffeine, stress, and probably too many years in New York.

"The Army Corps put out a news release on the seawall, saying that the pump stations shouldn't fail," I say. "How can they know they won't fail?"

"Math."

"Angela, if one of those systems goes down, Charleston will become a toxic bathtub."

"When that happens, we'll have a story. Just run a B-block voice-over on Spoleto."

Spoleto? It's a great arts festival but hardly front-page news. "It could be a feature—"

"Everyone is sick of hearing about the wall. Nothing has happened yet."

"Okay, fine, I'll do the Spoleto story, but one day Charleston is going to drown, and building a giant wall around the peninsula without wetland restoration and surface water storage is only going to sink it faster."

Angela smiles and rolls her eyes. We get along, but she makes it clear who is in charge.

* * *

At 5:40, it's time to head to the control room, which looks like a cave constructed from televisions. Justin once counted all the monitors: forty-two. I take my seat in the producer's chair and face dozens of talking heads from both local and national stations. I adjust my headset to check in with the talent. "Dan, you good?"

"Yep," he says in his usual cheery manner. Dan the Weatherman, like all TV weather presenters, is an agreeable guy. They're the heroes of live television, making sure our broadcast runs precisely twenty-three minutes and fifteen seconds. If breaking news happens, which can cannibalize precious minutes of our show, I speak through his earpiece to tell him he's got only eight seconds for his spot, when normally he's allowed three minutes. When the photog's camera breaks and we lose footage for a story and we suddenly have extra time that must be filled, Dan pleasantly yammers on about uneventful weather for as long as we need.

"Hi, Jasmine, doing okay?"

"Ready to roll." As Jasmine looks into a compact to check her teeth for lipstick, I make a mental note to ask her what toothpaste she uses. Jasmine normally anchors on the weekends, but one of our lead anchors took today off.

She was the runner-up for Miss South Carolina. Turns out, all those years of competitions prepared her perfectly for a career on camera. The problem is, she's stuck as a weekend anchor until one of our regulars dies. It's the same at all the channels.

Weekend anchors can end up waiting decades for their turn. A few lucky ones get a big break—a local story that has national legs—that can land them in the major networks. That's where Jasmine dreams of being. Though she checks the anonymous tip-line hourly, she still hasn't found her break. And while the Sonny story will be interesting to the locals, it won't make national headlines. I hope to find her a story that will.

A digital clock in the corner of the studio counts down to the start of the show. I press the "WEATHER" and "ANCHOR 1" buttons simultaneously. "All right, y'all. We're live in five, four, three, two."

The show starts with footage of Sonny's car, hazard lights flashing in the dark. Jasmine speaks over the video. "This morning, a judge was released from jail. At 4:12 a.m., troopers responded to a vehicle collision involving property damage just outside of the Coburg Community Apartment Complex in West Ashley. The car belongs to Judge Sonny Boykin. According to the jail log, Judge Boykin failed a field sobriety test. He was taken to the Charleston County Detention Center under suspicion of Driving Under the Influence. He was not administered a breathalyzer test and was released after a few hours."

We roll into the homeless man story, then after some national headlines, show the Spoleto festival coverage. Jasmine starts the C block with box-office hits and tosses to Dan the Weatherman. Camera Two pans wide as Dan covers every possible weather scenario. While he rambles on about the remote possibility of a tornado in the Upstate, my mind wanders back to Paul's message. Should I text back?

After the show, I check my phone and see a call from Trip. I phoned him Thursday afternoon when I knew he had a meeting. Somehow, I've managed to avoid speaking to him for almost five days now. I can't *not* talk to him for another eight hours.

I walk past the makeup room and through the kitchen to the break room. A fake flower arrangement collects dust on one of the tables. The old couch smells of burned popcorn.

"There you are," he says in his mild southern drawl. "Can you come up next weekend?"

"I'll be working," I say, suddenly grateful for my funky schedule.

"Then I'll come down. I've barely seen my fiancée since we got engaged."

"We really wouldn't get to see much of each other."

"That's okay, Cinnamon. We knew it would be like this for a while. I've got to finish this case anyway, so I'll just hole up in the library while you're at work."

"Sounds good," I lie, forcing a smile. I once read that if you smile while talking, your words can sound more positive.

"Did your mom find out if the William Aiken House is free that weekend? We've really got to secure a venue."

I was supposed to tell Mom to book our reception for the second weekend in May. Trip thought a party in that restored mansion, built in the early 1800s, would be the perfect place. "I'll talk to her."

* * *

Hours later, I return my socks to the drawer, pack my purse, and push the heavy door to exit the chilly, fluorescent-lit office. Outside, a wild night welcomes me to the natural world. Clouds sprint overhead, scudding across an endless indigo sky. A pop-up shower, by now out at sea, soaked the ground. The stirred, loosened earth smells like wild garlic and copper pennies, just the way it smelled in childhood when we excavated the back-yard, digging for porcelain shards, old apothecary bottles, and sharks' teeth.

The rain revived the tree frogs that live in the massive oaks. With no inhibition, no self-consciousness, they call raucously to each other. Animals don't fake smiles. They don't use sub-terfuge. They do as they want; they communicate what they mean. It's time for me to start living more like a wild, natural being, to start living in the moment, like Martha does. If I feel like texting Paul back, I should, right?

4.

Monday, Monday

While waiting for Martha in Kudu Coffee's courtyard, I spin my engagement ring around and around. It's a diamond solitaire with a gold band. The stone is as big as a pea. When it catches the sunlight, pink and yellow sparks of light flicker up and down the nearby wall.

When Trip got down on one knee to propose, I almost reached down to scoop him up. *Don't do it! I'm not sure if this is what I want.* But how could I say no? Here was this sweet boy, down on his knee, giving me a gift he had worked so hard to purchase. How could I end a relationship at the very moment he was asking to be with me forever? Who could look into such hopeful eyes and refuse?

"What up, Simian?" Martha scoots a metal chair over to a shady spot. Her ink-colored eyes match the black of her pupils, making her impossible to read. They're the first thing I noticed about Martha in the girls' bathroom. She's unpredictable and not at all cautious. Or maybe she seems that way because her expression is inscrutable. I find her fascinating. She's the freest person I've ever met.

She's also gorgeous: a good three inches taller than I am, with strong shoulders, a healthy C cup, a flat stomach, and long legs. She wears her raven hair in a bob like a 1920s movie star. She's almost perfect, except for her fingers and toes. Martha has comically large thumbs, and her toes are as plump as sausages. In the twelve years I have known her, I have never seen her in flip-flops. Even on a sticky day like today, she's wearing boots.

"Please tell me I didn't make out with that guy."

She removes her lid to drink her coffee, taking her time. "No, you didn't."

I collapse in relief.

"But you certainly acted like you were gonna go home with him. He was even buying me drinks."

"He texted me."

"And . . . ?"

"We're just talking."

She pinches a hunk of my muffin. "Maybe this is the guy you need to bang to figure things out."

Could I have an affair? And with that guy? "No, I don't think so."

"Well, you need to try something. Curiosity doesn't kill every cat, Simian."

Martha's parents got divorced when she was in middle school; she's pretty cynical about the institution of marriage—a view I've lately come to envy. She doesn't feel the pressure to marry and have kids. She's not looking for a birdie to build the nest. She has no ideas or prototypes for what a relationship should be.

Maybe it's because of her cynicism that she chooses the kind of men who scare me. Her men are older and hairier, with leathery skin that has creased into folds around the neck, revealing pink streaks when they swivel their heads. They smell like a hangover and have a look in their eyes that isn't always kind, is maybe even predatory.

It's not just the men she chooses who are different. It's also her approach to sex: Martha bangs and fucks. Those are the words she uses. I like to think I make love or, when it's a bit more perfunctory, I have sex, but never fuck. And when she does, it's on her terms. It often seems like a last-minute decision and usually happens sometime after 10:00 p.m. She'll straighten her back, squint her eyes in a knowing way. She'll switch from beer to martinis and play with the olives in a way only pretty girls can. Sure enough, some stranger finds an excuse to talk to her, and off they go.

I grew up differently. My parents are together and seem to love each other. It's not a passionate love; the standard, sturdy Charleston marriages seem too formal for lust. The locals are traditional about their arrangements, and this traditionalism bodes well for just about all of Mom and Dad's friends, and Weezy, too. So, when Trip proposed, everyone was excited. Our union fits neatly into a social construct that, apparently, keeps many people happy for decades. All I have to do is wear a floral dress, refrain from seconds, and maybe exile my zinnias to the far corner of our yard.

I wish I were more like Mom; she seems to have no need or desire that conflicts with Dad's. Her name is Caroline Ann Jenrette Middleton Smythe; everyone calls her Carry Ann. She briefly taught elementary school, but when Weezy was born, she decided to stay home and never really left. She keeps busy with her tennis matches and volunteer work at St. Paul's church.

This year, and on into the next, she's the envy of all her friends. Weezy is due in the fall with a boy. Shortly after, Caroline will make her debut, which is a series of brunches, cocktail soirees, and white-tie balls at which Charleston families formally present their daughters to society. The parties start in the summer and ramp up during the holiday season, when the debutantes are home from their senior year of college. The following spring, I am to get married.

Like most couples, Mom and Dad have their routines. They venture out to Edisto—our home in the country—one weekend a month. When they're in town on Saturdays, Dad golfs and Mom plays doubles. Every Sunday after church they stroll over to Battery Hall, where they have a standing 12:15 brunch reservation. Dad orders the shrimp and grits and a beer. Mom orders the quiche and a glass of chardonnay. That's been their weekend for the twenty-six years I've known them. No fights. No drama. Their marital life is a gentle meander through time.

This template never bothered me before. In fact, the mildness of their relationship paved the way for my idyllic childhood: swims at Laudie's, Wednesday night cotillion, my school days at Crescent Academy. Perhaps Mom sacrificed tiny bits of her freedom so that her children could lead such charmed lives.

After all, is it so hard to slip on a Lilly Pulitzer dress and avoid second helpings of potatoes au gratin?

Martha shoots up from the table. "I have an idea. It's brilliant, really."

"What?" Martha's ideas come suddenly and often have lasting consequences. When we were seniors, she got a tattoo on a lark. I went with her, gobsmacked as she selected a random picture off the wall. She chose a sparrow. How could she commit to something forever when she only just thought of it that moment? What did a sparrow mean to her, anyway? But I loved her for it—for making choices quickly. I couldn't decide on almond or oat milk for my latte. Martha doesn't hesitate. Her bold decisiveness landed her Bruno, too. She was smoking a cigarette outside Recovery Room—her favorite hole-in-the-wall—when a woman walking a foster dog strolled by. Now, he's hers forever.

"A gift. I'm going to bring you a perfectly fuckable gift, and you're going to love me for it."

"I don't want a vibrator."

"It's not a vibrator." She beams, then leans forward to touch the tip of my nose with her pointer finger. "You're going to love it."

5.

Surf's Up

Charleston's water babies have three beaches to choose from: Sullivan's Island, Isle of Palms, and Folly Beach. Sullivan's lies close to the harbor's entrance and near a rock wall called the jetties. This wall breaks up the chop from the Atlantic so cargo ships can safely roll into the harbor and tie up against its loading docks along the Cooper River. These tranquil waters are ideal for boats and boat-watching but terrible for surfers and surfing. Just north of Sullivan's is Isle of Palms, away from the jetties but more of a drive, and the waves don't get much bigger.

Folly Beach lies just south of the peninsula, east of James Island and away from the shipping channel. Because it's the only beach in the area with decent surf, it attracts a more alternative crowd. Shirtless beach bums with blond dreadlocks cruise the streets on oversize bicycles. Bumper stickers like "No Blood for Oil" and "I Love Small Waves" plaster rusty hatchbacks and funky storefronts. Station wagons are custom-painted with trippy images of mushrooms and fairies with rainbow-colored wings.

My secret parking spot beneath a towering oak is empty except for a growing puddle. I take a photo and send it to Angela. She texts back immediately: **"Breaking news . . . a puddle!"**

I reply, **"Clear skies. No rain. One day you'll see the light."**

My flip-flops squeak and slide as I make my way over the boardwalk. At the top of the stairs, the horizon stretches before me. Billowing cumulous clouds ride the hidden airstreams in a cobalt sky. The sand, as fine as Morton Salt, collects around posts, vegetation, and seawalls. Grain by grain, the sands gather together, forming modest but powerful barriers that protect the land from storm surges.

I squint to measure the surf. The tide just turned and is starting to go out; the waves are still big enough to ride and a bit more organized than they'll be two hours from now. For my feet to have traction on the board, I rub surf wax on its top using small, circular strokes. Because I'm goofy-footed, I Velcro the leash around my left ankle. A snarl of fishing wire, which can be deadly to sea turtles and other marine life, pokes out of the sand. Before heading into the surf, I wad it up and stuff it in my bag.

The early May air is warm, but the water still holds some of the chill from winter. Woolly fog lines the shore. I tiptoe into the ocean, then hop on my board to paddle out to the calmer waves beyond the surf. I lay my head on the board and listen to the ripples lap its underside while waiting for the next set. The rolling waves rock me gently; a sudden, unbidden thought of Paul makes me shudder.

I stalked his social media last night. In one photo, Paul pees on the wheel of a yellow Corvette. Mid-stream, he flashes a thumbs-up at the camera. In another, he clenches a knife between his teeth, ropy veins bulging from his neck. I didn't need to see more; I texted him back to tell him I'm getting married. Is this what's out there? Lone wolves pissing on cars and biting knives? What am I doing? Trip is so much better than Paul. He works late. He calls his mother. He donates to St. Jude and Ducks Unlimited. How dare I flirt with someone else?

A set comes in. I let the first wave roll underneath me and ready myself to catch the second one. I align my board with the shore, kick hard, and paddle harder. I drop into the wave, grab the rails, and pop up into a wide stance.

A beautiful storm of noises envelops me: the churning of the water underneath plays the melody; the fizz of the ocean spray chimes in. My board slices through the water, creating a sound as pure and whole as a tuning fork. I shift my weight to steer, heading south along the shoreline. And then . . . nothing. For a few sweet seconds, I'm so swept up into the moment that the world dissolves into the simplicity of movement.

Gliding over the water, I'm not engaged. There is no Trip. There is no Paul. I'm not even me. In the water, I experience pure freedom, a release from the guilt of having everything a girl could want, if only she could make some minor concessions.

6.

Dress Code

Mom and Dad wait for me in the atrium of Battery Hall. The club turned one hundred the year I was born. After all that time, the membership has remained white, male, mostly Protestant, definitely Christian, and—as far as I can gather—straight. Few Charleston newcomers know about this club; it doesn't even have a website.

Membership is capped at four hundred. Tito is a member. So is my father. My sister's husband is, too. Members' wives and their children are welcome as guests but only in the dining hall and only four days a week. Otherwise, the small but well-manicured compound is for members only.

The club was originally built as a sort of entertainment den: a billiards hall, an oak-paneled anteroom for cards and chess, a shuffleboard court outside. As Charleston grew in power, so did Battery Hall's members, and it has since become a place where decision makers gather. Partnerships are formed here, candidates are anointed, and deals are brokered.

To accommodate the changing nature of the club, Battery Hall removed the shuffleboard court sometime in the eighties and built the dining hall that doubles as a giant meeting room. Quarterly, all members gather for a surf and turf dinner and a talk from one of the South's leading politicians.

During the hot minute South Carolina had a woman for governor, the members debated whether to invite her to the annual gubernatorial supper. When the rules were written, the all-male membership simply never imagined a woman holding the top political seat in the state. In the end, they invited her to speak. How radical.

Dad mostly comes to have a glass of bourbon and play the occasional bridge game. In high school, I pressed him about the policy on women. "Why is Battery Hall just for men?"

"Oh, Simons," he responded in a calm, reasonable tone. "It's very normal for the sexes to separate. Your mother wouldn't want me barging in on her Ladies' Charleston Charities meetings. Besides, Battery Hall is nothing more than a boys' club. We just want a place where we can hang out with each other in our leisure hours. Where is the harm in that?" I found his points hard to argue; it was also the first time I wondered if he had wanted a son.

For the last few years, I've managed to dodge family meals at the club, always having to drive back to Chapel Hill on Sundays. Today, I don't have an excuse. Plus, we're here to celebrate Mom's birthday. Everything looks the same. On the far wall are portraits of the past twenty-five Battery Hall presidents. With his back to me, Dad studies the oil paintings, each rimmed by a gilded frame and stamped with a little plaque that notes their years of leadership.

The portraits are uniform. They all have the same inky background. Though they sit in slightly different positions, all men face the viewer. We see their heads, torso, and hands, all painted in the same scale. The presidents wear the Battery Hall tartan blazer, which is a plaid of moss green crisscrossed by thin white and red stripes. Only the presidents get to wear that tartan blazer. All are buried in it. While Dad, like all members of Battery Hall, was given a pair of gold cuff links on the day of his induction, I wonder if he ever dreams of his portrait on that wall. Does he want to be among these men, in a club within a club?

On the far left is the first ever president. Near the bottom of the fourth row, a younger version of Tito stares back at me. He was the nineteenth president. To the right, starting a sixth line of portraits, is a new painting covered by a carefully draped canvas. The current president's portrait has been completed. Soon, there will be an unveiling ceremony.

Dad spins around. "I kind of want to peek," he jokes.

To see what, another dude who looks like all the rest? What could possibly be interesting under there?

Mom wears a pale pink skirt and matching cardigan. She's looped a beige scarf around her neck. When she looks up from her phone, she inhales audibly. "Simons, you can't wear that jacket." She looks at me as though I stapled a bunch of tampons to my collar, some sort of super-absorbency accessory.

"I thought no jeans."

"Honey. No denim. Period. It's always been this way." She hurries toward me and tugs on my sleeve.

"I've got it," I whine, sounding like a teenager. Being here at Battery Hall—with its archaic, arbitrary rules for me to run afoul of—makes me feel like a child again. The twenty-five men on the wall glare at me, making me wish I *had* walked in with a tampon collar, maybe stuck a couple up my nose.

At least I am wearing an appropriate dress—sleeveless, knee length, spackled with red roses. I fold my jacket in half, drape it over my purse. Mom removes her scarf and tucks it over my jacket, hiding the illicit fabric as though we're smuggling contraband into the fancy-pants restaurant.

A hostess walks us to our table, which is set for six adults, plus a high chair for Francie. Along the wall is a high banquette. Above it, a mirror reflects our table; our snowy linen napkins have been folded into swans.

In the corner of the banquette, Weezy spoon-feeds Francie something orange and mushy. Weezy's husband stands to greet us. His name is Ashley, which is a normal and quite respectable name for a guy around here.

His younger brother, Clay, stands, too. Clay wears a candy-cane-striped bow tie stamped with the Greek letters of his fraternity. Pale freckles, as though applied by a pointillist artist, dot every inch of his face. When he smiles, his gums show.

"May I sit next to you?" I ask Clay.

"Totally." He lifts the menu to hide from the rest of the table and whispers to me, "Is this a boozy lunch? Or should I just order sweet tea?"

"I think one or two beers would be fine."

"Got it."

"How were exams?"

"Brutal. But one more year and I'm done. Where's Caroline?"

"At her internship in Charlotte."

"Oh, right. Cool. How's Trip liking Columbia?"

The air conditioning gives me goosebumps, but I don't dare put on my jacket. I open the napkin and flap the swan away, cover my thighs. "Good. He likes his new job a lot."

We order drinks. The server places an iced tea in front of me. Next to my glass, he sets a tiny pitcher of simple syrup and a long spoon. I pour and stir and taste, finding it impossible not to enjoy this little tea party for one.

Dad raises his pint glass. "I'd like to make a toast to your mother."

Mom straightens—her perfect posture even more perfect. Dad talks about her kindness, her patience, and her beauty. He says she's a lovely woman, an outstanding wife and mother, a devoted friend, a fantastic tennis player, and a helpful neighbor; everyone at the table nods in companionable agreement. Dad ends his speech by handing her a card—the same card he hands her every year, right here. And every time Mom opens it, she looks genuinely surprised to find a thousand-dollar gift certificate to Crawford's Jewels, hands down the best jeweler in town. Sometimes she treats herself to what she calls a bauble, though Crawford's doesn't sell trinkets. Other years she saves the cards, letting them stack up for when she wants to buy something extra sparkly.

Like a cloud sliding beneath the sun, casting a giant shadow, a blue blazer blocks my view of the right side of the table. A large hand lands on my shoulder. When I turn to see who it is, a leather belt becomes level with my nose. Button by button, my gaze inches up the towering chest of Sonny Boykin. *Shit.*

Dad, Ashley, and Clay stand to shake his hand. Generally, I stand when guests greet our table; it seems lazy for the women to stay put, and why are only the men expected to stand, anyway? Sonny's hand weighs me down, and I'm not sure I want to honor the judge by rising.

"Oh, please, sit down, sit down," Sonny says. "Celebrating the birthday girl, hey?"

Mom pats the banquette. "Join us."

"Oh, I can't. We're headed home. Nancy has a mile-long honey-do list waiting for me."

Dad remains standing. "Sonny, I'm sorry about all the fuss you've had to deal with."

"It's ridiculous. There were no charges and still the reporters are saying I'm some sort of criminal."

Mom shakes her head. "It's just awful."

"This too shall pass." Sonny lifts his hand from my shoulder to wriggle his fingers at Francie. She smiles. "Y'all take it easy. I'll see you at the unveiling on Thursday."

Mom leans over the table, her eyes following Sonny as he disappears into the lobby. "Honey, can't you do something for Sonny? He had to spend a night in jail. Isn't that bad enough? People should know he's an honorable man from a good family."

"He spent three hours in a jail, not a whole night. And even if that wasn't the case, I'm not going to write a fluff piece about him to make him look better. That's not how news works."

"You could make them stop running the videos about his little bump into a pole. They make him seem like a drunk."

"We report the facts. He got into a wreck, failed a field sobriety test, and then was taken to the station, where he was released without ever having to take a breathalyzer test. I think it's all a little odd, don't you?"

The table quiets. Weezy and Ashley inch closer to each other. Clay retreats behind his menu. Francie freezes; her fist stays high in the air, gripping a hunk of sourdough. Twelve eyes are upon me, all of them wary.

"He wouldn't drive drunk. We've known him our whole lives. He and Nancy have been married for thirty years."

I think of the portraits of the men on the wall, how images of Sonny, Dad, Ashley or Clay could be easily interchanged. These are the types of men my mother has known her whole life. Men who held the door open for her, vaccinated her children, sold her land on Edisto. These are good men. They are kind to her. They don't drive drunk, wreck their cars, and get magically released from jail.

I have a growing sense of unease that the wall of portraits represents far more than the leadership of the club. They are the figureheads of a powerful network; they look out for each other. These are the men who run the city, quietly, carefully, out of the limelight. And here I am, a modern woman—I like to think—stirring tea with a tiny spoon in the belly of the beast. "I don't think you should be so quick to be on his side."

When people are mad, they meet each other head on. They square off. But this look, where Mom cocks her head to the side, is a look of concern. Weezy and Dad are doing it, too. They wonder why I'm picking a fight.

"Simons," Mom says, brightening, "What if you got married at Battery Hall?"

Here's the thing about Charleston families: we regard civility above all else. No matter what is said or done, we remain in polite company. It's what we've been bred to do: hide our disagreements beneath the smiles. Not say what we mean. It's why Laudie never speaks up to Tito. It's why I said yes to Trip. It's why Mom changed the subject, and why I agree to move on as well, even though this new subject isn't a whole lot better.

"Remember we decided we needed a bigger venue?"

"Oh, that's right."

The server appears and takes our orders. I excuse myself to visit the powder room, weaving through tables occupied by Charleston's bluebloods. By the window, a couple of Laudie's friends, both widows, idle over after-lunch coffee. In one booth, a mother—maybe one of Weezy's old school pals—wipes ketchup from her daughter's gingham pinafore.

There isn't a hand-dryer in the bathroom; instead of using the single-use, high-quality paper hand towels embossed with the Battery Hall logo, I shake my hands dry. Dallying, I examine the prints that hang in the women's powder room.

The watercolors depict seemingly idyllic scenes of pre–Civil War plantation life. In one, enslaved women relax in the sun while their children nap, suggesting plantation life was filled with such languid afternoons—a visual denial that their babies weren't oftentimes snatched away and sold to other owners, never to see their mothers again. Another takes place just beyond the steps of a large plantation home. Enslaved people line up to shake the hands of a finely dressed white couple—their oppressors. In the painting, everyone is smiling. *Jesus.* Who chose these prints for the ladies' room? Why are they hanging in this club? It seems Battery Hall is even more backwards than I had feared.

7.

It's a Trip

A streetlight illuminates Trip's white Toyota truck; its motor hums. He's sitting inside, seat belt fastened, hunched over some documents. I can tell the AC is on full blast by the way it blows the papers. He looks up; I freeze. He doesn't see me on the curb, can't detect that just two weeks ago, I flirted with a man named Paul.

I slip off my shoes. My toes, cramped and cold from a long day at the office, soak up the residual warmth baked into the sidewalk. Raindrops from an afternoon squall linger on the plants, amplifying the scent of confederate jasmine that blooms riotously beside my house. It's twilight now, and Charleston is warm, seductive, and sweet-smelling. It's an evening ripe for springtime romance. So why can't I conjure up any feelings for the wonderful person inside that truck?

I stretch my arms overhead, trying to awaken my body. Maybe I can somehow physically summon the spark I used to feel when his truck rolled up to my apartment. I exhale, walk over, knock on his window.

"Agh!" He jumps, puts his hand over his heart. I notice the print of his bow tie: tiny palmettos. He bounds out of the Toyota and hugs me.

I lean into his chest. He lowers his face to reach mine. I tuck in closer to avoid having to kiss him. Undeterred by my hesitance, or perhaps just oblivious, Trip kisses my forehead. "Put on your shoes. You could step on glass."

It's something Dad—or Tito—would say, and in the same practical, no-nonsense tone. "I'm fine." I push from his embrace, backing away into the wet street.

He starts to say something but instead shakes his head. When he reaches for his bag in the passenger seat, I turn to scamper up the staircase, open the door to my apartment, and have the bizarre but delightful thought that I could just lock him out. I don't, of course.

Trip hollers from the bottom of the staircase, "Slow down there, Speedy."

He finds me in the kitchen and leans against the doorframe, watching me as I root around for a wine opener. I know he wants me to turn around and kiss him, do what normal engaged people do.

"Cinnamon, sweetie, you've got roaches." Trip rips a paper towel from the roll, picks up the dead one on the floor, tosses it in the trash can.

"I know. So gross. Charleston butterflies . . ."

He opens my countertop compost tin, releasing a fruit fly. "It's probably because of this."

"Well, I'm still going to compost." I hand him a glass of wine. "How's work?"

"It's challenging. In the best way. But I don't want to talk about work now." He puts his glass on the counter before taking a sip. "And I don't want wine. I want my bride." He steps forward, reaches his arm around my waist. Instinctively I stiffen, but not enough for him to notice.

He cups my cheeks in his big bear hands, bringing us face-to-face. His eyes are gentle, and behind that warm hazel gaze is a promise of safety. And perhaps, somewhere beneath the sheets of my bed lies my deep, wayward, long-buried promise of love. I take a breath and unbutton his collared shirt.

8.

Barrier Island

Edisto is one of the Lowcountry's many sea islands, and perhaps its most pristine. To the north are Johns, Sullivan's, Isle of Palms, Bulls, and Capers; to the south, Hilton Head and Daufuskie in South Carolina and St. Simons, Jekyll, and Cumberland in Georgia.

The islands in South Carolina closest to Charleston were developed first; Edisto Island's relative remoteness has spared it the rampant development that has befallen the others. Mom and Dad bought a house on a deep-water lot off Pine Landing Road about five years ago when Dad decided he wanted to become a better fisherman (instead of fishing, though, he's always working on some project, like taming the Edisto jungle that encroaches on the house, or nailing down balky boards on the dock).

Our isolated cabin on Flemming Creek is a sanctuary; it can also be a miserable place when you're stuck in a small house with your parents quizzing you about your career, wedding date, or anything related to the future. The good thing about a Wednesday to Sunday work schedule is that I can go to Edisto with my sister Weezy and her kid, Francie, sans parental units. Dad, like most people, works Monday through Friday, so he and Mom don't come when Weezy and I have our Monthly Monday nights here together. This will be our fifth Monday. And while we've gotten even closer since I've moved back to Charleston, I still haven't said much about Trip to Weezy. Maybe I'm like Laudie; I'm not ready.

It's an hour's drive to Edisto from Charleston. After crossing the Ashley River, Highway 17 South cuts through suburbia, down the Auto Mile with its acres of cars, past strip malls, generic shopping centers, and asphalt parking lots. Gradually, as the road narrows, the blight decreases; stands of pine trees and clusters of oaks appear. Instead of giant big-box stores, there are small businesses: a roadside tattoo parlor, a sandwich shop, a palm reader, tiny country churches. People sell live bait, crabs, watermelons, or boiled peanuts from their trucks.

On Toogoodoo Road, the trip becomes scenic as expansive stretches of river and marsh come into view. The last two miles to our house are on a winding dirt road. Gangly wood storks in the loblollies startle into flight when our car rattles down the bumpy road. As we drive farther into the low, flat maritime forest, the shadows thicken. Oak branches snake overhead. And although I can't see them, the white-tailed deer are resting in the rust-colored pine straw that serves as bedding for many of the island animals.

We pull up to the cabin, which sits in a clearing. Our screen porch overlooks the creek, which meanders and carves through estuaries of spartina grass.

The cabin has three bedrooms: a master, another room with a double bed, and a bunk room. Mom decorated the house with beachy knickknacks: framed prints of colorful umbrellas, duvets with seashells, cocktail napkins that read, "Cheers, Y'all." Weezy and Francie always take the double, with its starfish duvet and lighthouse-shaped bedside lamps.

We unload the car and divvy up the work. Weezy puts away the groceries. I open the windows and stash our bags in the bedrooms. "Wanna go with me to put in the crab trap?" I rummage in the freezer for some chicken necks.

Weezy glances at Francie, who beats a spoon against the recycling bin. "She seems happy now. We'll just hang here."

I drop the chicken in a plastic bag and head out the door. When I step onto the boardwalk, the pelicans at the dock's far end stiffen, taking stock of the interloper. Only after I walk halfway down the dock do they take flight, landing on the water's surface just down the creek.

Dad keeps the crab trap neatly bungeed beneath the bench on the green-roofed high dock. Made of chicken wire, the lightweight trap is about the size of a suitcase. I stuff the frozen chicken necks inside, close the hinge, check the knots at both ends of the rope, and fling the trap into the creek. The trap makes a satisfying whoosh when it hits the water and then rapidly sinks.

Blue crabs lurk on the creek bottom; the chicken oils will lure them inside the trap. On a good afternoon, five or six crabs will come in search of dinner. I always have to throw a couple back in the water, however, because it's family policy to return all the females to the creek, whether or not they are carrying eggs.

The simmering sounds of tidal zone critters grow in volume with the heat of the day. Marsh hens cackle; a stingray thrashes. With loud pops, fiddler crabs break the air seals from their underground homes. The crabs are each about the size of a quarter and practice courtship rituals that rival any daytime soap opera. I wait motionlessly; as soon as the crabs grow accustomed to my shadow, they resume business as usual.

The females have two identical small claws. They spend most of their time quietly picking at the microbial growth. The males, on the other hand, have one oversize claw, which sort of looks like a fiddle, that they wave to lure potential visitors to their mud holes.

This whole setup—where the males patrol the tight perimeter of their territories and the females roam, sizing up the lot, deciding which bachelor pad to visit—reminds me of college. Back at UNC–Chapel Hill, on fraternity row, the frat boys would drape large sheets across their houses, advertising themed parties. Drinking from red Solo cups, they'd stay put on their turf, not daring to enter another man's house.

The co-eds trolled the streets, chatting and laughing, deciding which place to go bum a few beers and maybe meet their husbands. It's how I met Trip, after all. Though we humans have evolved in some ways since we emerged from the primordial ooze, it seems we still practice the most basic, primitive mating behaviors.

As a gull's shadow passes overhead, the fiddler crabs scamper back into their holes. Some of the males get lucky, as the wandering females need shelter fast. Show's over. I head back to the house.

Inside, Weezy cuts into a seedless watermelon. "Here, Francie." She hands her daughter a dripping slice. Francie turned one last month. She has chipmunk cheeks. Freckles, like her uncle Clay's, dot her face. We all love Francie and believe she's a beautiful child, of course, but I think we were each privately disappointed that she looks more like a Townsend than a Smythe.

"It's still hot in here." I peel off my T-shirt. I am now in my Edisto summer uniform: a ratty red bikini top and jean shorts. "I'm going back outside."

"Can you take Francie?"

"Yeah, sure." I carry Francie down the steps. In the hummock, the cabbage palmettos stand ramrod straight. Their V-shaped bark rims the trunks in an elegant herringbone pattern. In contrast, the live oaks twist and knot like old hands. Within their cratered, splotchy bark, galaxies of aquamarine lichens multiply and divide. We wade through the underbrush—sedges and dead goldenrod—looking for bugs.

A car rumbles in the distance. As it comes into view, I'm stunned to see Martha's Volvo wind its way up the sandy road. There's someone with her. A guy. I squint to get a better look. *Holy shit.* Is that Harry?

I nearly drop Francie to the ground so that I can neaten my appearance. Pivoting away from the car, I swipe under my eyes to remove any possible day-old mascara streaks hiding in the folds. I tighten my ponytail and scrunch the crown of my head to give my flat hair some extra oomph.

The brakes screech, and the Volvo shudders to a stop. I wave as coolly as possible, as though old crushes randomly appear all the time.

"Surprise," says Martha flatly. She delivered on her promise—my gift.

"Hey, Simons." Underneath his thin T-shirt, I spy the same muscular shoulders I longed to touch in high school. He smiles his sideways smile, flashing the tiniest gap between his top two front teeth. He wears khaki shorts, low-cut socks, and green sneakers, much like the outfit he wore the day I first saw him.

Before he first noticed me, I had limp hair and a crop of chin zits. I rarely smiled because I didn't want to scare people with a mouthful of metal. Martha made me feel better by saying I had stainless-steel sex appeal, but still, who wants braces, especially as a high schooler? After my braces were removed, my hair was still limp, but a hairdresser determined that a chin-length cut on my soccer-ball-shaped head somehow worked. The tea-tree oil Weezy gave me cleared up the little bit of acne I had. My face had grown so that my wide-set eyes had become an asset, especially after makeup tutorials from Martha. With some experimentation with padded bras, I was pleasantly shocked to discover that I had started to turn some heads.

I caught Harry's attention that day. He was standing in the breezeway, his hands shoved into his pockets, his eyes downcast. I later found out that a teacher had caught him smoking in the parking lot before school and that he was waiting for his parents to take him home. He was surrounded by a handful of faculty and students who were in a heated discussion about individual rights.

A friend of his was arguing with the principal. "He's eighteen. He's legally allowed to smoke and even die for his country."

Through the commotion, Harry lifted his head to stare right at me. There he was, in trouble, and instead of shrinking, he had the audacity to flirt. No one saw that defiance but me. His gaze zapped me; it rewired me. Something about that look changed me internally. I'd had crushes on boys before, but never a full-bodied desire.

Somehow, Harry imprinted on me. It was indelible, and I was helpless. I decided right then and there that there was no other boy for me on the planet. Now, even after more than a decade, with a fiancé and work and time to muddle the memory, that feeling—evidently hardwired into the core of my being—is hard to shake.

He was suspended for a day. The next week, I found him by the water fountain at the start of lunch. "Hey," he said, tucking his lower lip.

"Hi." I imitated his tone, hoping I could match his nonchalance.

"I need a cup of coffee. Want to go to the Waffle House?"

The Waffle House? I'd always wanted to go. With its neon letters in square boxes lit-up in screaming, school-bus yellow, the sign seemed to target kids directly. Whenever Mom took us to West Ashley, I'd beg her to stop there. I'd tell her I was starving.

"Absolutely not," she always said.

"Why not?"

"There are places you go and places you don't go. This is a place we don't go."

"But, Mom, why?"

"It's dangerous, honey. It's full of truck drivers and drunk people eating breakfast for dinner."

I'd passed the restaurant many times on the way to school, wondering what was so dangerous about truck drivers, drunk people, and eggs and coffee any time of day. But even when I could go, when I had my driver's license and the occasional free afternoon, I never went inside.

Perhaps that day was the day, I thought. We weren't allowed to leave campus, but how would anyone know? We could sneak out at the start of lunch and be back before the bell rang for the next period. Besides, I'd never gotten in any real trouble before. This, I decided, was worth the risk. "Yeah, I could use one, too."

Without another word, he led me behind the upper school building. Teenage contraband littered the secret path: cigarette butts, candy wrappers, a worn copy of *CliffsNotes* on *Great Expectations*. We ducked under an ancient camellia, and voila! We were in the senior parking lot.

Out in the noonday sun, Harry slowed his pace. He stood tall. I mimicked his movements, feeling more invincible with each step away from the school grounds. I was brave. He opened his car door for me. "My dad made me get a stick shift so I wouldn't smoke when I drive." He lit a Camel and peeled out of the gravel lot.

The Waffle House rattled with activity. Grease crackled on the griddle. A waitress hollered an order to the cook. Silverware clinked. The jukebox played a Willie Nelson tune.

As I slid into a booth, I wondered if this counted as my first date. A server appeared with two mugs and a steaming pot of coffee. She filled our cups quickly but without making a splash. "What'er y'all havin'?"

I skimmed the menu, which was primarily pictures. Steak and eggs? Biscuit and gravy? I was too excited to eat. "Just coffee, thanks."

Harry didn't have to look at the menu. "I'll have the hash browns: smothered, covered, diced, and chunked."

"Okay, baby." She threw a handful of creamers on the table. I'd never had my own cup of coffee before, so I drank it black, like my mother did.

I was goofily, deliriously happy. I could do this every day. We did, for a while. But eventually he just stopped inviting me. I was crushed.

In my backpack, I carried around buttons I had made for him and his bandmates. They read: "I'M IN A BAND." It was the best I could come up with without seeming too desperate, though I never got the courage to give them to him anyway.

I later found out that while on a trip to check out Boston College, he had met a girl. "Never underestimate the power of sex," Martha told me while we sat in that same booth months later. I began to frequent that Waffle House, hoping I might bump into him. Martha was kind enough to indulge my obsession. I usually bought her lunch.

I spent the rest of the year wishing he'd break up with his college girlfriend. He still hung out by the water fountain, where I'd take a quick sip after French class. Occasionally he'd brush up against me when I pulled a book from my locker. His touch was thrilling.

But that was more than ten years ago.

Harry leans against the car with his hands in his pockets, his feet crossed at his ankles. He flashes his green eyes up to meet mine, and my heart pounds like it used to—before I had a nine-to-five, before my future was laid out for me, before I made a promise that feels impossible to keep. I ache for him, but I ache for that teenage version of me more. Almost automatically, I covertly use my thumb to spin my diamond to the underside of my ring finger.

Martha opens the back door to let out Bruno, her ancient pug. Francie drops her watermelon and screams. "Up! Up!" I don't blame her; Bruno is a rough-looking dog. His eyes drip a clear mucus onto his wrinkly face. His scabby tongue bounces up and down. He could use braces.

Weezy waves from the front door. Like any southern woman, she makes even uninvited guests feel welcome. Weezy would surely remember Harry from Crescent Academy. They didn't hang out in the same crowd, but with only a hundred or so in each graduating class, they at least were acquainted. I'm not sure if she ever knew about my intense crush. When I walk past Weezy to get some Coronas from the fridge, she looks at me as though she might have some inkling. I avoid eye contact.

I still haven't told her a word about my feelings for Trip,

or lack thereof. If I tell her, the problem becomes real. We'll have to dissect our relationship, and she'll suggest counseling and self-help books. And though she means well, she'd tell my parents.

I hand Martha and Harry a beer. "Y'all go down to the dock. I'll be right there." Martha slings her bag over her shoulder; Harry follows her out the door. The screen door bangs behind them.

I wait to speak to Weezy until they are out of earshot. "I'm sorry. I didn't know they were coming." Our Monthly Mondays are reserved just for us. We had decided in January, when they began, that we didn't want to have to entertain each other's friends.

"It's okay," she says with the tiniest hint of resentment.

I should say something like, *Really? Are you sure?* but I leave good enough alone.

I head down the hall and flick on the bathroom light to study my reflection, something I've desperately wanted to do since Harry arrived. I pull open the drawers and sift through old toothbrushes, travel-size tubes of toothpaste, and bobby pins. I find some old waterproof mascara and some blush, but no brush. I pump the mascara tube and apply. It's dry as a biscuit, but it will have to do. I tear off a couple of squares of toilet paper, dab it on the blush, and rub that on my cheeks. I purse my lips and look straight into the mirror. Just like a bird with a song or a fiddler with a giant claw, I, too, enact the rituals of the mating game. When Weezy sees me run past wearing makeup, she arches an eyebrow but keeps her mouth shut.

Bruno greets me on my way out to the creek. He wags his stubby tail but stays put at the foot of the boardwalk. Like a lot of little dogs, he's afraid to leave solid ground. After giving him a quick, reassuring massage, I stroll toward my friends, using this extra time to gather some confidence and hopefully scrounge up something clever to say.

Harry sits on the western railing, shaded by the dock's roof. Martha reclines in a pool of sun. She leans back on her arms, her legs stretched out in front of her. She's still wearing her boots. Oversize sunglasses frame her face. The sleeves of her T-shirt are neatly rolled up and folded around her strong upper arms. She ashes into an empty Corona.

"Nip?" Harry passes me a fifth of bourbon. I hate shooting liquor, especially without a chaser, but I'm glad for this social lubricant. I take a gulp and try not to look overcome by the burn in my throat.

I desperately want conversation, but I'm afraid if I ask too many questions, I'll seem nosy. Why is Harry in town? And how did Martha convince him to come all the way out here? Did he come here to see me? Does he know I'm engaged? Does he care?

The only way to quiet this tsunami of questions is to take a fast, vigorous swim. I walk down the rickety wooden ramp to the floating dock, push the swimming ladder into the water, and dive in. The water's warm on the surface, but just a foot underneath, it's chilly. And the current is swift. I hear everything: the grunts of the red drum, the cackling of tiny shrimp, the metallic whir of a crabbing boat in the distance. Then, a splash.

I swim to the surface to see Martha. She's fighting the current, jockeying her way to the swimming ladder. Martha isn't a great swimmer, but she knows enough to know that if she doesn't start heading toward the dock immediately, we'll have to hop in a jon boat and fish her out downstream.

She manages to beat the tide to the swim ladder and climbs out looking like a biker-babe version of *The Lady of Shalott*. Her wet T-shirt clings to her body: voluptuous breasts, flat stomach. She peels off her shirt to wring it out; her petal pink nipples show through her lacy bra.

I steal a glance at Harry, sure to catch him sneaking a peek, but his eyes are fixed on me. It's not until she waves at Harry that he turns his attention to her. He shakes his soft pack and hands her a cigarette.

Before climbing out, I rub the creek silt from my face so I don't look like the bearded lady. Harry offers me the bottle with an outstretched hand. I take another sip. So I'm not tempted to take a third, I check on the crabs, hoist the trap. When the cage surfaces, the crabs raise their claws aggressively, opening and closing them. I jostle the cage to get a look at their pearl-white underbellies: six males and two females.

"Dinner?" Martha asks as she exhales a stream of smoke. She's put her boots back on.

"Yeah, or at least an appetizer." Rotating the trap, I release the two females, which tumble into the creek. I shake the males into a bucket, dump the leftover bait into the water, and set the trap back on the dock. Once, unthinkingly, I left the bait in the trap. I returned a few weeks later to find one dead crab and seven dismembered claws. They starved when they ran out of chicken neck meat and couldn't escape, so they started eating each other. I turned them into cannibals. I felt criminal for weeks afterward.

I lead the way down the narrow dock back to the house. Martha and Harry trail close behind. Bruno yips and stomps in the salty grass, thrilled that we're returning to solid ground. The sun's warmth fading, it might even be cool enough for a bonfire. We could make a beer run . . .

Harry drapes an arm over my shoulders. I jump, electrified by the unsolicited touch.

"I've got to go. I've got a gig tonight."

Oh. My heart sinks. This is goodbye.

"He's playing at Tin Roof tonight. You should come, Simian."

I want to go. I can't, though. Weezy didn't come all the way out here to hang out by herself. "Sounds like a blast, but I'm gonna chill here with Francie and Weezy. Y'all have fun." I shoo them off, like I don't want Harry to scoop me up with his big fiddler claw and carry me back to his hole.

9.

Backpedal

Charleston's weekend bar scene has slowly crept northward up the peninsula over the years. Back in the nineties, tourists trolled the Market to get drunk. In the early aughts, gentrification began to move uptown, spurred in part by reviews from the *New York Times*, *Travel + Leisure*, and *Bon Appétit* waxing poetic about our okra, heirloom tomatoes, and she-crab soup. Once-seedy, derelict buildings are now restored. No more shabbiness, boarded-up windows, broken glass. Instead, newly planted palmettos line the streets. Sleek new bars offer signature farm-to-table cocktails. Monolithic hotels rise from the spaces between little nineteenth-century buildings rescued and protected by the Preservation Society.

Trip texted he'd be waiting for me with some of his friends at a new bar called Spill. I told him I'd arrive right after work. The pine walls, counters, and tables are made from salvaged pine and soaked in a glossy stain. The website advertises a boat-like, high-seas atmosphere; instead, this place gives off a casket-like, funeral vibe. Or maybe that's just how it seems to me.

Trip sits at a high-top with two girls; an overhead bar lamp shines on them like a spotlight, soaking them in gold, as though they are in a display case. The brunette wears a fitted dress made of Jacquard—slim over her shoulders, tight at the waist, ladylike as the rich fabric spills over her knees. Her eyes are brown but glittery. The blonde wears a silky peach dress that ties in front at the neck, not revealing any cleavage but inviting any passerby just to try to see. Their hair is loosely curled. They wear makeup, but not too much. I can see why Trip might want me in nicer clothes—these women look gorgeous, sophisticated, important even. And suddenly, I want to be like them. This is the type of woman Trip wants me to be. I get it.

Trip chose his standard lawyering uniform—a button-down shirt and freshly pressed khakis. He looks up from his lager and spots me by the door. "There's my bride." I reach for his hand while mentally checking my bank account. It would be a stretch, but I could afford a couple of nice dresses. Maybe Mom and I could go shopping together; she'd love that. And the next time Trip comes to town, I'll set the alarm early to curl my hair before work.

I turn toward the brunette. "Hi, I'm Simons."

"We've met before," she says. "I'm Bennett. I'm friends with your sister."

"Yes, of course," I backpedal, though I don't recall ever seeing her pal around with Caroline.

"Bennett interned over winter break where I clerked," Trip adds. "She's a senior at College of Charleston." He says the blonde went to law school with him.

"Nice to see you."

Trip stands. "Cinnamon, it's about time for dinner." When the two girls reach for their purses, Trip places two twenties under his empty glass. "I've got it. Glad y'all are in town."

I wish I didn't find that gesture so sexy. Trip is already making more money than I ever will, at this rate at least. As my husband, he would make sure we had a fine home with airy front rooms, renovated bathrooms, and real art on the walls—oil paintings with gilded frames. Just as he will tonight, he'll take me to dinners at fancy restaurants my whole life. Our children will have the option of private school. There will be orthodontia for them, summer travel for us, maybe even a house downtown. I have some money tucked away and imagine my parents would leave some for me in time, but life on my own would be very different than the life I know now. Isn't it just sensible to factor financial security into the calculations of eternal love?

We have a reservation at Muse, maybe the most romantic restaurant in town. As we walk into the warm night, Trip wraps an arm around me and fiddles with my ponytail. "Long day at the office? You're a bit greasy, sweetie."

And just like that, the spell is broken. I think of Laudie and Tito's comments about her clothes, her cooking. I stand a bit taller in my jeans and T-shirt, ready to pick a fight. "Is that how you want to start the night?"

"What do you mean?"

"The first thing you said to me is that my hair is greasy."

"Actually, the first thing I said to you was, 'There's my bride.'"

"Of course. You're a lawyer. Your job is semantics." I know I sound nasty. I don't care.

"What's the matter, Simons? Look, I'm sorry I said your hair was greasy."

"Trip, I'm never going to be like those girls. You know that, right?" What was I thinking? Curlers?! What's next, bleach my butthole?

"Is this about moving to Columbia? It's not forever. People make sacrifices, Simons. It can't just be your way all the time. Charleston is great and all, but it's not perfect. And even you know Columbia is a bigger news market. If you just gave it half a chance . . ."

"I have a job here. A good job. Just because I don't make a ton of money doesn't mean it's not worthy."

Trip throws his head back. "Simons, yes, it's a good job and I'm proud of you. But it seems like every time you're not at work, you're running around reliving your teenage years or something. I mean, what *are* you doing?"

The question isn't rhetorical. He waits for me to answer, but I don't tell him about late nights at the bars with Martha, accepting drinks from random guys. I don't tell him I feel trapped, that I have feelings for Harry, that I gave a man my number. After all these years of blaming Trip for the fracturing of our relationship, I realize I'm the bad guy. Like any creature cornered, I go for the attack. "You've changed."

"You're right. I have changed. I'm glad for it. I've grown up,

Simons. What about you? Are you becoming who you want to be?"

Am I? "I'm afraid I'm not becoming someone you want me to be."

"Shit, Cinnamon. I love you. I can't help it. Frankly, sometimes I wish I could. You're stubborn, and you always have something, I don't know"—he swirls his hand near my head—"brewing in there. Like you have a secret life. Or secrets from me. I'm giving you everything. Everything, Cinnamon. What more do you want to take from me?"

"Trip, I'm sorry. I don't know."

"Where has your confidence in us gone? Doubt is a real problem, and it's starting to get to me. It's got me thinking differently, and I've never done that before."

He doubts us, too? What does Trip think? A small but frightened part of me wonders if there is another reason he chose Columbia, not Charleston, after I had moved back home. What goes through his mind as he drinks with beautiful women? Could he possibly want something different? I'm not sure if it's my heart or my ego, but I can't stand the idea of his thinking of other women, of his even considering that toxic idea.

As though Trip senses it, too, he pivots abruptly and nearly marches down the street. I scurry behind him, scarlet letter and all. I don't ask where we are going because I'm pretty sure he won't answer me. I sneak my hand into his. He lets me hold it. After a few blocks, I see we're headed back to my apartment. Okay. No dinner? Fine.

Home, I fling open the cabinets in search of something

to feed my husband-to-be. I find a sleeve of whole wheat Ritz crackers, a jar of salsa, and some pasta. I open the fridge: wilted lettuce, moldy marinara sauce, rubbery carrots, and a suspicious-looking chunk of cheese.

"What are you doing in there?" Trip calls from the couch.

I cut the cheddar into slices and lay them on top of a plate of crackers. "I'll be there in two secs. I'm making dinner," I say as cutely as I can.

When I bring over the plate, he takes it and slides it onto the coffee table, out of my reach. He wants me to kiss him. In the quick moment before I lean in, I take stock of the man I almost pushed away. His features have matured a bit since I've last really looked at him. His face is thinner. The fine lines around his eyes are deepening. When he looks at me, it's as though he sees me differently, too. He used to look at me with dopey, love-struck eyes; now they've hardened. It makes me feel frantic.

I place my hand behind his neck and kiss him on the lips. He kisses me back and then quickly slides a hand between my legs, stroking a finger against the cotton underwear I got from Target.

Maybe this is the way all married women go about lovemaking. This isn't Martha's kind of lip-biting, ass-slapping, vertical fuck against the bookshelf. I wrap my arms and legs around him like a vine to a tree. I cling to his warmth, his steadfastness, his promises of tradition, place, and order.

His breathing quickens as he braces himself to lift me from the couch. He carries me to my bed—all white linens on a white wire frame. I painted the walls a silvery gray so that my bed looked like a pearl in an oyster. But instead of feeling like Venus on a half-shell, I feel like a blow-up rubber doll—a vessel of pleasure only for him.

Trip grunts above me, then collapses. For the first few years of our relationship, at the moment after sex, I'd run my fingers over the tiny hairs on the curve of his ear or kiss his back until he fell asleep. I'd reach for his hand, fold our fingers together, and marvel at how wonderful the heat generated by our skin felt.

Tonight, I pull the covers over my head and feign sleep. A while later, Trip gets out of bed and walks to the bathroom. He turns on the light and closes the door. While he urinates, I swallow hard to keep from crying. Why can't I love him?

From beneath the covers, I hear him walk to the foot of the bed. I hear the soft clink of a belt buckle and the rustle of fabric. He sits next to me; the mattress squeaks. He peels the sheet from my face. "I have something for you."

In the low light of my room, illuminated by the streetlight outside my window, I can see he is holding a rectangular felt box. "Open it."

It's a gold necklace with about a dozen pearls spaced evenly apart. "Sit up. Hold your hair back." Trip lifts the necklace from the box and loops it around my neck. I feel him clumsily fidgeting with the clasp. "I think I'm going to need help."

Pinching the ends of the delicate chain, I reach behind my neck. With my head bowed, I open the fastener with my thumbnail and hook it to the minuscule loop. Though the necklace is the right size, it feels tight around my throat.

10.

Secret Dances

I grew up on the west end of Atlantic Street, which is not on the water, but the tide slaps the seawall just a couple blocks away. My parents' yellow Charleston single is typical of the houses on this street: spacious but not gigantic, with porches on both stories supported by simple Ionic columns.

The closer to the harbor, the grander the houses become. Many of these single-family mansions have sweeping piazzas, expansive wrought iron balconies, or rooftop widow's walks, where sea captains' wives once scanned the horizon for sight of their husband's ship. Flickering lanterns flank the giant front doors. Sprawling live oaks shade the prosperous streets, their sinuous roots erupting through the slate sidewalks.

I peel a hard left onto South Battery, roll down my grandparents' oyster-shell path, and lean my bike against the crepe myrtle. Before visiting Laudie, I make my way to the zinnias.

Throughout my summers, while Weezy practiced her front crawl for swim team meets and Caroline sunned by the pool,

I worked in the garden with Laudie. She would stoop over her flowers, always zinnias, but she toyed with other varietals, too. One summer we planted delicate cosmos. Another year we grew scaevola nipped from a neighbor's bush.

When I was very young, it was my job to pick up stray oak leaves that had fluttered on top of the bark-lined beds. When I reached elementary school, she taught me how to weed and showed me how uprooting even healthy flowers can make the others grow hardier. By the time I reached middle school, she gave me my own pair of gardening shears and designated a spot for them in her potting shed. They're still there.

Over the last few growing seasons, as Laudie's vigor has waned, her semisecret garden has suffered. Still off-limits to the professional garden service she and Tito employ, her small, wild sanctuary shows signs of neglect. She can't keep up. In the few weeks since I last checked, weeds crowd the hydrangeas. The twisting tendrils of a jasmine vine meander through our seashell collection. She did plant some impatiens, but she didn't bury the roots deep enough and they're not thriving. She knows better. The zinnias still command the center of the garden, but they grow in thick batches. Some have gotten to be so top-heavy they fall over, smothering the new growth. I retrieve my shears from the potting shed and prune the zinnias, cutting some for a flower arrangement, and head inside.

The house is quiet, save for the ticking of the kitchen clock. I put the flowers in water and wander into the living room. Empty. The muted TV broadcasts a golf tournament. Large captions for the hearing-impaired scroll across the bottom of the screen. The screen switches to a commercial for a bladder medication. I turn the TV off and head toward the grand foyer.

Light leaps through the long, vertical windows that flank the main door. Two giant mirrors hang on opposite walls, multiplying the natural sunlight. The mirrors' gilded frames graze the old heart-pine floors and nearly touch the fifteen-foot-tall ceilings. As I make my way up the stairs, running my hand along the worn banister, I catch sight of my grandmother.

Dusty sunlight slips through the slatted second-story shutters, striping the floor. Laudie stands at the barre, her back toward me. A fuzzy haze frames her silhouette: her long legs, the curve of her hips. She stands in first position—heels together, toes pointed out. Her right hand rests on the barre. Her left, firmly wrapped into its removable wrist cast, extends out into the room. She dips into a plié; a diamond of light flashes between her legs. The armless chair Mom gave her for practicing senior yoga stays unused in the corner.

Since her fall, doctors have said "no ballet," at least until her wrist gets better. Mom and Tito have told her more than once she should quit for good. I walk around Laudie, careful to give a wide berth to her sweeping, injured hand. "Did Tito come around?"

"We're not going to tell him." She raises into a relevé. Her legs tremble, but she manages to stay lifted. "I'm looking forward to our ballet date."

"I'm guessing we're not going to tell Tito about that, either." She nods.

We didn't tell Tito when I snuck her out to hear bluegrass at

a local brewery. We didn't tell him when I took her out to try su-
shi. (She liked the miso soup, but said her nigiri roll tasted raw.)
And we definitely kept quiet about the day we sat in the front
row at a drag queen brunch. But she's frailer now, and Tito
rarely leaves this house; she's more closely monitored. Things
have changed. Lately, a lot of things have changed. "Laudie, can
I talk to you?"

"You can always talk to me."

"You promise you won't tell Mom?"

"Simons, we all have our secrets."

"I'll take that as a yes." I trace my foot over a floral medallion
on the old Oushak rug. "I'm thinking of calling off the wedding."

She stops, her feet still in second position. Her attention is
completely on me. "I was worried about this." She reaches for
her towel on the barre, gently dabs her forehead.

"What, you thought this might happen?"

She laughs lightly. "You hadn't picked a venue or bought a
dress or done anything the brides do these days. And, Simons,
you and Trip live more than one hundred miles apart. It hardly
takes a gumshoe."

"Maybe I just need a separation. Some time apart to think
about things."

"But you're separated now; you don't live in the same city."

I don't want to be like you and Tito, I want to say. I don't want
to be squeezed into some mold for a model wife. I also want to
date and kiss and sleep around, to sow my wild oats, as they say,
if that can be applied to women. With a clean break, I could do

it all guilt-free. And if it's a separation, I can always go back to Trip. It gives me options. "What would you do?"

"Well, honey, I can't make that decision for you," Laudie pauses, puts the towel back on the barre, "though I do have my thoughts."

"Just tell me!"

A door slams shut. Laudie checks her watch, still on her right wrist. "Your grandfather just got back from Battery Hall." She unties her ballet skirt as she hurries to her room to change. She stuffs it deep into a chest of drawers and then slides on a long, Tito-approved skirt. She switches out her canvas ballet flats for her Capezio heels, folds them into her sock drawer, and shuts it tight. She grabs her towel from the barre and hands it to me to hang on a rack in her bathroom. We've covered our tracks before Tito makes it to the bottom of the stairs. Laudie hollers down to him, "I'll be there in a minute."

When she faces me again, her face is solemn. "Come over next Saturday, but earlier so we have time to talk while Tito is at Battery Hall. It's time I tell you about Atlanta."

11.

The Little Death

Harry plays tonight. For days, I've been mapping out the evening, minute by minute. I'll freshen up at my apartment in fifteen minutes flat. When I get to the bar, I'll drink a gin and tonic to loosen up and sip water the rest of the night so that I'm not in absolute shambles for work tomorrow. I'll try to re-create the eyeliner I once (and only once) totally nailed. I painted my toes midnight blue and bought a toe ring at the Walgreens on my way to work. I'll wear sneakers to the concert, of course—but who knows where the night could take us?

Martha still hasn't texted me back. **"See you at 8:15?!"** I stare at my phone, impatient for her reply.

My script waits at the copier, neatly collated and warm to the touch. I swing by the bathroom for a pit stop before taking my seat in the control room. I put on my headset and stare at the digital clock as the red numbers count down to the start of the show.

Sixty seconds. What happens if Harry wants to kiss me? Am I capable of being a cheater? *Thirty seconds.* But what if a kiss is all I need to decide whether to stay with Trip? What if I could finally know for sure how I feel? *Ten seconds.* What if I already am a cheater because my heart isn't where it should be? "Going live in five, four, three . . ."

We air the news without a hitch. Dan the Weatherman recaps his predictions for the weekend. No rain. Forget the umbrellas. Remember the sunscreen. The anchors wave good-bye. The credits roll. *Badda bing, badda boom.* I'm outta here.

The second I enter my apartment, I turn on the faucet to get warm water running. I eat a spoonful of peanut butter, wash my face, reapply deodorant. I pull on my just-washed dusty-red corduroys and a soft black T-shirt, put on the toe ring, lace my sneakers.

My phone chirps. It's Trip. I decline the call.

It chirps again. This time, it's Martha texting back, finally. "10–4."

It's already 7:50. Time for the pièce de résistance: cat eyes. I pump the tube and swipe the liner over my right lid. Nailed it. I try again on the left. Damn. After a few more attempts and six Q-tips, I am pretty close to having the look I want: nonchalant, don't-give-a-damn, what-the-hell, take-me-or-leave-me sexy.

Before leaving, I place my engagement ring in my medicine cabinet, behind an old tube of Retin-A. It could fall off at the concert, right? Better safe here.

At Dudley's, the bar closest to the Music Farm, Martha waits for me. She sits at the lacquered bar, poking at a green olive in her martini glass with a teensy straw. She's wearing lipstick. It's a burgundy-wine shade. "That's a new look," I say.

"I do it all the time," she says.

Never, in all our years together, has she worn lipstick.

The bartender slaps a cocktail napkin in front of me before I have the chance to speak. His bicep is covered by tattoos, mostly of cartoonish monsters with goofy, bulging eyeballs. "What'll it be?"

I consider a martini but don't want olive breath. I stick with the plan. Isn't that what successful generals of invading armies do? "I'll have a gin and tonic, please." Martha lifts a freshly painted fingernail to signal she's ready for a second. "And another martini for her." I pull out my credit card to start a tab and glance at my ticket to double-check the start time of the show.

"You bought a ticket?" Martha asks.

"Online. I printed it out," I say. "What now?"

"Nothing . . ."

"You can't just say that, Martha. *What?*"

"You know what." Martha plays with her straw against her teeth. She should bleach them.

"No, I don't."

"Just be careful. He plays in a band, Simons. I know you and your little fairy-tale princess romances. I just don't want you to get hurt, that's all."

"It's not like that," I say, but I can feel my flushed cheeks betray me. "And what does that have to do with my ticket, anyway?"

"They're not a big band, Simian. They won't sell out or anything, that's all."

"I like this kind of music. I love music . . ."

"Simons, you couldn't name one band that doesn't get radio play." She eats her olive and licks the juice from her fingers.

* * *

A dozen people loiter near the entrance of the Music Farm, nearly all of them sucking on cigarettes with laser-like focus. The crowd is mostly college-age. The bouncer checks IDs with a flashlight. He draws black X's on the hands of the underage girls ahead of us.

Martha's right: the concert won't sell out. There aren't even eighty people here. Neon lights flash and swirl overhead; a large disco ball spins and throws shimmery squares of light all around us. We find a spot near the bar. Martha orders a Budweiser. Sticking with the plan, I ask for a water.

Harry appears onstage, walking toward his drums. Before he sits on the circular seat in the middle of his drum set, he pulls two drumsticks from his back pocket. He presses rhythmically on a foot pedal, creating a steady, tribal beat that awakens the room.

"Hello. Hello." A velvety voice booms. The lead singer of his band, Stone's Throw, cups a microphone in his hands.

A few girls in the front row cheer and lift their beers. "We love you, Jason!" one screams. Jason plucks out a few bars from

"The Star-Spangled Banner" on his cherry-red guitar. The girls in the front hoot some more. Jason turns back to look at his bandmates. "Y'all ready?"

I recognize the third member. It's Harry's best friend, Randy, from high school—the one who spoke in Harry's defense when he got caught smoking cigarettes. Randy plays the electric bass. He nods to Harry, who strikes his drumsticks overhead.

A gritty sound pours from the stage and pools into the empty spaces around me. It enters my mouth, my bloodstream. I let it overtake me.

Harry doesn't bother to look up for most of their set. He wears a Braves baseball cap pulled low; it hides his eyes. His lower lip glistens in the passing flashes of light. His arms and legs seem to move independently of each other. I'd never studied the movements of a drummer before, and I'm transfixed. I could watch him for days. In what feels like minutes, their set is over.

"Thank you!" Jason waves and lifts his guitar. The crowd has swelled now to several hundred who have come to see the headliner.

Martha heads toward the wooden staircase alongside the concert pit. It's cordoned off. She removes the rope and sails confidently up the stairs. I follow closely behind, nervous that a bouncer will bark at us. No one says anything, though. At the top of the stairs, she pushes open a dingy door and enters the green room.

Jason, Randy, and Harry are already seated, fresh beers in hand. Jason and Randy sprawl at either end of a ratty couch.

Harry's against the far wall in a torn leather armchair. Martha takes the only open seat in the room, between Randy and Jason.

A guy with a Music Farm badge enters the room. "Good show, guys." He lights a cigarette and reaches across a low table to hand one to Martha. She takes it without saying a word and falls back into the couch like she's watching *Jeopardy!* reruns in her living room.

Unsure of where to stand, I lean against the wall. I'm exposed. Perhaps unwelcome. I change my strategy. "I'm going to get a beer."

"We've got free beer up here," Harry offers. He disappears into a storage room and quickly reemerges with a PBR and a metal folding chair. I try to look as disinterested as possible when he hands me a cold one and opens the chair, placing it next to his seat.

The guys discuss the Music Farm's new sound system. Martha coolly chain-smokes, giving occasional, surprisingly tech-savvy advice on how to control the reverb. She and the guy with the badge exchange thoughts on something about "settling." I guzzle my beer, hoping to think of something helpful to say.

Thankfully, the thrash of a guitar fills the room. The main act has started. There's a hole in the wall that gives a profile view of the stage. I walk over to it. The band performs one song, then another, and I sink at the thought that Harry might not join me. Without warning, an arm grazes against mine. I jump.

"Whoa there, didn't mean to scare you." He moves in closer, stands behind me. His hot breath tickles my ear. "So, are you going to come to my show and not talk to me?"

I wriggle my empty can. "I'm just here for the free beer."

"Oh, really?" He traces a finger along the outside of my arm.

This would be a time to win him over with my wit, if I had any. "Yep."

We spend the next hour watching the show, moving apart only for Harry to fetch more PBRs. Every now and then our bodies touch; each time an electric charge surges through my core. I drink another beer, then another; with each swallow I suppress the voice that says, *Simons, what if Trip saw you? You know you still have to go to work tomorrow, right?*

Harry runs a finger down my neck, unzipping my inhibitions. He presses his pelvis into my back, reaches his hand around my waist. His hand rises up to my throat, pulling my head back to kiss him. I'm aware of this, but more as an observer than as a participant. I follow the lead of my body, of his body, and we kiss.

I feel young, gorgeous, and brave. I feel daring and sexy. I also feel drunk.

"Thank you, Charleston!" The lead singer waves and the crowd cheers, jerking me back to reality. The floodlights turn on over the stage and in the greenroom. The invisible becomes visible: stains on the carpet, cracks on the walls, dried paint peeling from the ceiling. Everything looks dirty, defiled, and profane. *Fuck.* I just kissed another man. "Harry, I've got to go."

Harry moves to block my exit, his large shoulders a citadel. "Stay."

I want to stay, but this is not how I want to start my new life without Trip—as a drunk cheater. I'm not being brave; I'm being a coward. "I have to go. I'll see you soon?"

"I don't know."

Is he teasing? With his eyes shaded by his ball cap, it's hard to tell. The room starts to spin. A wave of nausea rises from my gut. I swallow hard. "Goodnight." I spin toward the staircase, gripping the railing on the way down. My head throbs, the pulsing of my temples intensifying with each step. But beneath the beat of pain is a thought that's clear, pure, and unequivocal: now is the time to end it with Trip.

On King Street, there are no private places to make a call. Around the corner is an empty back alley, quiet, lonely, anonymous. I sit on a small stoop beneath an awning and dial Trip. The phone rings and rings.

Well, shit.

I stand to leave but am tossed back to the steps by crushing nausea. A gripping force seizes my body. I throw up, heave over and over. Soon, mercifully, there is nothing left. When I lift the back of my shaking hand to wipe my sticky face, the name of the store comes into view: Lowcountry Bikes. It's one of the few remaining independently owned businesses uptown, and the small group of retailers running the joint help lead the charge in converting our dangerous roadways into safer biking routes. *Oh my God*, I'm such an asshole. I find a couple of dead magnolia leaves to scrape my throw-up off the steps. With my stomach empty but my head still pounding, I stumble home.

12.

Breaking News

The ceiling fan grinds above me. A lavender light shoots through my blinds. Beeping assaults my ears. I punch my alarm off. It's 7:30.

I'm still wearing my dusty-red pants and black T-shirt from the night before. When I pee, my urine spreads like bright orange dye in the bowl.

My stomach rumbles. I'm ravenous. With trembling hands, I fry two eggs in olive oil and toast some bread. I chew with my mouth open; I gulp my water—all the bad eating habits Mom trained me to avoid. I have no extra energy for formalities. On my way back to bed, my gaze settles on the vase of wilting zinnias. I set my alarm for 8:20 and fall back to sleep.

What seems like seconds later, the alarm blares again.

* * *

At the office, the news team gathers for the morning meeting. I dry heave when a videographer walks past with a microwaved burrito. Justin sniffs me out. "Late night?" he asks. "I have some Ensure if you want it."

"Oh, no—thanks, though," I say, almost gagging at the idea of drinking anything other than water. Besides me and Justin, there are four people at the meeting: Meghan, the six-o'clock producer; the technical director; and two production assistants. We are waiting on Angela.

Meghan looks up from her phone. "Isn't that for old people?"

"I drink it before I lift. It's also good if you don't have time to eat or something."

"Oh." Meghan returns to thumbing a message. One of the production assistants yawns. Justin's knee bounces at a furious pace as he reviews his notes. I pass the time hoping for a good burp to settle my stomach.

My phone vibrates: four missed calls from Trip and a text. **"Are you okay?!?!?"**

Before there is time to process, Angela arrives, shaking a breakfast drink. "What have you got?"

Justin pitches a story about the shortage of skilled workers in the restaurant industry. He adds that he plans to follow up on the murder case we ran at the top of all the newscasts yesterday. Meghan wants to give an update on the Isle of Palms residents working to save baby sea turtles from disorientation caused by renters leaving the lights of their beach houses on all night. She suggests the story could tie in nicely with the Sullivan's Island controversy over the resurgence of the coyote population.

"Simons?"

My stomach somersaults. "I think it would be interesting to

interview the independent store owners, to see where they fit in with all this new development." Perhaps a story on the district could give Lowcountry Bikes some more business and help my karma.

She shakes her drink. "You mean on upper King?"

I nod, because she's right, but also because I'm afraid to speak; I might throw up. My phone vibrates again. It's Trip. I need to call off the wedding, to salvage what little integrity I have left. But I can't do it here, not while I'm at work. Why does he keep calling?

"Okay, let's start with Justin at the top of the six to cover the murder. We'll do some national news and then segue into the restaurant bit. Meghan, give what you have about sea turtles to our resident tree hugger." Angela winks at me. "Run the King Street story at the seven, too." We wait for more instruction, but there is none. Angela waves us away, and we scatter like roaches.

I sit at my desk to begin the long slog of research and writing. My work phone rings. *So shrill.* "WCCC News 14."

"There you are!" It's Trip, and he sounds more annoyed than relieved. "I've been trying to reach you since last night. I heard this awful noise, like maybe you were hurt or . . ."

"What? I can't talk right now."

"You called *me*, Simons, at eleven fifty-four last night. I heard all this noise and was practically screaming through the phone to get your attention . . ."

"Trip, I am so confused. I'm at work . . ."

"I know. I called your work phone."

"Yeah. Oh." *Oh.* The details of last night swim into focus. I did call him last night. I must have left the phone on while I was puking my guts out on the threshold of a bike store. Oh my God, I am such a mess. "Trip, I was sick, but I'm okay now. I need to talk to you, though. Can we talk later?"

"Simons, what's going on? I deserve to know."

I'd rather wait a day, giving me time to talk to Laudie, to hear her story, get her advice. But Trip is right. He deserves to know. Now. I tell him I'll call him back from my cell once I'm outside the office and at a spot where I can have privacy.

"Simons." It's Angela, who's surprisingly agile when it comes to popping up out of nowhere. This time, she arrives with a swoosh, still seated in her rolling office chair. She plants her feet inches away from my desk. "There's more to the Sonny Boykin story, I just know it. He was leaving an apartment complex. Judges don't live in apartments." She chews her thumbnail, raw and wet from anxious gnawing. Still, she wears a smile on her face.

"I've got to take a personal call outside."

"Okay, well, hurry up."

Past the break room, on the opposite side of the building's parking lot, there is a small clearing next to a retention pond. My only company are the geese trolling the fresh-cut grass, shitting as they go. I find a spot in the shade of the lone willow tree and phone Trip. It's not where or how I'd planned to make the call, but it will have to do.

"Trip, I want to call off the wedding." There, I said it. No backpedaling. No excuses. I wait for him to speak. Nothing. My phone shows we're still connected. "Trip, I said—"

"I heard you." A long silence is followed by the creak of an office chair. "You'd better be sure. You can't unsay this."

"Trip, I'm sorry." What else is there to say? I *am* sorry. I am sorry I am not in love with him anymore. I am sorry I have this aching need to be apart from him. I am sorry I have a wandering eye. And I am so sorry I kissed Harry.

"So, what does this mean? Are we single?"

"We could take break for a while. Like, six months or something."

"Ha. A break. From our relationship? Like a gym membership?"

"I'm not trying to be funny. I'm just trying to figure this out."

"Let me get this straight. You want to break up for a while and try to get back together in six months."

"Then we could have a talk. See where we are."

"Okay, well, *wow*." After another long pause, he says, "I'm not sure what else to say right now. I need some time to process this."

"Okay," I say, thankful that he's the one ending the call.

"Goodbye, Simons," he says, sounding a bit more ominous than I'd like.

And then, it's over. We're separated. I tilt my head up to the sky and spread my arms, opening my chest to the universe to cast off guilt and receive the thrilling gift of sudden freedom. I did it. I answer to no one. I'm untethered. Unburdened. Unleashed into this wide world. Yet there's a heaviness—in the atmosphere, in my heart—that lingers.

13.

Prima Ballerina

Laudie invited me for lunch at 1:00 p.m. on Saturday, the time Tito plays chess at Battery Hall. I haven't told Laudie about the breakup yet, but it seems she somehow knows. When I walk into the kitchen, she hugs me tight and lets me cry. "I did it, Laudie. I called off the wedding. I had to. I kissed someone." I can't see her face. I'm not sure if I want to.

"Do you love Trip?"

"I care about him so much."

"But do you love him?"

"Not as much as I should."

"Oh, sweetie." She hands me a tissue. "Life gets messy when our hearts don't feel like they're in the right place." She guides me to a seat at the table. A pitcher of iced tea sweats on the sweetgrass place mat. She places a bowl in front of me: cantaloupe topped with cottage cheese and raisins: a feast for a prima ballerina. She retrieves her lunch from the counter and takes a seat.

"Do you think I made a huge mistake?"

"It depends on what you do next. Whatever you decide, don't do it out of fear."

"Be brave, huh?"

"That's right, the moral of the story. And now it seems like it's more important than ever for you to hear." She slides her bowl, untouched, to the side, clearing the space between us. "I was nineteen. Your grandfather and I were dating at the time. Girls got married young those days. We weren't engaged yet, but I knew he had marriage on his mind. And I knew if I ever wanted to be on my own, I had to leave before he proposed. I had read about this woman, Dorothy Alexander, in the paper. She had founded the Atlanta Civic Ballet. There was nothing like it anywhere else in the South, and she was looking for more dancers. I told Mother and Daddy that if they didn't give me their blessing, I'd go to the tryouts anyway and take a bus in the middle of the night to get there.

"They knew I was serious. Mother rang the Pruitts to ask if I could ride with them when they went to drop Mary off at Agnes Scott." She chuckles. "Oh, we had a grand time driving there, packed like sardines with all our suitcases, singing show tunes and eating egg salad sandwiches. As you can imagine, Tito was furious."

"For leaving."

"Yes, for leaving him. Of course he never knew about all the fun I was having."

"Like what? What did you do?"

"I went to the theater whenever I felt like it. I'd go to the river. I even jumped off a train trestle."

"What? How high?"

"Must have been twenty feet."

"You daredevil."

"One night, on a full moon, some of the boardinghouse girls and I went skinny-dipping. There was a big house across the street with a pool. I had noticed the family must have left town on vacation, so we all did it on a dare."

"Wow."

"If your grandfather found out, he would probably have had me committed."

"Just for having fun?"

"I think it bothered him that I wanted to see if I could make it on my own."

"Why would that bother him?"

"Because girls from good families didn't go off and work."

"Tell me about your job."

"My roommate at the boardinghouse helped me get that job as a secretary for a manager at Coca-Cola. I typed letters and ran errands and all that sort of stuff. I got a paycheck and was proud of it, but I was still just a little helper like the rest of the girls. In the end, most of them were there to meet their husbands, anyway.

"I had other aspirations. I wanted to be onstage. I wanted something different for my life. I think your grandfather found that threatening. A lot of people found that threatening."

I take the last bite of my doll-size meal. "It makes perfect sense to me."

Laudie leans across the table to cup my chin. "I knew you'd understand." She covers her lunch, which she never touched, with cling wrap and puts it in the refrigerator. "Come upstairs with me so I can get some time in at the barre before Tito gets home."

We walk to her room, where she changes into her ballet clothes. I wonder if I should stop her, but I can't. It would be like stopping a person from prayer. She lays her day skirt at the foot of her bed and places her Capezio heels on the rug just beneath it. She ties on her ballet skirt and uses her finger to hook the heel of her ballet flats around the back of her feet. Her movements are slow but deliberate and graceful. A quiet peace surrounds her.

I follow her to the hallway, plop onto the floor. From here, Laudie looks taller, prettier, robust even. She floats her left arm up, still in the removable cast. She dips into a demi-plié. "The dancing in Atlanta—I'd never seen anything like it. It was just wild."

"The ballet?"

"Oh no, that was different. I practiced every day for those auditions. I used my windowsill as the barre and kept hitting my foot on the bed." She laughs to herself. "I loved ballet, but I loved to go out dancing, too.

"The kids danced differently in Atlanta, not like they did here." Her eyes dart around the room, as if to catch sight of the memory. "They did the jitterbug and the Lindy Hop and all that, but they danced like banshees, like they had a fever or something. The boys twirled the girls so fast their dresses stayed lifted above their knees for the whole song." She cocks her head to the side, as though someone is watching her, and she's allowing him the pleasure.

"That's where you met someone." This, I knew, was the real secret.

"Yes, I did. His name was John. And I remember thinking his skin glowed, like a golden idol's. He looked heavenly, Simons. He really did. And he had an easy way about him, a sort of lightness I had never seen in a man. He danced that way, too. Light as air. I'd never danced like that before, but my body knew what to do. I could handle any turn he could come up with. Soon we were going steady. He'd take me out to dinner, and then we'd go to the nightclubs. The music there, it put everyone on fire. We'd dance all night, drinking gin. Then on the way home, we'd end up necking by the cemetery." She turns to me with a luminous smile. "Do you still call it that?"

"No," I say with a laugh, "but I know what you mean."

She extends her right leg toward the barre, but it doesn't catch the first time. I uncross my legs and tent my fingers on the rug, readying my body to sprint toward her. She tries again, dipping backward ever so slightly, before hooking her foot in place.

Part of me knows I should stop her; she could fall and hurt herself again. But the other half, the braver half, knows that ballet is her passion. Her first love, however, must have been John. Where is he now? After all these years, do they keep in touch? Is she hiding a stash of love letters somewhere? "What happened to him?"

"What happened to who?" A voice floats up from the first floor, feet pound on the stairs. When Mom's face emerges just above the top step, her eyes widen with alarm. "Mother! What are you doing at the barre?"

"Oh hush," Laudie says, but something causes her body to pitch to the side as though she's been pushed. Mom darts behind Laudie to steady her. I race to other side. We prop her up, like legs to an easel, and lift her back to standing. "Simons," she hisses, "were you just going to watch until Mother fell and sprained her other wrist or something worse? Help me put her in her bed."

I drape Laudie's right arm over my shoulders. Mom takes her left. Laudie walks, leaning heavily on us to make it to her room. We lay her on the bed. Mom swipes some extra pillows from Tito's side of the bed and stacks them behind Laudie.

"I'm fine. Y'all go on now. I just need a little nap." Laudie flicks her good wrist at us, waving us away, insisting we're not needed.

But I can't go yet. If Tito finds her in bed in this state, wearing her ballet flats and skirt, he'd rip the barre from the wall himself. "Laudie, scooch your hips over." I untie her ballet skirt and slide it from beneath her. I wish she would protest, say she can do it herself, but she's too tired. I walk to the foot of Laudie's bed to pull the ballet flats from her feet.

Arms crossed, Mom watches wordlessly while I tuck the contraband items deep inside Laudie's chest of drawers. When I reach for Laudie's day skirt, Mom surprises me by getting onto the other side of the bed. "Mother, lift your hips up." Together, we hike the skirt over Laudie's willowy, exhausted legs.

"You have to promise me you'll stop going to the barre," Mom says.

"Y'all quit fussing over me. I just need some rest."

Mom closes the curtains and motions for me to follow her out into the hallway. "Simons, I know you mean well. But one bad fall could kill her. Promise me you won't let her do that again."

I can't promise that, so I say the next best thing. "I'm sorry, Mom."

14.

Crab Crack

Six blue crabs rattle in a white bucket at my feet, blowing bubbles and pinching one another's legs. A gigantic stainless-steel pot boils on the stove. Steam billows overhead, making the already-toasty kitchen even hotter. I dump the blue crabs inside. They die instantly, I hope. When they pinken, I drain the pot and carry our Monthly Monday dinner to the porch.

For the crab crack, Weezy and I have assembled newspapers, paper towels, heavy spoons, and a bowl of water. Weezy wears an old nursing bra and some stretchy biker shorts. Her growing belly pokes out beneath a tank top. Our legs need shaving. Dirt collects in the spaces between my toes, beneath my nails. We've wrapped our hair in careless buns, high off our necks. We sit on the floor.

Weezy goes for the claws first. She cracks the shell open with a mallet. I start by prying off the carapace. Warm goop drips from my fingers to the newspaper. I use a spoon to scrape away the gills. I swish the carcass around in the water bowl to clean off excess innards. After I break the body in half, it strikes me that everything about cooking and eating crabs is somewhat violent.

A small pile of smashed, broken shells accumulates between us. We take turns feeding Francie pieces of the sweet flesh. She asks for more, and we give her as much as she wants. I sink into the rhythm of our picnic, enjoying the companionable absence of conversation as we hammer on the shells and suck the legs hollow.

"Simons, you have something you want to tell me?"

"What?"

"You've barely said a word since we left town."

Four days have passed since I kissed Harry, three days since my phone call with Trip. I haven't told a soul other than Laudie, and Laudie keeps her secrets. I guess Trip hasn't said anything either, because in the insular world of Old Charleston, news travels fast. I was going to tell Weezy about the breakup; I've been waiting for the right time, but there will never be a right time. Best to get it over with. "I told Trip I don't want to get married."

"What?!" Weezy is all eyes. "What happened?"

"I think we just grew apart. Or at least I grew apart."

"It's the long distance. Most couples can't survive it. I said that. I said you should just quit your job and move to Columbia."

"I remember."

"Columbia isn't that bad. It's actually a lot of fun. There's that river running through the city, and that art museum is really top-notch."

"I know."

Crab juice pools on the funnies section. The ceiling fan churns noisily above us. "It's not about Columbia, is it?"

"No."

"Why didn't you tell me?"

I keep my head down, avoid eye contact. "I didn't want to upset you. Or disappoint you. Everyone seemed so happy."

"Yeah, but you are the one who is getting married. You are the one who is supposed to be happy."

"Thanks."

She gasps at a new thought, holding her spoon high like a weapon. "Did he cheat on you?"

"No. Of course not." I wipe my chin with a paper towel and debate whether to tell her about the kiss. I don't think she would ever understand; she'd never look at me the same. "Weezy, can we not talk about this anymore?"

"I'm your sister. I'm supposed to know these things. How did I not know y'all were having problems? I feel terrible."

"Don't feel terrible."

Weezy scoots over and pulls me in for a hug. "Are you sure this is what you want?"

"I think so." My voice has risen into a high, mewling register and won't come down. "It felt wrong to be with him. Something wasn't right. But not being with him doesn't feel exactly right either. Did it feel right with Ashley?"

"Yes. I have to say it always felt right." She lifts her shoulders as though Ashley is behind her this very minute, giving her a squeeze.

"Like, you never felt you had to change to make your relationship work?"

"Change who I am? No. Definitely not." She bangs open another claw with a spoon. "Don't get me wrong. We have our moments."

"Like what?" They don't get along sometimes? They seem to always get along.

"Like when he watches Francie, he calls it 'babysitting.' And he leaves the toilet seat up. Little stuff like that. Of course, I'm not perfect, either. I'm a slob. I don't dress as nicely as I used to."

"Weezy, you're pregnant."

"Anyway, it's a give-and-take. But marriage is worth it, for sure."

"Hmm."

"What about babies? I've got at least two single friends sleeping with random men without protection they're so desperate to have kids. The biological clock thing is real."

"I don't know if I want kids. Francie is adorable, but I don't feel a strong desire to have one."

"Then what do you want?"

I pile the glistening white flesh on the newspaper. "I guess I need to figure that out."

Weezy half frowns, half smiles. "Mom's going to lose it when she finds out."

"I know."

"When are you going to tell her and Dad?"

"Tomorrow."

Weezy coughs out a piece of crab. "Dangit. While I'm here?"

"Jeez, Weez. I'm sorry to inconvenience you."

"Just kidding. You know I have your back."

"Thanks. That means a lot."

"I know."

* * *

After Francie falls asleep, Weezy and I slip on our flip-flops and ease open the creaky front door. I told Weezy we might be able to see some phosphorescence. She surprised me by saying she'd like to check it out. There are no other docks in sight, no houses, no man-made lights. We don't bring a flashlight; our eyes adjust to the darkness. It's a spectacular Lowcountry night. Beneath this dome of stars, we could well be inside a jewel box.

Weezy cranes her neck to look up. "Thanks for dragging me out here, Sims. I'm half thinking of waking Francie up to see this."

In single file, we make our way down the warped boardwalk planks. Beneath us, in the low plain of the marsh, tidal creatures treat us to a percussive performance. Shrimp pop as they leap from the water to escape predators. The oyster beds click, expelling old water for new. Marsh hens squawk in the spartina grass. Trolling stingrays splash in the shallows.

I guide Weezy onto the floating dock. We step carefully on the wobbly platform, its bobbing motion creating a wake in the otherwise still waters of the slack tide. I bounce on the dock's edge to agitate the water. The dinoflagellates ignite; tiny bursts of unearthly, surreal-green sparks flare and die—an entire cosmos at the tips of my toes. I dip a foot into the warm water to stir up more magic.

I fetch a paddle from an overturned kayak and hand it to Weezy. She drags the paddle through the water, making figure eights. The motion brings millions of microscopic creatures to life. What we see is an underwater fireworks show. "Wow," says Weezy. "I never grow tired of seeing this."

"I know. Magic." I don't just want to look at it; I want to be in it. I strip. A light breeze slides over my shoulders and down my spine. I jump high into the pewter night and plunge into the luminous water. It's like swimming in a liquid Milky Way.

Weezy lowers herself in from the swim ladder. "Oh my God, it feels *great* in here." She flips onto her back. Her bulging breasts and belly are radiant in the bath of starlight and phosphorescence. I watch her for a moment to be sure she's got her bearings. Because of the slack tide, she doesn't need to fight a current. But still, she's a pregnant lady. When it's clear she's floating comfortably, I swim toward the creek's center.

I turn onto my back, too, baring my body and soul to the world. A scintillating dome is formed by Orion's Belt, the Big Dipper, and a million other stars, visible and invisible. A shooting star courses overhead, slicing the sky. When is the last time Laudie saw a comet? I should take her out to see the stars.

"Simons?" The voice is faint. "I need some help, Simons."

Twenty feet away, Weezy struggles to pull her body out of the river. I race toward her. She's made it to the middle rung of the swim ladder, but can't manage to hoist herself up. I grip the rails and ram my shoulder beneath her bottom to give her a push.

"Ouch! You are so bony," she says, laughing.

"Are you okay?"

"I'm fine. I've just lost all my ab muscle already and I'm not even halfway done with this pregnancy."

"Just take your time."

"Oomph." She moans as she lumbers up the ramp. I scramble behind her to gather our clothes. Wet and naked, beneath the stars, we walk back to the cabin.

15.

The Talk

Mom and Dad arrive the next afternoon. Tonight, we feast on a classic Lowcountry summer supper: boiled shrimp, fresh corn on the cob, sliced Edisto tomatoes. Mom dotes on Francie, peeling shrimp for her grandchild.

Dad chews in silence, looking content but tired. He still hasn't changed out of his business suit, but he at least removed his jacket and flipped his tie over his shoulder. He worked through the weekend and just finished his case today, so he's taking the rest of the week off.

Mom sits to my left. She wears a tennis skirt and smells of sunscreen. Since the news about Judge Boykin has died down, conversations with my family are less strained, at least for everyone else. Mom is trying to pin down a day for wedding-dress shopping. Weezy locks eyes with me. I know what she wants me to do, but I'm not ready to make the big announcement. "Soon," I mouth.

Mom's eyes dart from Weezy to me. "What?" she asks. "What is it?"

Dad looks up from his plate. "Simons, answer your mother."

In our life as a family unit, we've been fortunate not to have to share much bad news. When I wrecked Mom's car my sophomore year in high school, they changed my curfew to 9:00 p.m. until I paid off the premium with my babysitting money. I didn't make enough that summer, but they took what I had and said they were just glad no one got hurt. When our dog, Spot, died, my parents mourned for a few weeks, but then Mom found she didn't miss the dog hair and Dad was thrilled he no longer had to scoop poops from the garden. My parents will bounce back from this news, too. Surely. Well, here goes nothing.

"I broke up with Trip. We're taking time apart." I don't know why, but I laugh. Nerves, probably.

Mom spins in her chair to face me. "This isn't funny, Simons."

"I'm not trying to be funny."

Weezy reaches for my wineglass; Mom bats her hand away. "It's not good for the baby." She turns to Dad. "Ed?"

He's sitting straighter now, looking a little more awake. "Is this true, Simons?"

"Yes."

"So you are calling off the wedding?"

"For now," I state, though it comes out like a question.

It's Dad's turn to speak, but he doesn't say a word. He doesn't even look at me. Instead, he drops his napkin on his plate, rises from the table, and walks down the hall. I'd rather be yelled at.

In silence, we watch Dad disappear into the bedroom. Even

Francie watches. Mom pushes her half-eaten dinner to the middle of the table and plunks her face into her hands. "I just don't understand."

What is there to explain? She never had to make her relationship work. It just worked.

"Have you thought this through, Simons?"

"Yes, I have thought this through! I have been thinking about it for a long time." As gently as I can manage, I add, "Don't you want me to be happy?"

"Of course I want you to be happy. But you don't know what happy *is*, Simons. Happiness comes from stability."

"Yeah, but, Mom . . . you've never lived life on your own. You don't know what you're missing. You've always either been taken care of by Tito or by Dad. Maybe you don't know, either . . ."

Weezy, often the umpire during bouts of disagreement between me and my parents, shoots me a warning look—a yellow card. I just stepped over a line.

Mom's voice rises. "What do you know about taking care of other people? You think we're all an island? There is nothing more important than family, taking care of family. Something you seem to have forgotten. Your job is to protect Laudie from that death trap of a ballet barre, not encourage it."

"Mom, I—"

"No, you listen. I'm your mother. I don't know what's gotten into you, but I don't like it. You're being foolish and stubborn. You have an amazing future with Trip, a future most girls only dream of, and you are about to throw it all away."

"I just need some time."

Weezy shuffles around the table, wraps her arms around Mom's shoulders. "Mom, Simons is trying to do what is right for her. We should give her our love and support. People make better decisions when they feel supported. We can all agree we want her to make good decisions, right?"

In Weezy's embrace, Mom calms down. She twists the stem of her wineglass. "Simons, I want you to seriously consider re-thinking your decision. There's still time."

I want to tell her that what's done is done. A fait accompli. I can't go back now. I finally had the courage to listen to my heart, or some sort of distant thrumming of it. Still, I know what I have to say. "Okay, Mom. I'll think about it."

Mom leaves her corn and shrimp unfinished. Before she disappears down the hallway, she warns, "Not a word to your grandmother. It will put her in her grave."

16.

Fences

Martha told me about a house party. She didn't specify if Harry would be there, but my heart quickened at the possibility. It's the weekend, so I don't get off work tonight until 11:30. I told Martha I could be there by midnight.

The eleven-o'clock show moves smoothly. Per usual, our weekend audience gets the full weather report. "Showers later this week will cool things off a bit, but the next few days will be in the high nineties. Put on that sunscreen and make sure to keep Fido and Kitty hydrated. It's hot out there, folks!"

Thank you, Dan the Weatherman.

The party is on James Island, two bridges away. I pull off Folly Road and enter a subdivision named, elegiacally, Carolina Parakeet Manor, for the now-extinct birds that once flourished here. They were hunted for their feathers, which haberdashers used to embellish ladies' hats in the nineteenth century.

I drive in circles through the subdivision. I should have turned on the GPS. House after brick ranch house rolls past.

Each has an identical lawn stretching to the street. Each has an attached garage. Only one is lit. Cars are parked on both sides of the street. Finally. Bingo.

I tap the brass knocker. No one hears me, so I push the door open. A few heads spin my way. None are familiar faces, but they do smile back.

The minuscule living room is ablaze with light. It's easy to tell a bachelor lives here. First, the room has just one sofa but two enormous flat-screen TVs. Bare floor. No rugs. No potted spider plants or fiddle-leaf figs. A Bud Light poster hangs above the mantel; a busty blonde in a bikini winks at me. Air conditioning pumps furiously from a window unit. Scented candles flicker on a coffee table. The air reeks of a Yankee Candle flash sale.

In the kitchen, I find Martha, alone. Is she waiting for me? She leans against the sink beneath the only light in the room—a buzzing fluorescent. Still, her hair shines like obsidian. Her skin reminds me of Mom's porcelain claw-foot tub—white, smooth, cool to the touch. "There you are." She lifts her cup, a 1920s-looking coupe, and purses her mulberry lips over the rim to take a dainty sip.

"Martha, I did it. I called it off with Trip."

"Holy shit, Simian." She reaches for my head and tousles my hair. "Who knew you could be such a rebel?"

"Yeah, I can't believe it myself."

"Nothing like a little gift from Martha to get the ball rolling." She winks.

I want to ask if Harry is here, but for some reason I feel that asking that question will downshift the mood. "Thanks for being my friend through all of this. You've had to listen to me talk about Trip a lot."

"Well, now you're going to talk to me about all the kinky sex you're gonna have." Martha gestures broadly around the room. "Welcome to the wild and fucked-up world of the single life. The booze is out back on the table under the tree. Grab a drink and come back immediately."

"You want to come with me?"

"Too fucking hot."

"You won't get lonely?"

"I've already talked to every loser here. Just hurry back."

I open the back door and enter a scene that makes me glad to be young, single, and free: people talking, laughing, and making music. I run my thumb over my third finger, left hand. No ring. No Trip. I am unattached. I am my own woman. I enter my brave, new world.

A glaring floodlight blanches the faces of a crowd milling around a keg on the patio. My eyes take a few moments to adjust. Eventually, I make out at least a dozen people under a towering longleaf pine tree that grows smack-dab in the yard's center. The night air is humid, piquant, alive with possibility. My nose detects a trace of salt and sulfur; we're not too far from the ocean.

I walk toward the bar, into the anonymity of the shadows. I lift one bottle after another trying to find one with enough wine to fill a glass. I feel around until my hands alight on the contours of a coffee mug.

"That's mine."

Harry. I'm zapped. Weak-kneed. On fire. At the Music Farm,

in the greenroom, I was an adulteress. Not now, though. He stands behind me, close enough for me to catch the commingled scent of Ivory soap and mint gum. "Would you like to share?"

"Sure," he reaches for the mug. Our fingers touch; I can almost see sparks fly.

I start to ask him about how he ended up back in Charleston, but he says he can't hear and that we'll need to move farther away from the music to talk.

Martha is waiting for me. I should return to the party to clink glasses with my best friend, celebrate my new independence. Instead, I let him lead me to a secluded spot along a wooden privacy fence. "My lounge." He gestures to some overturned buckets. A crabbing net leans against the far wall.

Harry takes a seat on the taller bucket, taps on its sides. Drumming to the music that's coming from the party, he explains he lived in Boston after college. He joined a band for a couple of years. When the lead guitarist broke his arm, he moved to Nashville for a year but couldn't find a good band to join. "Most of the gigs were for country pop bands, anyway." He eventually moved to Savannah, where he reunited with his high school pal Randy and together they formed Stone's Throw. They've been on tour for four months, and now they are taking a break.

"What about you, Lois Lane? I hear you're a reporter." He passes the mug of wine to me.

"Yeah, that's pretty close," I say.

"But it's not right."

"Right," I say. "You're right that you're wrong, I mean."

He laughs.

"I'm a producer for News 14. I basically spend my days writing what the anchors say."

"They don't write that themselves?"

"Producers do it. We decide what goes on the news, like what's in your refrigerator that's going to kill you . . . tonight at seven."

"You're funny."

Am I? Above us, the tree stretches so high that it's impossible to see its upper boughs. It seems to reach above the troposphere, into the stratosphere, and beyond into outer space itself. Time dissolves into the drumbeats, the wine, the moist night. We drink from the same cup.

He stands, takes my hand. I follow without question. He leads me into the farthest leafy reaches of the long suburban lot.

The earth beneath my feet is pliant. He's moved us to some swampy otherworld that's dense with possibility and unknowing. Placing his hands on my hips, he presses me against the fence. He rubs his hand over my breasts and up my throat. He bites my neck just behind my ear; my head tumbles to the side in absolute surrender. He kisses me. His lips are generous, supple, fuller than Trip's. Harry's tongue confidently sweeps through my mouth. He tastes like wine and an irresistible, thrilling kind of danger.

"I found you." Martha's dark figure blocks us from the party. She takes a step closer, into a sliver of moonlight. Her skin is ghostlike. She pats me on the shoulder and turns to Harry. "You hear she's newly single?"

Harry steps back from me, his strong arms limp at his sides. "Martha."

"She is, really. Hot off the press. We were going to celebrate with a drink, but then she just disappeared. But here she is, our darling southern belle."

"I'm sorry, Martha." In high school, Martha drove me to the Waffle House for chance encounters with Harry. She hand-delivered him to me at Edisto. She took me to his show, walked me up to the greenroom. Then I abandoned her when she was ready to celebrate my big leap to independence. I'm a bad friend.

All that pleasure—the energy of the starry night and the magic of the tree—now just makes me feel jittery. I made a self-ish choice, and I'm busted. The moment is over. The magic is gone. "I'd better go. I have to work tomorrow."

Harry pushes past Martha. "I'll walk you out."

I look to Martha, my decisive friend, to dole out my punish-ment. She lights a cigarette. "Better get going, then." Though she smiles at me through a stream of smoke, I can't read her eyes. I can never read her eyes.

I follow Harry but pause to yell back to Martha. "I'll call you for drinks soon. My treat."

Harry moves fast, not slowing to talk to anyone. When we reach my car, I don't immediately get inside. I hesitate, give him a chance to give me a proper goodbye kiss. Instead, he taps the hood of my car twice. "Drive safe."

* * *

It's impossible to sleep. My mind replays our kiss, Martha's inscrutable face, and how Harry patted the hood of my car. What does it all mean?

The AC hums. The ceiling fan revolves overhead. The streetlight illuminates my sheets; its white peaks and valleys look like meringue. My eye catches the gold-and-pearl necklace Trip gave me. I had draped it over the side of the vanity mirror the second Trip left and have not touched it since. At the time, the necklace felt like an exchange for my freedom. I felt that if I were to wear it, I might as well get my towels monogrammed and develop my own recipe for cheese biscuits—more cheddar, less buttermilk. But now, after another confusing night, the necklace looks like what it is and has always been: a thoughtful gift from a bighearted guy.

Tears prick my eyes. *Shit.* I can't go back to Trip now. I can't cave after finally making a bold, resolute step toward my future. I jump from bed, grab the necklace, hurl it across the floor. It slides somewhere underneath my bed, out of sight.

Back under the covers, I grab my phone to avoid thinking about Trip or Harry. The screen shows three missed calls and a voicemail, all from Mom. The voicemail begins with an audible inhale. "I know you think it's none of my business, but I just need to say that I hope you called Trip. I hope and pray it will all work out. I really do. And Caroline's debutante brunch is the last Sunday in June. I'm reminding you now so you'll have time to buy a nice dress."

17.

Ham Biscuits

Like Mom, Louisa Lachicotte married a local lawyer. Also like Mom, the only time she didn't live South of Broad was when she went off to Vanderbilt University. Louisa has been Mom's BFF since they were first graders at Crescent Academy. Mom even named Weezy after her (Louisa got shortened to Weezy). Now, they're doubles partners and both have leadership roles in the Ladies' Charleston Charities. They host parties for each other's children to celebrate major occasions. Louisa hosted a debutante brunch for both Weezy and me. Now, she's doing it for Caroline.

Louisa's house appears frozen in time. Nothing ever was—or ever will be—out of place. Perfectly manicured ficus vines grow on the risers of the steps leading up to the front piazza. In the planting bed that runs alongside the driveway, the Ligustrum must have been trimmed with embroidery scissors and a magnifying glass.

A single row of blue agapanthus provides the one touch of

color in an otherwise monochromatic landscape. "Too many colors would compete with one another, don't you think?" Louisa once asked me. While I can see her point, I prefer the bombastic, exuberant blooms of Laudie's mismatched zinnias.

Because I'll spend the better part of this day in a windowless newsroom writing stories about beach options for the July 4 weekend, I take a moment before going inside to sit on the joggling board.

Lots of Charlestonians have a joggling board on their piazzas; it's a long, thin, flexible plank of southern pine supported on either end by rockers, which moves the joggler up and down, side to side. It's traditionally painted "Charleston green," a green so dark it is barely distinguishable from black. The story goes that young, aspiring lovers would each sit demurely at one end; as an evening of bouncing and rocking wore on, girl and boy would gradually find themselves side by side at the dip in the middle.

"I'm glad I caught you," Mom calls from the front door. She wears a pleated lavender dress and kitten heels.

"Hi, Mom."

She sits next to me. The joggling board sinks a bit farther; we slide a little closer together. The Ashley River glitters in the distance. Pillowy cumulous clouds drift overhead. "Have you called Trip yet?"

"No."

"I haven't told anyone about you two. You could get back together, you know. Plus, we want to keep the focus on Caroline."

"It's a special day for her."

"It is." Mom studies her hands; she toys with a cocktail ring on her right hand.

"Is that from Dad?" She must have cashed in a few birthday gift cards.

She lifts her hand. "It's a tourmaline. Do you like it?"

Tiny white diamonds encircle a pink stone. Part of me wonders if those are blood diamonds. Another part of me wants to wear it. "I think it's pretty." I pat her skirt. "Let's go inside."

We enter the foyer. An enormous bouquet of Madonna lilies and white roses perfumes the house. A curving staircase draws my eye up toward the crystal chandelier, which, refracting light, scatters jewel-like rainbows over the crowd.

Caroline's friends look like professional models: tiny waists, shiny hair, good bones. Mom's friends also look lovely, though it's likely many have had facelifts—discreet ones, of course—and probably all have been recently Botoxed.

Young, old, and in between, we all wear dresses. Some debutantes push the hemline, but for the most part, we wear what we'd put on for an Easter service. The dresses are either in solid colors—lemon, cantaloupe, raspberry, pistachio—or else patterned with flowers. No black, brown, or beige in sight. I'm no exception. I purchased a floral dress—one with pink peonies—from a consignment store. Since Mom didn't comment on it, the dress passes muster.

The food is arrayed on old silver and Delft china platters that have been placed around the mahogany dining table. Everything on offer has been miniaturized, downsized, feminized: baby ham biscuits, mini tomato pies, itty-bitty crab cakes, and—essential at all South of Broad events—Mrs. Harley's crustless tea sandwiches on white bread. Each sandwich is bonded with liberal amounts of mayonnaise and then quartered into soft triangles. Most parties serve all four types of Mrs. Harley's sandwiches: chicken salad, pimento cheese, shrimp, and cucumber.

"Where's Laudie?" I pop a mini tomato pie into my mouth.

"She's not coming."

"Why?"

"Because Tito doesn't want her to get hurt. As I'm sure you recall, she nearly collapsed at the barre."

"You told Tito." It's hard to swallow.

"Of course I told him. He's there all day and can keep an eye on her."

"But she wants to be here—"

"It's not worth the risk, Simons."

In a rustle and blur of aquamarine silk, Louisa appears. "How are you?" she asks in the familiar drawl of a woman with a proper Charleston pedigree. Her smile exaggerates the ligaments in her neck. She flings her arms wide for a hug.

I lean in, careful not to muss her hairdo. "Hi, Louisa. It's such a lovely party. Thank you so much for doing this for Caroline."

"Of course!" She blows me a kiss, dispatching me toward the bar.

In the creamy white living room, a pair of mint-colored tufted chairs has been pushed beneath the window. A couple of Mom's friends roost on the chairs' edges, legs crossed, skirts tucked over their knees. Directly beneath a brass chandelier is the bar. On it are cocktail nuts, cloth napkins, and bottles of white wine dotted with tiny beads of water. A ladle rests in a scalloped punch bowl, which is filled to the brim with the shimmery cocktail I recall from my debutante days—the Pink Panther.

Because I need to be at work in a couple of hours, I help myself to iced tea. But then I think, *When will I ever have a Pink Panther again?* Just as I pour myself the mix of champagne, cranberry juice, and maraschino cherries, Caroline appears.

Her cheeks are naturally rosy. Her tan is even: no strap marks. And it's not sprayed on. With her yellow dress nipping in at her waist, she has a Barbie Doll figure. She comes by it authentically—she's the sister who got Laudie's figure. "Jeez, Sims. Double-fisting before noon?"

Well, that's annoying. I start to tell her that only one hand holds alcohol, but instead I go on the offensive. "I need to loosen up for your debutante striptease." I churn my hips.

"Hilarious," Caroline huffs.

"Hola, sissies!" Weezy appears behind us. Francie clings to her mother's shapeless aubergine dress. It looks out of place among the flowery frocks, but it's probably the only thing that still fits her these days. Weezy turns to me. "I just saw Laudie. She says you're taking her to a ballet in a couple weeks. That's really thoughtful of you."

Caroline coils a long, shiny lock around her slender finger. "She can't go. She nearly died the other day, Simons. Plus, Tito has her on lockdown, anyway."

"She didn't nearly die. She had a dizzy spell because she hadn't eaten her lunch."

"Well, if she can't come to my brunch, she certainly shouldn't be going to a ballet."

"She has a point, Sims," Weezy adds reluctantly.

I agree but try not to think about it.

Weezy brightens. "On another note, I've finally made a decision. I'm having this baby at a birthing center."

"Gross," says Caroline, only half-playfully. "Y'all have fun talking about that."

She spins toward a friend. I recognize her; she's the one I met at the bar who interned with Trip. Bennett. A strange flash of dislike flickers over me. I shake it off. "Aren't all babies born at birthing centers?"

Weezy sinks into the love seat, swinging Francie from her hip to her lap in one smooth, maternal motion. "You have no idea what I'm talking about, do you?"

"I'm sorry." I drop down next to her. "I've been a little preoccupied."

"So, remember right after Francie was born, she had to go back to the hospital for four days?"

"Yes, of course." It was awful. The wires and monitors attached to Francie's little body terrified me.

"Well, I've been doing some research. I found out about something called HAI, hospital-acquired illnesses. She got sick *because* she was in the hospital."

"You mean right after she was born?"

"Yes! Hospitals are where sick people go to die, Sims. It's not where healthy people should go to have babies." She taps on her belly. "I don't want this nugget to be exposed to all those germs."

"So, you're going to have the baby at a birthing center. Is that where they deliver in a tub?"

"Yeah, but you could do it on the bed or anywhere in the room. Or on the toilet, but I don't want to do that."

"No," I say with a laugh. "I wouldn't do that. Will there be a doctor?"

"A midwife." She reaches for my champagne glass.

"Take it. I don't want it."

"Good ol' Pink Panthers." Weezy takes a tiny sip. I know she's feeling a little guilty, but it's just a sip. She didn't even allow herself that in the first trimester. She's such a good mom. She's a good sister, too. I'd fall apart if anything happened to her.

What if something *does* happen during delivery? I stamp out images of Weezy taking her last breath in some blood-soaked pool surrounded by midwives rattling their amethysts and rose quartzes. "What if"—I think carefully about my phrasing— "something doesn't go as planned?"

"There's a hospital two miles away. They take you there if they think you need to go. They have a protocol and everything."

That makes me feel better. "What does Ashley say?"

"He thinks I'm nuts."

Ashley thinks gourmet coffee is nuts. He thinks going anywhere for college other than Clemson is nuts. He thinks eating any other nut than a peanut is nuts. "Well, I'm sure you've done your research. I support you."

"I know. Thanks, Sims." Weezy smiles, looking wistfully at the ceiling. "Did you know that being in warm water during delivery feels almost as good as an epidural?"

I love being in the water. Nothing's more relaxing. That makes sense. Natural. Natural is good. "What does Mom say?"

"I haven't told her." She flashes me a cheeky smile. "What the hell, maybe I'll tell her right now."

"Dangit. While I'm here?"

* * *

Mom, Caroline, and I head over to Laudie's after the debutante brunch. Mom carries a plate of Mrs. Harley's sandwiches. Caroline holds a bouquet from the party. We enter through the kitchen. "Mother?" Mom calls into the den.

The TV is on but muted. The room is otherwise dark. Laudie naps on a recliner, her face turned away from the screen. Mom places the plate on the coffee table and removes the Saran Wrap. "We brought some goodies for you."

Laudie straightens and smooths her skirt. "Thank you."

Caroline crosses the room with the bouquet. "Here, smell these lilies. They smell so good."

Laudie inhales with her eyes closed. "They're heavenly."

Mom clicks on a lamp and turns off the TV. While the room should be cheerier, it feels the same. Static and subdued. She and Caroline stand side by side, waiting for me to speak. In the car on the way over, they hatched a plan. It was up to me, they decided, to tell Laudie.

I do my best to sound positive. "Laudie, Mom and Caroline are worried that going to the ballet might not be a good idea. But we can still see it. Caroline found a video of *La Sylphide* online. We can watch it here on your TV. I'll bring snacks."

Mom clears her throat, reminding me to add another point. "It will be like having front-row seats."

My stoic grandmother—always composed—bows her head ever so slightly. A single tear rolls down her face. I can't bear to look.

18.

The Tonic

It's nearly three o'clock, and I haven't yet left the house. I slept in, ate breakfast, and then took a nap. I'm finally getting around to starting the day.

I imagine Harry would have called by now. He hasn't. What's the rule now these days? Wait a week? It's been nearly a month since the house party. Was it the kiss? I press my mouth to my forearm and test my Frenching skills like I did as a bored eighth-grader. Still good. Harry must be busy.

As I wash my face, I wonder about the other men. Surely some guy would have sniffed out my recent singleness. The last time I was single was in college, where troves of hormone-packed students flowed in and out of academic buildings and campus quick-marts. We practically rubbed up against each other to order burritos or check our mailboxes. I'm afraid in my new life, at this rate, I'll run into a potential mate about as often as I change my toothbrush. When I pick it up, fruit flies fly out from the bristles. Not good.

I head outside to my porch. The summer is quiet. Little noises—a buzzing mosquito, a distant wind chime—sound exaggerated these days. Occasionally, some kid lights a firework left over from the holiday weekend. Many residents have decamped to the Blue Ridge Mountains or up north to Cape Cod or Maine to cool off. Those who remain retreat indoors into the air-conditioning. But after long days inside my windowless office—working through the holiday weekend—I'll take the heat. I sit on a wire chair; just over the rail is a panoramic vista of quaint buildings, terra-cotta rooftops, quirky chimneys, and plenty of sky. The air is sticky hot. Every few minutes, a gust lifts my shirt, as if to try to see what's underneath.

Martha's voice pierces the silence. I lean over the railing, look through the branches of a crepe myrtle. She's walking beside a man. It's Harry. She didn't return my calls inviting her out for drinks. We haven't spoken for weeks. But here she is now, bringing him back; she's forgiven me.

Dashing inside, I whack my couch pillows into shape, kick the rug straight. I stash the dirty dishes in the oven, hide my half-eaten pasta in the back of the fridge, and run a damp rag over the countertops.

I fly into my bedroom, scoop up my underwear and inside-out pants. I shove everything in the hamper, clean or dirty. I'm straightening the sheets when I hear the knock. "Coming!"

The bathroom situation needs assessing. When did I get so messy? I ball up loose strings of dental floss and swipe the toilet top's dust bunnies with my bare hand. My engagement ring remains hidden on the top shelf of my medicine cabinet.

More knocking. *Shit*. In front of the mirror, I rake my hair with my hands to volumize it, make sure nothing is stuck in my teeth. No time to change. Opening the door, I'm careful not to sound breathy. "Well, hello, strangers."

Martha stomps past me and walks up the stairs; a six-pack of PBR bangs against her thigh.

"Hey, Simons." Harry's smile is mischievous, lopsided. His faded orange T-shirt reads "Georgia Made." It's emblazoned with a large peach that sports a provocative crevice. Leading Harry upstairs, I add a little sway to my hips.

Martha shuts the door to the porch and cranks up the window unit to full blast. "You keep it too hot in here, hippie." Her shirt, a feminine button-down with tiny polka dots, flutters in the draft of the AC. She wears lipstick again, but it's worn off a bit. "I stuck the beers in the freezer. They need some time to chill."

"I think I've got the ingredients for a gin and tonic. Want one?" They both say yes.

When I return to the living room, Martha is staring at Harry, her head dipped to the side, revealing her swanlike, creamy neck. Harry stares back at her. I feel like I've walked in on a conversation, but a soundless one, with no words exchanged.

My phone, facedown on the coffee table, buzzes. I reach for it, but Martha snatches it first. "It's Trip. Our little princess has two gentleman callers."

I grab the phone from her and silence it.

"Aw, come on. We could put him on speaker, have a little group chat."

The room temperature rises twenty degrees. I look at Martha, my eyes boring into hers, imploring her to shut up.

"Don't look so worried. I'm leaving." Martha heads for the door. Her boots pound down the hollow stairs. The old street door bangs shut. And just like that, it's me and Harry. I blink stupidly, carrying three glasses in my hands, trying to figure out what the hell happened.

Harry appears unfazed. "Cheers."

"Cheers." Now what to say? In the wake of the bizarre delivery of him by Martha, I'm utterly confused. But here he is, the man who first made me feel what it was to want a man. He snuck me out of school. He took me to the Waffle House. Then he stopped calling. But now he's back in my life. The universe has granted me a chance for bravery—with a rebel, to boot.

He lifts a shoe box of CDs off my shelf.

"The guy who had the apartment before me said I could have them."

His fingers walk over the spines of the cases; I imagine those fingers walking between my breasts, past my belly button. I cross my legs.

"The *Dookie* album. Muse. Whoa, Alien Ant Farm? I haven't heard these in forever. Here, put this on." He hands me a White Stripes album. "The drummer is a chick."

He taps a foot to the rhythm. The sun starts to set. I suck on my lime. The CD stops. He moves to sit closer. I ask him about the concerts he's played. We share Martha's drink. The bony sliver of a moon slides to the middle of a windowpane. He touches my neck; my cheeks burn. I stand to make another round.

"Uh-uh." He snags a finger through my belt loop.

I pause, frozen. What do I do? Well, I certainly can't make any decisions unless I collect some data. Experimentation is the prudent choice to make, right? He leans back, slides me on top of him. I run my hands over his shoulders and chest. It's impossible not to compare his body to Trip's. It's not better or worse; it's just not Trip, which feels traitorous. Best not to think. We kiss; he tastes like gin. His mouth finds its way to my ear; his hot breath melts what's left of my rational brain.

He peels off his shirt, then mine. With one hand, in a quick snap, he expertly removes my bra. We look at each other, eye to eye, skin to skin, soul to soul, for a short but thick moment. Am I ready to have sex? We haven't even been on a proper date yet. The cherubs on my mantel watch me with judgmental eyes. I'm no angel, I decide. I take his hand and guide him to my bedroom.

"Are you on the pill?"

I am, but I am afraid of STDs. I've never had sex with anyone other than Trip. "Do you have a condom?"

"No," he says, and I am glad he's not the kind of guy to be going around with a condom in his wallet. I think? "I'll pull out."

I feel a twitch of uncertainty. "Okay." I nod, and with that his strong arms seize my sides. He flings me onto the bed.

I am disoriented by his strength, scared and excited. He climbs on top of me, but just when I think he's done tossing me around, he lies on his back. "I want you on top."

A trace of light reaches from the lamppost and into my room, just enough to put me on display. In this grayscale light, Harry can probably see that my left breast is slightly bigger than my right, and that I haven't shaved my bikini line in a week. I suck in a little to shrink my stomach.

"Mmm . . . right there." He lowers me onto him. I wince for a moment. It hurts a little, but don't people talk about the mix of pleasure and pain?

I find myself moaning and gasping for air. I see flashes of green and white, shooting stars. He moves quicker and quicker; I become nothing but a vessel of pleasure. Soon he quits thrusting and lifts me off him. He turns to the side, his body quivering, and then is still.

While sex is—generally—a two-person deal, in this moment I feel alone in the best way, like the first-place winner at the top of the podium, gold medallion and all. By having sex with another man, I've halved some sort of claim Trip had over my body. I was his alone. Now, I've shared myself with someone else, of my own accord.

I did it. I had sex, and with a sexy musician. The big moment is over, and I'm A-okay, happy even. I still have ten fingers, ten toes. Everything turned out just fine. Martha's right: curiosity doesn't kill every cat.

* * *

Early-morning sun blanches the floors and walls, enveloping the room in a temporary haze. Harry is not in the bed. Through the slit between the door and the frame, I see him lean into the sink, bend over, and suck water from the faucet. I wonder if he used my toothbrush.

He emerges from the bathroom, his eyes puffy, fully clothed. "Good morning" I say, as casually as possible.

"I thought you were asleep." He crosses the room, his eyes on the floor. "Have you seen my shoes?"

I sit up and summon a big smile, conjuring an independent woman who can have sex—or not—and not get attached. "They're probably next to the couch."

He walks over to give me a hug, the kind of side-hug I was taught to give to campers when I was a junior counselor at Camp Ton-a-Wandah. "I'll call you soon."

I gather the covers just sloppily enough to reveal a little boob. "Bye," I say, biting my lower lip and giving him what I hope is a super-sexy look. He smiles back, and I see his eyes catch sight of my left breast—the bigger one—before he pivots and heads out of my room, down my apartment stairs.

I wonder when he'll call. Tonight?

I pick up my phone and see yesterday's missed call from Trip. He had sent a text then, too: "**I heard Laudie isn't doing well. Please tell her I say hello.**" I wait for a twinge of guilt to trickle over me, having completed the most visceral step in our separation, but I feel nothing other than tenderness for Trip. How sweet it is of him to think of her. But *wait a minute*, how would he know about Laudie?

19.

News Tip

It's another day at the office—hectic but normal. We wrapped up our morning meeting; I'm at my desk, having traded my flip-flops for wool socks, writing a story on South Carolina's miserably low rank among national school systems. Our state has wallowed in the bottom ten—and often in the bottom one or two—for decades, ever since such statistics have existed. South Carolinians often say, "Thank God for Mississippi." The latest abysmal ranking is hardly news, so this story shouldn't be difficult to write, but so far I've managed only a couple of sentences.

Instead of doing my job, I've been reviewing Harry's exit in my mind. Flashbacks replay as kaleidoscopic fragments: my twisted sheets, his no-big-deal exit, a desperate side-boob.

Today is Friday, and Harry still hasn't reached out. We had sex, for goodness sake. No flowers, no note. Doesn't copulation at least warrant a phone call? Trip and I dated for months before I took off my clothes. Maybe if Martha told me everything, I could get the facts about Harry, compartmentalize them, and finally get some work done. I reach for my phone to text her; she'll tell it to me straight. "**Can you call me?**"

She texts back immediately. "**Camping.**"

Martha camping? "**Have a sec to talk?**"

"**Need to save battery.**"

Who is she with? Could she possibly be with Harry? Maybe the whole band is going camping. Harry could have invited me. I can camp. I'm sure I can . . .

"Simons." Angela snaps open a Diet Coke. Behind her, the normally frenzied newsroom swarms like a kicked hornets' nest. "A woman is accusing Sonny Boykin of pressuring her for sex. She's young, like twenty-three, and she lives at that apartment where he wrecked his car. We're going to run it in the A block and tease the hell out of it. Justin's trying to reach her now."

Meghan runs up to Angela. "Justin got hold of her. She said Boykin texted her a dick pic."

Angela's head whips around. "We need that dick pic!"

"Justin asked her to send it. She said she was going to."

"Ugh!" Justin yells from his desk. "Sick!" We run over to Justin's desk and look at his phone, which he holds away from his body like it's a dead animal. The image is shaky, and, other than the chin, the face is completely cropped from the photo. Still, it's clearly a picture of a big, old dude with an erection.

Angela smiles a Cheshire cat smile and heads to the control room. "Blot out his dick and let's go live."

"Wait, what do we say?" Meghan asks. "That he's accused of texting a dick pic?"

"Say 'sexting,'" Angela and I respond in unison.

Back in my chair, I hope to settle my mind enough to process this craziness and write a story about it. I am grateful to be swept up in a communal commotion—away from my mind's endlessly looping images of Harry—even if it is to televise a pixilated dick pic to the citizens of South Carolina.

My fingers hover over the keyboard, but I feel . . . stared at. I spin in my chair to see Angela studying me, her head cocked to one side. She plucks the tab of her Diet Coke can. "Simons, you're a Charleston native. Aren't you related to the Boykins or something?"

Surprised it took her this long to ask, I'm relieved I can answer honestly. "No. I am not related to the Boykins," I say firmly.

She stares at me expectantly, like a dog waiting for a treat. Finally, she gives up, or maybe she decides to strike another time. She takes off, charging through the maze of cubicles. "We're going live at the next break!" she yells at everyone and no one. "We're going live!"

The control room, with dozens of monitors blinking and flashing, doesn't look much different than NASA's mission control. Sitting in the producer's chair at the back of the room, I slide on my headset, wriggle my fingers over the bank of lit-up keys, and punch the one labeled "TALENT 1." "You ready?"

On the monitor, beneath the warm studio lights, our lead anchor studies the script. She straightens the collar of her blazer. "Yep."

Justin is also in the newsroom, but he's staged away from her, giving the appearance that News 14 has more than one studio.

We don't. He stands against the far wall in front of our glossy News 14 logo, hurriedly swiping foundation over his T-zone. I ask him if he's ready. He snaps the compact shut and smiles toothily into the camera. The man does have good teeth.

The large digital clock in the corner inches us closer to the big moment. When we're within ten seconds, I start the countdown. "We're live in ten, nine, eight . . ."

Justin's face grows somber, telegenic. "We have breaking news. A sexting scandal. Judicial intern Rachel Ronan accuses Judge Sonny Boykin of pressuring her for sex and texting her lewd pictures. Earlier this summer, Judge Boykin wrecked his car outside of the Coburg Community Apartment Complex, where Ms. Ronan lives. Judge Boykin failed a field sobriety test and was taken to the station under suspicion of a DUI. He was never charged and was released without having to take a breathalyzer test. WCCC News 14 has the story. Stay tuned to hear it first."

Angela pumps her fist. She flashes Justin a thumbs-up and dashes out of the studio into the control room to scan the TV monitors tuned to our competitor stations. She wants to find out if we broke the story first. For her sake, I hope we did.

I should stay at the station at least another hour. It's what producers do when there's a story to be sniffed out. But lately I've been feeling more like a lapdog than a newshound. I don't care about Sonny. How does this information help anybody? The Army Corps of Engineers used an outdated study to determine the height of the eight-mile seawall proposed to be built around the peninsula. That miscalculation should lead the night's news. And why on earth are local authorities even thinking of approving the massive Wildcat Acres proposed development ten miles outside of the city? Those wetlands are already struggling to absorb the runoff of the suburbs nearby. Sure, the developers will make millions, but who will pay for the flood damage? Already the federal government has purchased and razed nearby homes that were constantly flooding. And yet the Department of Health and Environmental Control just agreed that developers can excavate and fill in more than two hundred acres of natural wetlands. How is that possible? Putting a bunch of houses on a floodplain is like dumping concrete into a clogged drain. I should be writing about environmental issues, not dick and balls. I wave goodbye to Angela, who's sitting at the news desk, gnawing on her thumb, her right ear glued to the police scanner.

20.

For the Birds

Giant thunderheads gather strength north of the peninsula. Shadows flicker overhead; a flock of brown pelicans flies south. I count twenty-four. They travel single file along the shoreline, using the updraft created by the sea breeze that bumps up against the dunes and beachfront houses. Somehow these gangly birds figured out that the airstream propels them along their daily commute from the rookeries to the ocean. The birds keep their expansive wings open and arched to maximize lift and minimize effort. They go with the flow. They make life seem easy.

I wrap the leash around my ankle and walk into the ocean; it's as warm as Francie's bathwater. The strength of the outgoing tide has not nearly reached its max, making the paddle past the break effortless. In the mellow waters, I slide into a seated position on my board and watch the vacant horizon.

A gelatinous purplish globe bobs by. Then another. At least a dozen float around me on the water's surface. Cannonball jellyfish: they're about the size of a cannonball, a unit of measurement any Charleston child understands. Pyramided stacks of cannonballs cemented together are another part of the statuary at White Point Garden; generations of kids have climbed on them.

A couple of days ago, hundreds of jellyfishes washed ashore. I begged Angela to let me run the story—I was sure this beachside graveyard had something to do with global warming, and I hoped maybe dead jellyfish could scare people into taking notice of the plight of our natural world. "Go ahead," Angela had said. "People love to freak out about jellyfish."

It turns out these sea creatures washed up because an onshore wind pushed them ashore. "All very normal," explained the fish and wildlife expert at the Department of Natural Resources. Today, the carcasses are mostly gone, having been eaten by crabs and gulls.

"Hey!"

A surfer paddles toward me. It's not the first time I've wandered into some surfer dude's imaginary territory. Once, I stood my ground (so to speak, since we were in the ocean), only to have my leash yanked just as I was dropping in a wave. I was a victim of some idiot's concept of a territorial pissing match. I slide my stomach onto my board and paddle parallel to the shoreline, away from him.

My thoughts wander back to Laudie's conspicuous decline; they often do these days. I know I should dwell on other, more positive things, like how she's had eighty-six good years. She lived to meet a great-grandchild. Sure, she might have missed out on a great love, but how many people really do live storybook romances?

And what about Harry? Does he ever think of me? Does Trip?

Ever since we broke up, I've felt unraveled. I'm growing tired of floating like a jellyfish through life, getting pushed around by Harry's vague gestures and unanswered calls. I want to be anchored. Maybe I should listen to Mom, ask Trip to take me back. It wouldn't be an epic love, but I'd have a life partner. Stability. We'd have children, and grandchildren, and maybe I'd live long enough to meet my great-grandchild, too.

A decent set rolls in. My board rises and falls, a toy on the belly of a waking giant. I align my board perpendicular to the shore, ready for the ocean to suck me in and shoot me out. I kick hard and paddle harder to catch the moving wall of water. I hop to my feet, lean left to steer my board along the wave. My body is propelled by the water, the wind, and—by way of the tides—the moon.

I ride the wave. For these blissful moments, my mind is in free fall, untroubled by doubts and second guesses. I am not wanted or unwanted. I am not wet or dry. I am not Simons. There is no Trip. There is no Harry. Laudie's not deteriorating. Life is pure movement.

Until it isn't.

My fin digs into the sand. The ride is over. I lift the board up under my arm and run as fast as I can back into the ocean. Maybe if I keep moving, I can keep ahead of this sinking feeling.

21.

Crumbs

At Kudu Coffee, I order an iced latte and find a seat under a tree. After ten minutes of watching the clouds and picking at my nails, I give up on Martha. Fine. I'll find something to read.

Past the ordering queue, near the bathrooms, a little shelf holds a motley assortment of abandoned books and local periodicals. I grab a copy of the *City Paper*.

"Simons?" Behind me is a lean, muscular guy. He wears fitted dark jeans. His V-neck shirt reveals some chest hair and a silver chain. Jet-black eyelashes rim his ice-blue eyes.

I have no idea who he is. "Oh, hey. It's good to see you." I fumble to make the connection. A reporter? One of Caroline's friends? I give him a smile: friendly, but not flirtatious.

"It's been, what, four, five years?"

That puts us back in college. Now I remember. Kevin. I think he was from Florida. Or was it New Jersey?

He stacks three packets of Splenda and tears them open above his coffee. When he lifts his arm to drink, a current of cologne assails my nostrils. "We should go out sometime. I just bought a boat."

He holds his gaze an extra beat. I'm sure those baby blues have won over women before, but chemistry is chemistry, and I don't feel any. Go out with this guy? Naw . . . not my type. Except when I flip through my Rolodex of polite excuses, my social calendar—full of white space—appears in the foreground of my mind. What the heck. Who knows—plenty of outstanding men wear perfume and jewelry, I'm sure. And I haven't been out on a boat yet this summer. "Sure. That would be fun."

He takes a moment to read my business card before sliding it into his wallet. "I'll text you." I know he will, and there's a comfort in that. With my copy of the *City Paper*, I return to the courtyard, feeling slightly more optimistic about life.

Outside, Martha sits at our favorite table. I messaged her to apologize for my behavior at the party, and I also thanked her for bringing Harry to my house. She didn't acknowledge those texts. She wouldn't talk on the phone or meet me in person until now. She wears a black tank top, a black maxi skirt, black boots. Leaning back, she stretches her legs so that her body is one long, dangerous line. "Who was that?" she asks, not turning her head.

"Some guy who went to Chapel Hill. He wants to take me on his boat."

With her head tilted up to the sun, I can't decide whether her exposed white throat looks vulnerable or daring. "That sounds like fun. A zipless fuck will be good for you right about now."

"Ew. I don't even know what that is."

"It's the perfect one-night stand. No expectations."

I turn that thought over like a piece of licorice on my tongue. How is it possible to have sex with no attachments? I wish Harry would call. I was sure he would. "Listen, I'm really sorry for ditching you at the party."

"Water under the bridge."

I'll take it. "How was camping?"

"Outdoorsy."

"Who did you go with?"

"What is this, twenty questions?"

"I'm just making conversation."

"I went with the band. They were recording at a studio in western North Carolina, so we camped afterward."

Surely, after the drive up and back, plus a night or two by a fire, she would know what Harry's thinking. "Can I ask you something?"

"Shoot."

"Do you think Harry will call?"

Martha sits up, removes her oversize glasses. Her eyes are red and puffy. There's a scratch on her chin where she picked at a zit. Her black fingernail polish has been nibbled away at the tips. She's human again. "Shit, Simian. Don't ask me that."

"Jesus, Martha. I'm reaching out here."

"So am I. You get everything you want. You wanted Trip, so

you had him, nice rock and all. Then you didn't want him, so now you don't. You had sex with Harry. I *gave* him to you, even after you ditched me, by the way. Now that's not enough? What, you want him to propose, too?"

She's trying to connect, but instead she manages to make me feel no bigger than the courtyard finches scavenging for crumbs. I drum my fingers on the metal table. All along, deep down, I knew Harry wouldn't call. And as stupid as it is to want him to take me to dinner, I still do. And I'd like Trip to phone, to check in. He hasn't reached out since he asked about Laudie. I've thought about calling him. I've picked up the phone, scrolled for his number, put the phone back down. I'm afraid he might tell me to leave him alone. I wouldn't blame him.

I stiffen, fighting the instinct to collapse into a ball and cry, to dissolve into something boneless and leaky. If I don't want freedom, what is it that I need? A cage? No. I want to be a free agent, not some spineless southern belle prone to the vapors. "You're right. I expect too much."

"Don't expect anything. That's the way to be free." She places her hand on my knee. I stare at her strange thumb, which is wide and flat and doesn't seem to be a part of her at all. "Don't forget Harry is a musician; they sleep around. And they can because they're free. It's the only way for people like us." She scoots her chair out from the table; it rakes noisily against the concrete. "I'm going to get a coffee." She nearly flattens a finch on her way to the door.

I rub my forehead. Does she mean "us," as in Martha and me, or is she talking about herself and Harry? Maybe I don't want to be *that* free, anyway. I want my family—my roots. And my most important relationship right now is with Laudie. I'm going to lose her soon, probably in a year or two. I know this. And while nothing and no one is permanent, that's no reason to cut all ties, to live life with no attachments. Even when people die, their stories remain. Our stories, generation to generation, are intertwined. The stories live on.

22.

The Last Dance

A storm churns out of the south, whipping the branches of oaks, ripping off the older leaves; they skitter down the dry asphalt and get caught along the curb. A gush of cool air flings a floppy hat off a tourist; a plastic bag takes flight. Thunderheads gather in the distance. Later this afternoon, it will pour.

As Mom and Caroline suggested, I've come to watch a streaming version of the ballet with Laudie. I packed us a ballerina-approved snack: bottles of Perrier and a bag of low-fat popcorn sweetened with stevia.

Just as I reach the bottom of the back staircase, a horn blows. Tito's ride to his weekly chess tournament has arrived. My grandfather emerges from the back door and begins his careful descent, one hand on the railing, the other gripping a cane. I should offer to help or at least wave hello, but instead I set the bag of snacks against a topiary and make a detour to Laudie's garden.

As I walk through a tunnel of greenery, long-tongued aspidistra lick my ankles. Camellia branches bump against my back. The needle-sharp leaves of the sago palms rake my forearms. When I enter the garden, my stomach turns.

What was once a fairy-like landscape of free-spirited, joyous shapes and colors is now a ramshackle knot of weeds and dirt. Our shell collection lies half-buried under decaying magnolia leaves. The ficus vine she had trained to crisscross the back wall has grown so unruly and heavy that it's started to peel away from the bricks, like a blanket being stripped from a bed.

And the zinnias. They're all but dead. Their petals have browned. Caterpillars have banqueted on the leaves, leaving them riddled with holes. Invasive weeds—crabgrass, thistle, and nightshade—usurp their water supply.

Even the little potting shed in the far corner looks slumped and tired. I grab a trowel and some shears. I drop to my knees to rip up the Bahia grass. I rake through the hot soil to hook roots of renegade spurge and chickweed. I toss clumps behind me in fistfuls, and when the pile is big enough, I dump it in the shade of a sago palm. Methodically, I work left to right, removing every errant plant from this little plot. Eventually, all the messiness— the decay and mutinous weeds—are gone. The dozen or so zinnias that remain stand erect, stalwart, restored—at least partially—to some semblance of order and beauty.

* * *

Laudie waits for me at the kitchen table. A beam of light, slicing through the coming storm and into the window, blanches the left side of her body, halving her into shadow and light. She wears a tweed skirt suit. She's dabbed on peacock-blue eyeshadow to match her outfit. A gold jaguar with ruby eyes slinks up her lapel. Her hair is tied back in her signature low bun. A string of fat pearls encircles her neck. Her pocketbook rests squarely in front of her, straps neatly folded. Next to it is a pair of tickets. *Oh, shit.*

"You're taking me to the ballet."

"Laudie . . ." My throat goes dry. Even if I take her and nothing happens, we won't get back until after Tito gets home. He'll know. My family will know.

"I'm not asking you, Simons. I'm telling you. I'm not going to wither away in this house, waiting to die."

"But, Laudie, I can't." Mom and Tito forbid her at the barre, let alone out on the town.

"Yes, you can. You definitely can. Besides, if I can go through all the trouble of getting this dressed up, I can certainly sit for a couple hours in a theater."

"You do look magnificent," I admit. But extra rouge and shoulder pads don't fully camouflage her weakened frame, her pallor.

She straightens as she sees me size her up. "I won't tell you the rest of the story if you don't take me." She gestures to the spread on the table—another measly dancer's feast: some crackers and fruit, iced tea. Still, it's a place setting, like the one she made when she first told me about John. Typical of Laudie: even for just saltines and grapes, she has set the table with place mats, cloth napkins, and sterling silver cutlery. "Do we have a deal?"

I feel myself relent. Sitting across from her and reaching for my glass, I recall that old expression: better to ask for forgiveness than for permission. The ice has melted a bit. After the first watery sip, her no-calorie instant tea tastes as it always has—strong and bitter. "Tell me."

She grins. "We'll start where we left off, with John. He and I went steady for months. Even though I phoned Mother once a week, I never told her about him." I notice that her watch, given to Laudie by her mother to remind her to call home, is now back on her left wrist. The cast is gone.

"Because you knew she wouldn't approve?"

"Well, yes. But mostly because John was my secret, a part of my life that no one else owned. He was dashing, Simons. Any woman would have fallen for him. Many women did. I did. And when we walked into a dancing hall together, the crowd parted. Oh, we were horrible show-offs. We had the best time hogging the spotlight.

"We were an item those days. We joined the other boarding-house gals and their beaux by the river or at drive-ins. We sat on the hood of the car and drank hooch and ate boiled pea-nuts. We were madly in love, and so, well, we did what lovers do. People talked, of course, but none of them knew my family in Charleston. So I didn't care."

I compute her age at the time and realize that she first had sex at a younger age than I did. How on earth did that happen? I suddenly feel better about my fling with Harry, even if he never calls back. "Do you miss him?"

"I miss the idea of him. But he wasn't who he seemed. Or maybe he was. I don't know."

"What do you mean?"

"Back in those days, we didn't talk about birth control. I thought I was pregnant."

"You must have been so scared."

"I was terrified. How could I face my family? How could I dance with a big old belly?" She laughs, but I find it hard to join her. "I called John and told him I thought I was pregnant. He told me he would come pick me up immediately, that we would figure it out." She twists her lips. "He never came."

"I'm so sorry. He abandoned you."

"That's what it felt like. I felt so foolish, Simons. No one said it, but everyone predicted it."

I wonder if she had an abortion, but decide to avoid leading with such an invasive question. "So, what did you do?"

"I had my period. Or maybe it was a very early miscarriage. I'm not sure. But I was so relieved. Still sad, but relieved."

"Did you tell anyone?"

"No. The girls just thought I was sad about the breakup. I let them take care of me, reading to me or rubbing my back or combing my hair. Those were thoughtful girls."

"They sound nice."

"Maybe a month later, they finally convinced me to go

dancing. They were always trying to cheer me up. And when I walked in the door, I saw John in the corner with another gal. He looked at me as though he had never seen me before."

"Oh, that's awful."

"Your grandfather was never perfect, but he is loyal. So I telephoned him that night and asked him to please fetch me."

"Wow. You were heartbroken?"

"Oh, yes. I was heartbroken, but I got over it. Mainly I was just so glad not to be pregnant. And, after all, if I hadn't come home, I wouldn't have you. Or your mother. Or Weezy and Caroline and Francie. Plus, I still have my secrets."

"*Have* secrets? There's something more?"

"Of course." She winks. "Always. It's my granddaughter bait."

"You said you'd tell me the whole story."

"I will"—she taps her watch—"but we need to get going."

"No fair," I tease.

"What I want you to understand, Simons, is that the worst part of the story was that I lost my confidence. I think that's what happens when people have a big scare: they run back to what they know, even if it was what they were trying to get away from, even if they had a bright future ahead of them. I don't want that to happen to you."

A ripple, quick and disturbing, races across her face. I think of a riptide—water moving lightly on the surface but roiling ferociously underneath. She blinks hard; the filminess returns to her eyes. To speak, she forces her words. "I stopped being brave."

I place my hand on Laudie's arm—more bone than flesh and as dry as chalk. "Laudie, are you okay?"

She jerks her hand away. "Yes. Don't you start treating me like a baby, too." She takes the tiniest sip of tea, the glass seemingly as heavy as a milk jug in her shaky hand. "Oh, that helps." She presses her hands against the table to push herself to standing. After raising her body just a couple of inches, she flops back into her chair.

I look away, not wanting to embarrass her. She can do it on her own. She must. At the second attempt, she hovers between sitting and standing, her legs shaking with effort. She is suspended in a strange halfway posture, unable to stand or sit. She's not going to make it on her own. I hurry around the table, put my hands around her hips, lift her upright. Neither of us speaks, tacitly agreeing that to acknowledge the moment is to admit going to the ballet is a bad idea. "Get my keys," she commands.

We walk to her car, which sits unused except for our excursions. In the passenger seat, she struggles to fasten the seat belt. After a few attempts, she lets it snap back to its cradle above the door. Instead of buckling her belt for her like she's an invalid or a child, I resolve to drive extra carefully, my hands gripped tightly at ten and two.

I notice dirt between the folds of my knuckles. A plumbago leaf clings to my dress. A faint patch of sweat lingers at the back of my neck.

I pull into a handicap spot, parking tickets be damned. Overhead, the clouds converge. The wind gathers strength, blowing hard from the south. Ravens and crows crisscross the sky. I hurry to the passenger side to retrieve Laudie.

We walk carefully from the car to the Gaillard Center, our

arms interlocked. I'm entirely focused on getting her inside safely, one step at a time. My eyes scan for obstacles: curbs, tree roots, uneven pavement. The tips of her Capezio shoes flash in and out of my narrow field of vision.

But once inside, on the smooth marble of the lobby floor, Laudie slides her arm out from mine. She pulls back her shoulders and lifts her neck with all the elegance of a great egret rising from the marsh. She pauses for a moment, inhaling deeply, as she does just before her exercises at the barre. Her feet are turned out into first position.

Some old Charlestonians weave their way toward us to give Laudie a kiss. I want to shoo them away, afraid they might knock her over, but Laudie receives them like a queen greeting her subjects. They comment on her outfit and her beauty; she charms them with her knowledge of the dancing troupe and scenes from *La Sylphide* she's particularly excited to watch. I stand proudly beside her, watching my brave and bold grandmother hold court, until the house lights flicker a second time.

The grand performance hall is cavernous. A massive velvet curtain shields the stage. When the curtain is pulled back, the recessed stage looks like the back of a monster's throat, ready to swallow us whole.

Thunder cracks and booms. Rain drums on the roof and lashes the building. Laudie, finally safe in her seat, turns to me. "Isn't it grand?"

I turn to look at my grandmother—at the gleam in her eyes and the determination behind them. "Yes, it is grand."

The lights dim. A single violinist plays a few haunting notes. Soon, the whole boisterous orchestra joins in. The tempo gains momentum. The horn section blasts, cymbals crash, and the timpani drum rumbles. To my right, Laudie waves her hands in the air as though she's the conductor.

The curtain opens. Onstage, a man sleeps in a regal chair beside a giant hearth. *La sylphide*, a ghost fairy, appears. She wears white, her tutu so delicate it could have been spun from cobwebs. He wakes from his reverie, or maybe he's still in a dream. They dance together, but she's the star. She floats across the stage as though the laws of gravity don't exist for her. Her movements appear effortless: she seems wholly an otherworldly spirit. When she stops mid-twirl to stretch into an arabesque, Laudie seizes my arm. "Stunning."

The first act concludes with the man's fiancée weeping; she is heartbroken because he loves someone else. Still, the music is happy. The corps de ballet gathers, maybe forty dancers in all, leaping, twirling, flirting, and spinning onstage together. The curtain closes for intermission. The Charleston audience, known worldwide for its often wildly enthusiastic applause, leaps to its feet. I join the standing ovation and turn to Laudie to help her up, but she's slumped in her seat.

"Laudie?" I lift her up by her shoulders, try to read her face. Her eyes are open but vacant. If I were to let go, she'd collapse to the floor. "Laudie, are you okay?!"

Laudie mumbles, but I can't hear anything over the applause. *Don't leave me! Oh my God, what did I do?* She was fine, better than fine, just moments ago. Wild panic overtakes me. "Is there a doctor?" I yell louder, desperately. "Is anyone a doctor? I need a doctor!" Soon, people nearby join my call for help.

An usher jogs toward us, his flashlight winking as he hurries over. A woman appears and squats at Laudie's feet. "I'm a doctor." She pulls her glasses from her shirt pocket; her eyes scan my grandmother. She presses a thumb against the inside of Laudie's wrist. "What's your name?"

Laudie mumbles. Her head slumps like a wilted zinnia after weeks of drought.

The doctor's face, stitched with concern, tightens. "Look at me. Can you smile at me?" Laudie doesn't move. The doctor turns to the usher. Firmly but calmly, she says, "Call an ambulance."

23.

Sick as a Dog

The newsroom is nearly anarchic. Multiple phones ring at once. The normally silent TV monitors are on full blast, making it seem as though the anchors from different news channels are in a yelling match. Police and fire scanners screech like herring gulls fighting over a chicken bone at the beach.

In my peripheral vision, an object is ballooning in size and headed right for me. Before I can step out of the way, I'm nearly run over by a photog the size of a linebacker. He pivots just in time to keep from knocking me flat on my back, but he still somehow manages to stomp on my foot. *Ouch.* He might have crushed a tiny bone.

"Shoot, I'm sorry," he says, but keeps on running. He shoves open the door to the parking lot and bolts into the sunshine.

"Simons!" Angela hollers for me from her desk. Making my way to her, I walk on the outside of my right foot; it minimizes the pain. While the rest of the newsroom swirls in chaos, Angela is cool—a black hole among comets.

She brushes crumbs from her chest. A few remain on the shelf of her bosom, caught in the pilled ribbing of her sweater. "We already had our morning meeting. Everyone came in early. I just sent Justin and a photog to the courthouse. If there's no traffic, they should make it in time."

At least that explains why the photog was in a mad dash. My right big toe throbs, but the pain is nothing compared to the knot in my heart that tightens each time I think of Laudie and my supreme idiocy. I saw the signs. Any sane adult would have known it was foolish to push a fragile person beyond her limits, and all for what?

* * *

The press conference starts at 5:30, when most people are commuting home. In the control room, Angela stands next to me, her arms crossed. She smells like coffee and dog. We watch the wall of monitors. All the stations, even the national ones, aim their cameras at an empty lectern with a dozen microphones propped up along its rim. People milling in the background of the frame look awkward and self-conscious, like strangers in a crowded elevator waiting for their stop.

My mind wanders to the hospital. When Mom entered the room, she stopped abruptly as though blocked by some invisible wall—a force field generated by her reaction to the scene. Laudie lay asleep in the bed; the overhead fluorescent lights heightened the contours of her face, accentuating her hollow cheeks and sunken eyes. Her lips looked as rubbery and dead as chicken skin. A clear tube ran across her face just beneath her nose.

She was dressed in a blue-and-white hospital gown so voluminous that it swallowed her. Laudie would never wear anything so ill-fitting. I had tucked the fabric around her shoulders in an effort to give the gown some shape. I readjusted her socks and gathered her sheets neatly around her legs, trying to make her look more like the real Laudie, the strong-willed young woman who ran off to Atlanta to dance, not some feeble old sack of bones who just suffered a stroke.

Mom raised her hand to her mouth as two fat tears slid down her face. After a long moment, she spoke. "Oh, Simons."

I started to get up from the chair, the backs of my bare legs sticky from the nylon cushion. "Mom, I'm sorry."

Mom put a hand up, signaling me to either stop talking or stay put. I wasn't sure, so I kept quiet and stayed in my corner.

Mom walked over to Laudie and took her left hand from beneath the sheets, revealing more tubes. "Mother, it's Carry Ann."

Laudie opened her eyes. They were still a crystal blue. She patted my mother's arm and turned to me. "It's okay," she said weakly. "It's okay."

Those two words are all that have kept me going the past seventy-two hours. *It's okay.*

Sonny Boykin approaches the podium, snapping my attention back to the newsroom. He's assailed by the rat-ta-tat-tat of clicking lenses and the blinking strobe of the cameras' lights, but he doesn't react. A tiny American flag is pinned to his lapel. I strain to see his cuff links, with the telltale mark of "BH," but it's impossible to make them out. Before he speaks, he furrows his brow like men do when they want to look intelligent.

He begins in medias res. No opening statement. Just chitchat about his boyhood in Beaufort, South Carolina. "As many of you know, I backed my car into a utility pole. It seems this little incident has made headlines across the state." He smiles ingratiatingly, chuckles even, implying we are silly for all the fuss. "There's all this talk about the failed field sobriety test. I was so shaken by the wreck, I couldn't see straight. Once we got to the station, they came to their senses and let me go." His tone grows stern. "I'm not a perfect driver, but mark my words, I'm also the victim here. For whatever reason, that woman wants to drag me through the mud. It's a smear campaign. And the media is so desperate for content, they'll broadcast anything, even disgusting pictures." He shifts his gaze; I'm sure he's scowling at the bank of reporters in the back of the room. "Shame on you. And shame on her. Her story is false. It's completely untrue, ridiculous."

"Total denial. I should have guessed." Angela spins on her heels, heads back to her desk.

* * *

With clips of Sonny's press conference dominating the news rundown, it was easy to write a script for the seven o'clock broadcast. My draft has been cooling in Angela's inbox for nearly a half hour—eons in the news world. She reviews each script daily, one of her myriad duties as news director, and normally she can never get the scripts early enough. When I go to check on her, she's staring at the wall.

"Angela?"

"I just got a call back from the vet," she says finally. "Cooper has cancer."

"Oh, no. I am so sorry, Angela." Pictures of Cooper surround us. Cooper at the beach. Cooper sacked out on a divan. Cooper with trick-or-treaters. Cooper shaking hands with a fireman.

"He's not that old. He's only eight."

"Is there anything I can do?"

"Make this summer go away." She absentmindedly scrolls over the script. "Or help me sell my house so I can move back home."

She's my boss, but she's also human. Unsure if it's what she wants, I dip low to hug her. She stiffens at first, but then she lets her head fall on my shoulder for a moment. "You want to leave Charleston?"

"There's nothing for me here."

The beaches, the ocean, the historic houses, the secret gardens—how could anyone ever move from Charleston? "Sure there is."

"You've got to go, too, you know." I must look bug-eyed, because she tells me not to look so surprised. "Listen to me. I believe in you. You're actually a really good producer, and you'd be even better if you got to write about puddles and fish or whatever it is you want to write about. Charleston has never been your market. You have to go to a bigger market for an environmental science reporting gig. You can't get anywhere here, at least not yet."

Leave? I can't leave Charleston.

24.

If the Dress Fits

Mom dressed up for today's outing. She wears a pink gingham dress, low spectator pumps, and pearl earrings the size of june bugs. Every now and then she slips out of view, disappearing behind billowing white dresses.

We are at Elegant Evening, Charleston's go-to dress shop for balls, cotillions, weddings, dances, proms, galas, and black-tie events. I am sitting on the bridal boutique stage—a raised, carpeted platform bordered on three sides by full-length mirrors. My reflection, framed by hundreds of lavish white dresses, is repeated over and over—shattered fragments and vivid reminders of the way my life could have been. I remind myself that it was my decision to call off the wedding. This is what I wanted.

While our relationship has cooled since I broke my engagement to Trip, Mom still swung by to deliver the occasional basket of Johns Island tomatoes or soft peaches from the South Carolina upstate, but our visits hadn't been much more than a quick embrace and a hand-off. After Laudie's stroke, however,

Mom hadn't said a word. Nor had Tito or Dad said anything. So, when Mom texted to say she's taking Caroline dress shopping, she was extending an olive branch. Somehow, this shopping trip will right some wrong, if only a little. I'll do what it takes to be accepted back into the tribe. For her, I put on foundation and some pearl studs from my debutante days.

Laudie is still hospitalized. Doctors confirmed an ischemic stroke; she had a blood clot in her brain. They say most of the recovery will happen in the next three to four months. She has already regained most of her speech, but they are not yet letting her walk around unassisted. She has spent five nights at the Medical University of South Carolina. She'll be discharged any day, her doctors say.

Our family has developed a routine. I visit her in the early mornings. Mom comes at lunchtime, and Dad often stops by on his way home from the office. Tito visited the second day but since has stayed at home, apparently too busy hiring a handyman to remove the barre.

Afraid of catching some nasty virus in the hospital, Weezy opts to video chat with Laudie through Mom's phone during her visits. Afterward, Weezy calls me to report on Laudie's afternoon status: "She's tired. She still slurs her words a bit, but her spirits are good."

Last time I checked, she didn't seem too tired to me. Even though she was stuck wearing a hospital gown, she refused to look like a patient. Her hair was coiled in a dancer's bun; she even dabbed on the peacock-blue eyeshadow she wore to *La Sylphide*. Although confined to bed, she sat up straight, ready to receive company. Her speech sounded fine, too. When I pressed her for the end of the story, she said, "You'll have to wait until we can do it over lunch."

"I'm sorry you're stuck here, Laudie."

"Simons, listen to me, I'd rather die going to the Gaillard than wither away at home. Really."

That statement raised my spirits. "We were brave, weren't we?"

"We were."

Caroline emerges from the dressing room with the gait of a princess. She holds her arms inches away from her body, her wrists flicked upward. The ivory gown cinches in at her waist, balloons out just below her midsection. She steps onto the stage and engulfs me in a whirlwind of fabric. I have to scoot over so I won't be devoured by her massive skirt. "Jesus, Caroline. Just a sec." I bat at the layers of her dress.

Caroline gathers up handfuls of fabric to clear the space between the two of us. "Simons!" she whispers above the rustle of crinoline and organza. "Why do you have to sit in the one spot where I am supposed to stand?"

"I didn't think—"

"I know. You weren't thinking at all. Seems to be the theme these days."

"Caroline, don't you think I feel horrible enough?"

Mom appears behind me, or at least I think that's her behind another blizzard of fabric. "Caroline, what do you think about the dress?"

My sister returns her attention to the mirror. "I don't know. It's pretty, but I want something a little more . . . fun."

"Oh, but, honey, that one is so elegant on you."

"Thanks, Mom. Why don't you help Simons find a few dresses to try on?"

My dress? I glare at Caroline, angry at her for bringing up the fact that I was originally supposed to be buying my wedding dress on this shopping trip. Though, I'm sure, Mom hasn't forgotten that minor detail.

"You still need a dress to wear to the ball, Simons," she clarifies.

True.

"I'm buying you one," Mom says, more of a statement than an offering. "Just don't tell your father."

Another olive branch. An expensive one, too. "Thanks, Mom. Will you help me pick it out?"

We gather a half-dozen non-white dresses—in tulle, lace, organza, silk—and I carry them over my arm to the dressing room. I start with the navy-blue one—the one she picked out. I slide it over my head. The heavy lace dress is itchy. I wouldn't normally pick out a dress like this anyway; who under the age of fifty wants to wear a high boat neckline?

Now it's my turn on the stage. I'm surrounded again by hundreds of copies of myself.

"It's lovely, Simons. It's flattering." Mom is pleased with her choice. She climbs on the platform and adjusts the bodice so there are no creases. "You haven't told me who the lucky man is."

"Who?"

"Your date for the ball, Sims," Caroline hollers from the dressing room.

"You can't just pick anyone off the street, honey. He's got to be able to do the foxtrot at the very least."

"I know."

Caroline steps onstage in a different dress. This one has a mermaid cut and is far sexier. "How about Clay?"

Oh, Jeebus. Clay? First, he's Ashley's younger brother. Second, he's Caroline's age: a rising senior in college. And third, we're plainly not each other's type: he can't drink a beer without his camo koozie, and his main topic of conversation is his recruitment duties for Chi Psi. Besides, I doubt he'd want to go with me, anyway.

Mom shrugs. "Well, I know his mother did send him to cotillion. He must own tails."

True as well. Clay would be a fun, easy date. But I hold tight to the idea that the evening has potential for romance, a new start even. "Give me a week and if I can't find someone by then, I'll see if Clay's free."

A desperate electronic jingle bleats from inside Mom's purse. Mom drops the dresses and digs for her phone. "It's the hospital," Mom says and retreats to a corner of the showroom. "Hello? Yes, this is Mrs. Smythe." She hunches over the phone, every fiber of her being tuned in. "Well, is she okay?"

Caroline and I follow her, lifting our dresses so we don't step on the hems. Caroline places a slender hand on our mother's back. "Mom, what is it?" Caroline asks.

Here's the thing about Charleston women—the true-blue bloods: They are not dramatic. They do not scream or sob or faint. They do not cry tears of joy when their children marry, and they don't squawk like chickens over gossip about a friend's divorce. They don't fall to pieces in public at a funeral. They act with decorum. They respond politely. They do not draw attention to themselves.

Instead, they focus on the moment—the marriage, or maybe news of an accident. As members of the tribe, these women ready themselves as support troops, to celebrate the wins and to collect the fragments of loss to help put a member's life back together. So, when Mom reports the hospital's news about Laudie, she remains composed and dry-eyed.

"Mother had another stroke," she says neutrally, though she looks as though she's made of dust.

25.

Prescriptions

The kitchen is as cool as a vault. The wall clock ticks. The dishwasher hums. The second-floor hallway is warmer, quieter. Normally, sunlight pools onto an ivory hall rug speckled with pastel roses. As children, we would jump from flower to flower, pretending we were fairies while Laudie practiced her arabesques a few feet away at the barre. Now, there are scars on the wall where the barre was attached. With the curtains drawn and the wall sconces dimmed, the playful atmosphere has vanished.

"Hello?" I knock tentatively on the bedroom door. No answer. I gingerly open the wide door and enter the tomblike stillness of Laudie's room. Dust particles hover, unmoving, in the weak light that escapes the heavy draperies. The room smells of rubbing alcohol and ammonia.

A bouquet of zinnias sits on her vanity; the blooms are doubled by the mirror—a trick my mother taught me, one that I'm sure Laudie taught her. A few flowers—those with cherry-red and marigold centers—are still perky. Most are dead.

Laudie sleeps. Her body looks as though she's fallen from the sky and landed in the mechanized hospital bed. She arrived home by ambulance this morning. Three days after the second stroke, the doctors agreed it's best now to keep her home. Keep her comfortable. It's time for hospice.

Laudie's hairline has retreated to the very crown of her head. Her temples sink into her skull, craters as big and round as eggs. Her skin is nearly translucent, like a jellyfish's. Her movie-star lips have twisted into an involuntary snarl. My dear, sweet, beautiful grandmother. I'm so sorry.

The antique wingback chair, the one she draped her evening dresses over while she did her her makeup for a night out, is next to her bed, ready to receive visitors. I take a seat; my foot knocks an empty bedpan. Seven prescription pill bottles and several tubes of ointment clutter the bedside table.

"I'll give you some time."

I jump at the sound of a woman's voice. She emerges from a dim corner of the giant bedroom. She wears pink scrubs and white sneakers.

"What's your name?"

"Shaniece."

"I'm Simons. I'm the granddaughter."

"Simons?" Laudie turns her head in my direction. After a moment her milky eyes, which had seemed drifty and unfocused, alight on me. "They wanted me," she says, or at least I think that's what she says.

"Who? Who wanted you?" I lean close, turn my ear to her mouth.

She emits a high wheezing noise and struggles to sit up. "The letter."

"The letter, Laudie? What letter?" I try to spin the Rubik's Cube of clues my grandmother left for me. Who wanted her? What letter? A love letter . . . from John?

Laudie tries to speak, her mouth opening and closing like that of a fish out of water. She kicks at her coverlet and arches her back. It just might kill her to say another word. If she dies now—because I'm pressing her to tell me something—how could my family ever forgive me?

Shaniece comes to my side. "It's okay, Mrs. Middleton. You just need to rest." She lays a hand on my grandmother's chest and slowly adds pressure. "Would you like to read to her? Seems to calm her down."

"Good idea."

"I'm going to run downstairs. Will you be okay?"

"Yes. Thank you."

Shaniece studies me for a moment before gathering a couple of pill bottles from a metal table. As she leaves the dark room, a wink of daylight flashes inside, disappears. The door closes behind her with a soft click.

I look for something to read. On Laudie's nightstand, beneath a glass of water, is the Bible. The leather cover bends easily in my hands. Traces of burned coffee and sandalwood scent the air. I begin reading aloud at the bookmarked page—1 Timothy, chapter 2, verses 7 through 15.

This is why I was chosen to be a teacher and a missionary. I am to teach faith and truth to the people who do not know God. I am not lying but telling the truth. I want men everywhere to pray. They should lift up holy hands as they pray. They should not be angry or argue.

Laudie pedals her feet. Is that a good sign? I press on.

Christian women should not be dressed in the kind of clothes and their hair should not be combed in a way that will make people look at them. They should not wear much gold or pearls or clothes that cost much money. Instead of these things, Christian women should be known for doing good things and living good lives.

Women should be quiet when they learn. They should listen to what men have to say. I never let women teach men or be leaders over men. They should be quiet. Adam was made first, then Eve. Adam was not fooled by Satan; it was the woman who was fooled and sinned. But women will be saved through the giving of birth to children if they keep on in faith and live loving and holy lives.

What the hell? What other ghastly rules are written about women in the Bible? I look at Laudie, who appears to be resting. But her hands are curled. I pull out my phone for a quick search.

1 Corinthians 11:9: "For indeed man was not created for the woman's sake, but woman for the man's sake."

Proverbs 12:4: "An excellent wife is the crown of her
husband, but she who shames him is like rottenness
in his bones."

1 Corinthians 14:35: "If they desire to learn anything,
let them ask their own husbands at home; for it is
improper for a woman to speak in church."

Colossians 3:18: "Wives, submit to your husbands, as is
fitting in the Lord."

Jesus. What is this stuff? No wonder women are subjugated.
Why is any of this misogyny okay to preach today?

My poor mother. Is this what she hears every Sunday before
brunch at Battery Hall? Has Trip wanted a Christian woman
all this time? Is that why he wants me to dress modestly, eat
moderately, have more self-control?

In what ways have misogynist concepts like these molded
Laudie? How could she have the confidence to try out for a
ballet troupe when her lover, who very well could have been
the father of her child, abandoned her in a time of need? No
wonder she came home.

From what I've observed, she was submissive to Tito exactly the way the Bible prescribes. And now here she is, on her
deathbed—at the end of her story, whatever it is. She's taking
that story to the afterworld with her, so I'll never truly know.

Laudie stirs; her labored breathing grows louder. "Simons,"
she says, though I only hear the second part of my name. She

somehow steadies her breathing. She stretches her fingers. The milkiness of her eyes retreats like a tide, revealing a crystal blue. There's strength behind her gaze, an energy incongruent with her decaying body. The next thing she says I hear as clear as a bell: "Be brave." She tumbles back into sleep, into another world.

"Laudie?" I start to cry. "What do you mean? Does this have anything to do with the letter? What do you want me to do?"

She doesn't hear. She's drifted off to some liminal space between here and the afterlife.

Light blasts into the room. Dust particles swirl around Shaniece, who is backlit. She carries a tray with little plastic cups and bottles. "Did you have a good visit?"

"Yes. No. I don't know. I think she's trying to tell me something."

"Did you try reading to her?"

"I did, but I think I just got her worked up." I close the Bible. It shuts with a thud.

Shaniece scans my grandmother. "Well, she looks relaxed now." She points to a book at the foot of the bed. On the cover, a boy with a red cape flies on a broom. "Maybe next time, though, try *Harry Potter*."

26.

Love Scandal

School started. We run a two-minute package on back-to-school tips for families and tie that in with a story about a local charity that feeds hungry children on the weekends. I stack the show so that our sports reporter can kill time talking about football season. The whole Sonny Boykin story comes and goes, depending on whether more compelling news surfaces on any particular day. Since not much is happening around town, we're digging up the dregs of that story; we know it can pay the bills. People love scandal.

Meghan finds me at my desk. "Justin found some old photos of Ms. Ronan on Facebook. We're running some of them at six."

"Any pictures of her with the judge?"

"Yeah, at some law event. The rest are random party pics and a few of her at the beach."

I click on the shared office file labeled "Sexting Sonny Boykin." In one shot, they're at a cocktail party. She's petite; standing next to Judge Boykin, she looks even smaller. She wears a maroon dress, black stilettoes. The judge is in a gray business suit. His arm is around her waist. They both smile.

In another photo, she wears a bikini, her breasts sugar-coated with sand. She's on Sullivan's Island—I can tell from the lighthouse in the background. The last is a selfie taken in what looks like a restaurant bathroom. While they're all normal photos for a twenty-three-year-old, when paired next to a pixelated dick pic, they suggest something seamy. "Do we really need these other photos?"

"Well, Sonny's accusing her of libel, and she won't talk to us."

"Yeah, but I feel these photos suggest that she's slutty or something, like she might not be totally believable."

"Well, Sonny could be innocent. Two sides to every story."

"What does Angela say?"

"She took the day off to be with Cooper."

"Oh."

* * *

Before my seven-o'clock show goes live, I sneak into an editing suite to tweak the lead story. South Carolina is a Bible Belt state; we know many of our viewers attend church, where versions of male power and female submission are preached and ratified every Sunday. Many of our viewers will be predisposed to doubt Ms. Ronan's innocence just because she is a woman.

Not on my watch. I pull the video of the story, which will run beneath the anchor speaking live, from the shared office files and drag it into the desktop trash. I scan through my show's video-editing files and load the original back into the editing software. With a quick click and drag, I remove the solo images of Ms. Ronan at the beach and in a bathroom. I leave the photo of Judge Boykin and Ms. Ronan together in the package, stretching its time on screen to nearly twelve seconds. Normally, an image stays up for three seconds, five tops, so anyone who knows video editing would see this as sloppy, but I don't care. Ms. Ronan could be lying, but why would any woman want her personal life pried open like an oyster at a Lowcountry roast?

For good measure, I add a story about Wildcat Acres, the proposed six-thousand-home development on a floodplain. The latest is that the city's planning director moved forward with the infill proposal approved by DHEC.

The lead developer is a Charleston local, the son of the owner of the Coast Company. I recognize both men as members of Battery Hall. But who is the planning director? My search pulls up the image of a handsome blond man in his fifties with his hair brushed back into a sort of modest pompadour. Charles Boone. That could certainly be the name of a local, but I don't recognize him. And if he were a member of Battery Hall, he certainly wouldn't advertise it on his bio. Whoever he is, he should know that the lead cause of flooding in that area will be the fill dirt. Will the federal government bailout these new homebuyers, too? What a mess.

While I'm at it, I toss in the plight of Gadsden Creek, a tiny finger of water reaching into the peninsula off the city's west edge. Developers plan to fill this wetland and are getting the city to use tax dollars to help them do it. The last time I pitched this story idea, Angela said that maybe ten people care about a shallow tidal creek next to a poor Black community; the story would waste airtime. News is still a business—I get it. But this one time won't hurt.

27.

The Kicker

Weezy rolls to a stop beneath the crepe myrtle just outside of my apartment. She drives just like my mother, with her body hunched over the steering wheel, her elbows bent like wings.

Weezy insisted I accompany her to a prenatal checkup. She said I needed to get out of the house, to do something other than work or visit Laudie.

I've learned that as long as I'm too busy to think, I don't feel absolutely terrible about taking my grandmother to the ballet. My shirts now hang in color-coordinated sections. The mantel cherubs shine after a Q-tip-crazed scrubbing session. All questionable condiments lurking in the recesses of my fridge now lie discarded in the bottom of my trash can. So when Weezy phoned to tell me she was picking me up, whether I liked it or not, I told her I'd be ready in five.

Slow and steady, Weezy eases on the gas. She juts out her chin, peering over the dashboard, methodically searching for moving objects, left to right, like reading a book. I twist around to say hi to Francie. She gives me a cheeky smile and returns to eating Cheerios, one by one. Just as we turn the corner, my eye catches a strangely familiar silhouette. Trip?

If he were in town, he surely would have called. At least as a friend. I hope we're still friends. What are we? Maybe we should have had our conversation sooner. As I stare into the side-view mirror, he slips from the frame. I unbuckle to swivel completely—my knees on the seat, hands on the headrest—and catch sight of his profile as he disappears behind a house on the corner. Definitely Trip.

"What are you doing?"

"Nothing." The radio plays another Michael Jackson song. I change the station.

"Aw. Why'd you do that?"

I've enjoyed MJ's songs but never considered myself a fan. Weezy, on the other hand, had a poster of him in her bedroom. "I'm sorry. I've hit my limit." Yesterday was August 29, Michael Jackson's birthday. A production assistant played *Thriller* on his phone during commercial breaks. Jasmine wanted to close out the last news broadcast of the day by waving a sequined glove. I said no, absolutely not. Didn't she see the documentary?

Weezy checks her blind spot and pulls off down a side road. We roll past one anonymous development after another. Finally her Volvo bumbles into a gravel parking lot. She taps on her window, indicating a small brick building squatting beneath some pines. "It's right there. Doesn't it look much more user-friendly than a hospital?"

I didn't have any expectations as to what a birthing center

is supposed to look like, so I guess it does seem, at the least, less intimidating than a hospital. Just one story and modest in size, it was probably someone's ranch home in a former incarnation. Baby-blue shutters frame the windows. The front door is pink. Lavender vincas, probably tended by one of the midwives, grow along the walkway.

With Francie on my hip, I pull open the office door for Weezy. A receptionist doing Sudoku glances up. "Hey, Louisa. Have a seat. I'll let her know you're here."

The waiting room feels homey, but almost too homey, as though I'm in someone's living room. Amateur paintings of mermaids and fairies hang above the mismatched Goodwill furniture. Tendrils of potted philodendron twine around the window toward the exit sign. Weezy sinks onto the sofa, tossing a pillow at me to make room for her growing body.

I catch it. The hand-embroidered pillow simply reads, "Vagina." Ha! Would I dare to have that pillow on my couch, with that one fun and funny word? Why is "vagina" such a loaded word, anyway? Maybe because it's powerful. Maybe I need this word more in my life, but how? Vagina. Vagina!

A woman in dreadlocks appears to escort us to an exam room. Paisley curtains soften the casement windows. A matching duvet covers a daybed. Weezy shimmies onto the table and lifts her shirt up to her bra line. She still has a couple of months to go but is already more visibly pregnant than she ever was with Francie. The stretch marks from the first pregnancy have faded to faint streaks the silvery color of dolphins. A new patch of strawberry lines radiates like a sun star around her belly button. "He's been moving a lot lately. Get Francie to feel him."

I press Francie's hand against Weezy's stomach. *Gadunk.* We feel the thump. Francie looks up at me, and we exchange smiles. "Wow, Weez. That's crazy."

"You never felt Francie kick?"

"No." I shake my head. "I never did." Two years ago, when Francie was in the womb, the very idea of children made me feel trapped. I imagined myself with Trip, in the Upstate, spending my days picking Legos off the floor and talking to mommies about poopy diapers and daytime TV. Women who had kids, I thought, had surrendered their youth and their freedom. When they said goodbye to the pill or to pulling out, did they willingly say goodbye to wild nights, spontaneity, and all the possibilities that come with a life unencumbered?

Weezy's son will be born literally attached to her. Sure, Ashley will cut the umbilical cord, but then her baby will drink from her breast. Weezy will carry him, bathe him, clothe him, soothe him. She'll go back to work part time, eventually, but for many years her life will be defined by a tight orbit around her children.

I have chosen to live unfettered, at least for now. I do what I want, when I want, and I'm so grateful for my freedom I attempt a moonwalk across the floor of the examination room. In the words of Michael Jackson, "Hee hee!"

28.

Redneck Hairdryer

A day of low humidity is a rare summer treat in the Lowcountry. In the drier atmosphere, everything looks clearer, more precise. Laughing gulls swoop high above the marina, casting razor-edged shadows on the parking lot asphalt. The palmetto fronds look as sharp as knives in the high-def light. The reflections off the white hulls of sport fishers are so blinding that I need to look away. Today, the water glitters antically in the wake of two Boston Whalers that weave their way through the marina's maze of docks and out toward the river.

Kevin waits on the metal ramp. He wears a trucker hat, white tank top, and American flag–themed board shorts. He takes a swig from a Bud Light. "What's up, Simons?" He tilts his head back and squints hard into the sun, his nostrils two gaping circles. "Everyone else is already on the boat. Crazy assholes have been partying since yesterday."

I follow him down the ramp to the floating dock. We pass a family readying their boat for a day on the water. The children cling to the boat rails, trying to stay upright in their bulky life jackets. Their mother packs the cooler with Ziplocked sandwiches, juice boxes, brownies. The dad tinkers with the engine and checks the bowlines. It's a lot like the way my family prepared for a boat trip.

When I gave up Trip, did I give this up, too? I called him last night. I wanted to talk to him about Laudie, tell him about the ballet. He would make me feel better. He would remind me that going was her idea. He'd tell me to focus on how she looked in the lobby—like a monarch.

He didn't answer. At first, his phone rang and went to voicemail. I called two more times; he's the type to always have his phone nearby. Still no answer, so I texted: "**Can we talk?**" I knew I was entering dangerous territory—we had agreed to postpone our conversation until sometime in early winter, a full six months from the breakup, three months from now.

He wrote seconds later. "**I don't think that's a good idea.**"

I called him immediately. He had to answer; the phone was in his hands. Instead, he texted again: "**Sorry, I can't talk right now.**" He didn't even type those words himself. He chose that phrase from the multiple-choice response menu.

That night, I missed our relationship. I mourned it. Finally, though, it felt silly and self-indulgent to cry aloud, so I got a grip and stopped. In my quiet apartment, a singular thought entered my awareness: *The only one who can get me out of this hole is me.*

That's when I accepted Kevin's invitation.

Kevin's boat is tied up at the end of the docks. It's large—way larger than any motorboat I've ever been on. The center console is as big as a refrigerator; at the stern are three out-board motors.

Four women lounge on the bow. Each sports a glossy bikini. They're wearing makeup. They look like they showered this morning. My ratty surfing bikini feels childlike. The last time I painted my toenails was in anticipation of Harry's show. Now, polish covers only the top half of my nails.

Why didn't I think to put myself together more? Caroline would have arrived in a cute cover-up. She would have brought a stiff canvas tote bag, filled with a fluffy rolled towel and freshly cut cantaloupe for everyone.

He gestures to a spot next to two giant coolers. "You can put your stuff here." I drop my reusable grocery bag and in-troduce myself to each of the girls: Jessica, Taylor, Brooke, and Jen. There's another guy; with lazy curiosity, I wonder which of the girls he's dating.

Kevin revs the engines. I pull in the fenders and flake the stern line.

"At least someone here knows how to work a boat." It's the girl in the sequined cheetah bikini. Jessica? Brooke? They offer me a beer. At first I refuse, saying I have to work this afternoon; but then I think, *When in Rome.* My decision is greeted with cheers. I raise my beer with a smile. It feels good to smile.

Kevin drives the boat a bit too fast for the marina's "No Wake" zone; no one else on board seems to notice. Does he know about going idle speed? I chug half my beer, rinsing down any ownership of the boat's behavior.

We troll past the Charleston Marina's MegaDock, which is

appropriately named. Giant yachts of the world's super wealthy tie up here for a few nights before zipping off to the Caribbean or across the Atlantic. The girls on the boat wave to the crews scrubbing the decks. They wave their hands back and forth, which is the first sign to me that they are not locals. It's like spotting an artificial geranium or daffodil in a window box South of Broad—might as well put up a sign that says, "Hey, you guys, I'm from Off!" Instead, Charlestonians do more of a boat salute; when we see another boater, we extend a hand, hold it steady. We also drive Key Wests and Boston Whalers, not inboard wakeboarding boats outfitted with concert speakers that blast rap-rock.

We boat to get away from it all, not to carry it with us. We listen to the waves, look for dolphins, find a spot to swim. And even the most outspoken member of Battery Hall wouldn't hoist a flag bearing the name of his favorite political candidate.

Once we reach the Ashley River, Kevin guns the engines. Our boat hydroplanes effortlessly. We slice through the harbor, which is glassy on this nearly windless day. Still, there is some chop, bouncing all eight boobs in unison. The girls clasp the speedboat's metal rails. I hold on, too. We go fast, faster than I've ever been in a motorboat. If we were to hit something—if there were a shallow spot, a sandbar, or something large and submerged—we'd be flung off the boat like batter off an egg-beater.

I always felt safe when Trip took his family's boat out to the lake. At the beginning of every boating season, he checks the expiration dates on his flare, fire extinguisher, and fishing permits. Even for a quick outing, he snaps his navigation lights on and off to ensure they work, just in case the day doesn't go as planned. On the water, he's always cognizant of other watercraft, careful to keep a safe distance. When we return to land, he devotes a full hour to running fresh water through the engine and oiling down the motor.

My impatience flared during these fastidious routines; now I realize he was just being responsible. How could I have been so blind? If I had been paying attention, I would have observed his methodical mind in action as he backed the trailer into the water. I would have admired his strong hands as he cranked the winch. Instead, I looked away, annoyed, imagining some sort of better life, barefoot and untethered to the traditional, predictable world.

My face grows hot. Tears brim in my eyes. I root around in my bag for my sunglasses and stare straight ahead, trying to think about nothing.

"Redneck hairdryer!" Kevin shouts, his hair spiked straight by the wind.

A little self-deprecating humor. Nice. I give him a thumbs-up, trying to be in the present. I'm on a boat with fun-loving, carefree people. Why can't I have fun?

Kevin pulls back on the throttle as we approach the lee-ward side of Morris Island, an undeveloped spit of land near the mouth of the harbor, accessible only by boat. Looking at the mound of sand, held together by morning glory vines and needle-rush roots, I easily see how the land has shifted dramatically over the years. The lighthouse, originally built on land in 1876, is marooned fifteen hundred feet offshore. Several groups work to preserve this historic landmark. The question is, though, with nearly half of the construction in the United States built on shifting coastal zones, can our country save every structure near the water?

It's an incoming tide; we could simply beach the boat and be fine. But I don't say anything for fear that my guidance might be taken for mild castration. The guys figure it out, anyway. Kevin lobs an anchor onto shore. His buddy hops onto the beach and drives it into the sand.

It's hot now that we've stopped. The hummock of trees east of us blocks the offshore breeze. I tell Kevin I'm going for a swim. Only after he turns away do I remove my hat and sunglasses to jump in.

Underwater, I feel at home. Ancient horseshoe crabs crawl beneath me; stingrays glide nearby. I kick hard, swimming away from my thoughts to nowhere in particular. When I emerge, the shore is much farther away than I had anticipated. Kevin's boat bobs up and down at least fifty yards away.

Fuck. I'm in a riptide. A powerful current sweeps me out to sea. Surfers know to swim with the current, even if it takes them farther from the shore, until the giant stream relinquishes its grip. But the water won't let go.

I kick hard—going against all safety protocol—and use every bit of energy I can summon to beat the current. Breathing sharply, I glance up to gauge my progress. The island slips by.

I'm losing ground, but instead of succumbing to panic, I

yield to a pleasant thought: maybe it wouldn't be so bad to be carried out into the Atlantic Ocean. Where would the water take me? It might be nice for some other force to determine my direction in life. Lately, I've found it exhausting to do it on my own.

I let go.

The water, as it tends to do, folds my body into a fetal position. I float soundlessly with the tide. I don't struggle. I have no wants. This nothingness must be like death, weightless and peaceful. Maybe this is what Laudie dreams of at night—or even when she's awake. She's probably tired of the fact that everything these days is a struggle: eating, talking, hearing, being. As I am carried off by the riptide, I imagine Laudie being carried off to the afterlife.

Something large swims past me. It happens again. Curious dolphins have whipped by me before, but they always surface within sight, letting me know that they're dolphins. Yet on the surface, there are no arcing dorsal fins in sight. Surrendering to the whims of tidal patterns is one thing; getting bitten by a shark is another. I hammer my arms through the chop, catch myself groaning at the effort. I take a half-stroke to orient myself and am surprised to see that I'm actually headed back toward the beach. The riptide apparently makes a U-turn sooner than I'd calculated. In just a few more minutes of strenuous swimming, I reach the boat.

I hang on the ladder, every cell in my body tired and thankful for rest. I'm also thankful that no one seemed to notice that

I was missing, busy having a near-death experience. I take a moment to recoup before pulling myself up the little swim ladder attached to the boat's stern.

Just as I lift myself up from the water, a freshly waxed labia eclipses my view of the open sky. "Oh my God, I have to pee so bad!"

It's Taylor. Or Brooke?

She squats on the swimming platform, hanging onto the rails. She gives me a drunken smile. "I've been holding it forever."

I should move. I should just swim away and give this woman some privacy and maybe avoid a stream of hot urine flowing my way. But I'm exhausted and afraid that if I let go of the ladder, I'll sink right to the bottom, never to be seen or heard from again.

Finally, she's done. She slides her dry bikini bottom back on. Just before she climbs over the stern, she gives me an almost flirtatious look. "You're a little kinky, huh?" She laughs and tilts her head back.

I have no idea what to say to that. I am so weak from exertion I don't even smile, which probably makes me seem even creepier.

Mustering my strength, I haul myself up the ladder and all but collapse on the bench behind the center console. Kevin is at the steering wheel, fiddling with the music, his swimming trunks still dry. "What happened to your toe?"

I start to explain my work injury—which has now turned my toe a brownish-blue color—but instead say, "Shark bit it." Kevin laughs. While he digs around in the cooler for another beer, I take a moment to send a little prayer up to the heavens. I hope Laudie will be taken peacefully to the other side. I also send thanks for a good lesson: that where I want to go, I don't always have to go against the tide.

29.

Hot and Steamy

I hear scratching sounds coming from inside my apartment. I unlock the door and open it a crack. A scruffy head pokes out. Bruno. Martha asked me to watch him; she had to visit her grandmother in Florida. I nudge him back into my apartment and shut the door firmly so he doesn't escape or, more likely, tumble down the stairs. "Hey, little guy." He spins away to lick his genitals.

My phone buzzes. It's a text from Kevin: **"We're going to Stripes Saturday. You should come."** Stripes is one of the newer bars on upper King Street. There's always a queue outside the door. Worse, there is a red carpet for people to wait on, as if everyone is a sort of movie star.

I've never been to Stripes before. I've never wanted to go, either, nor have any of my friends. At the established bars, locals can expect to see a cousin, an old classmate, a friend's little brother. That's just the way it is around Charleston. But things are changing. We're becoming strangers in our own land.

Stripes is a bar for tourists and newcomers, where our rank as locals goes unnoticed. Perhaps that's why Dad and his friends value their membership at Battery Hall. Those males know one another; they've sniffed one another out, as did their fathers and grandfathers before them. And because of protocols and expectations, there has never been—and never will be—a fist-fight at Battery Hall. Men do not make passes at other men's dates or wives. No one gets sloppy drunk. Everyone's polite; good manners rule. And while all that social structure feels archaic and suffocating at times, in the recent chaos of my life, the order lately sounds appealing.

"Thanks for the invite. Can't. Dog sitting."

Bruno paws at my leg. "What is it? Are you hungry?" Martha left a satchel for him on my couch. I dig around to see what's inside: a couple of plastic chew toys, a pouch of dry kibble, and a letter with my name on it. That's sweet.

Simian,

I want to be honest with you. I'm not actually visiting my grandma. I'm on tour with Stone's Throw. They asked me to be their road manager. I didn't tell you before because I wasn't sure that it was going to be a "thing" until recently.

Thanks for taking care of Bruno while I'm gone.

XO,
Martha

A manager? How on earth is she qualified? Her work experience is piecemeal, at best. She assists wealthy old widows with odd jobs, driving them to funerals or organizing their photo albums. Her longest employment stint to date was when she was an administrative assistant at a downtown hotel. Still, that's not management. And with Harry's band?

I've heard the term "blood boil" before, but I have never experienced it until now. I'm actually feverish. Some ice water should cool me down. Bruno follows me into the kitchen, his nails clicking like castanets. I open the freezer to find that the ice maker's broken again, so I root around for an old ice tray possibly hidden behind frozen mixed berries and microwavable meals-for-one. I can't find it, but there is ice—in the form of exploded beer cans. They're the PBRs Martha brought over that fateful night. Poetic.

"Arrgh!" I yell into the frosty space, then slam the door shut, as if to lock up all the angst released from my scream inside the freezer.

Bruno is whimpering, scratching my legs. "Down, boy." I brush him away. He yips, racing to the front door and back.

"Okay, you need to go to the bathroom. Hold on." I change out of my work clothes and into some jean shorts and a tie-dye shirt.

Bruno relieves himself under the "No Parking" sign, and for a long time. When he's finally done, Bruno tugs on the leash. He needs a walk. I let him drag me for a few blocks until we arrive at a pocket park near a cluster of brand-new town houses.

There, Bruno trots to a patch of grass. He arches his back. *Shit.* I forgot to bring a poop bag.

I scan the park, looking for something to improvise with. I search the perimeter, under the sycamore trees and behind a lone park bench. Nothing. Where is litter when you need it? I spy a trash can at the front of the other entrance. Maybe someone tossed an empty plastic bag. I lean over the top to sift through it.

"Simons?"

I look up. It's Trip. I can't see his face. He's backlit, his silhouette rimmed by trees. Bruno starts to yap wildly, but I'm too stunned to hush him. I stand still, like a white-tailed deer fixed in a hunter's crosshairs. We haven't been this close since we were last in my apartment, before I called off the wedding. It is easier to ignore old feelings for him when he only exists through texts and unanswered phone calls. Now here he is, in the flesh, and my heart beats faster.

What is he is doing here, at this park? On a Tuesday evening? And why, of all times, did he have to catch me while I was rooting through garbage? I take a few quick steps from the trash can. I straighten my shirt, pull a stray thread from my jean shorts.

He walks toward me. Detail by detail, he comes into focus. He wears crisp khakis, a cornflower-blue button-up shirt, a navy blazer. Tiny beads of sweat dot his nose. His expression is both kind and slightly worried.

"What are you doing in town?"

"I had a work conference." He lifts a camel-colored briefcase as evidence.

"Where are you staying?"

He hesitates. A ripple of small dimples forms on his chin. "With a friend from work."

"Were you in town last week, too? I thought I saw you."

"I was. Are you doing okay?"

"Yeah. Good," I say as convincingly as possible, meanwhile racking my brain for clues. A friend from work? Who does he know who lives near here? Does he come often?

"I'm really sorry about Laudie."

"How did you know about her?"

"Oh. Um. I don't really remember. I just heard she had to go to the hospital."

"Actually, that's why I was trying to call you. She had a stroke. I took her to the ballet. The whole family told me to not take her, but I took her anyway. That's when it happened. She's been getting worse ever since."

"It's not your fault, Simons. I'll bet she insisted."

"She did. You know Laudie."

"It's not your fault, Simons," he repeats.

It feels so good to hear those words, delivered with such certainty. Though a part of me wishes he had called me Cinnamon. "Do you want to come over for a drink? Before you see your friend?" I try to say the word "friend" as neutrally as possible.

"What are you trying to do?"

"I thought it would be nice to catch up."

"Simons." He sighs. "You called off our wedding. You can't just pick me up again, like some toy."

"I'm sorry." I hang my head and stare at the ground. He wears freshly shined penny loafers. I scrunch my dirty toes. "Well, maybe we could have that talk sooner than later. What's six months, anyway? Just some arbitrary time line."

"I think time away from each other is a good thing right now. Let's stick to the plan." A tiny pinch forms on the bridge of his nose. "I have to go." He starts to walk away.

"Wait! Do you have a plastic bag?" It is a desperate plea for him to stay, but for what? His companionship? His forgiveness?

He digs into the pockets of his khakis and pulls out some tissues. "I have these," he offers and places them in my hand. He turns again to leave.

"I miss you," I yell and wait for some bit of reaction.

Before disappearing behind the corner, he calls, "Take care of yourself, Simons. You're a good girl, okay?"

I am left standing alone in a patch of grass. I'm not sure how many moments pass before I notice Bruno rubbing against my calves. He looks from me to his little doggy turd, which has somehow already established a colony of flies.

This, I tell myself, *is a freebie.* Everyone gets a poop freebie every once in a while, right? I pick up his leash and head for the exit.

"Uh-uh-uh." A woman walking a Great Dane wags an accusatory finger.

"I was going to pick it up," I protest. She is right. Dog poop pollutes. Enough of it can foul waterways and shut down oyster beds for miles. Still, even though it occurs to me to ask if she has an extra plastic bag, I don't want to give her the satisfaction of knowing I came unprepared. I'm going to have to pick up this steaming turd with Trip's Kleenex.

I layer the tissues, one on top of the next, hoping to create a barrier between my skin and the poop. It doesn't work. Immediately the feces soak through the Kleenex's flimsy layers. They're warm and sodden. I dry heave once as I toss the wad into the trash can.

When I get back to my apartment, I scrub my hands clean. Then I allow exactly one minute to feel jealous of this new friend of Trip's, not a second more. Next, I text Kevin: "**The dog said I could go out.**"

30.

Call Me Cinnamon

It's mid-September, and the city still stews. At 100 percent humidity, the air is saturated. (Which, I've learned, doesn't necessarily mean rain. Thanks, Dan the Weatherman.) My feet are so sweaty they slip down to the tips of my high heels, crushing my pinkies and reinjuring my right big toe. I'm wearing a tiny dress. The neckline is high, but so is the hem. It has little more fabric than a bathing suit, which should make me feel cooler, but every inch of it clings to my skin.

After seeing Trip and becoming suspicious that he might have another love interest, I did what any woman with a pulse does—I tried to look fabulous. I washed and even blow-dried my hair. I put on foundation. I swiped bronzer between my breasts—a trick to fake cleavage that Caroline once showed me. I doubled my mascara, and while waiting for my nails to dry, I put Crest Whitestrips on both my upper and lower teeth. If I were to run into Trip, I'd blind him with my very fucking happy shiny smile.

As expected, there's a line for Stripes. I queue up on the red carpet. The people in front of and behind me wear shimmery fabrics: Lurex, spandex, polyester. A muscular bouncer hooks and unhooks a velvet rope, admitting people one at a time. Calm down, everyone. We're in Charleston, not Miami.

The room is packed with people in their sexual prime—all round tits and square jaws. I scrunch my shoulders together and cut a path to the bar, which is two people deep. I find a space next to a young guy, smile, and nudge my way between him and the bar. He doesn't smile back but does let me in front of him. I shout my order at the bartender.

"Don't pay for that." Kevin's steel-blue eyes seem more intense in this light. He grabs my hand and drags me over to a cluster of orange couches. "We got bottle service."

The four girls from the boat crowd around the table. Their dresses don't cover much more than their bikinis did, but then again, neither does mine. I can almost see up their skirts and make a mental note to keep my legs crossed when sitting.

Taylor turns toward me. She's the one who urinated on me. Not on purpose, of course, but still. That face, those labia, were imprinted on me forever.

Kevin tugs on my arm, pulls me down to sit next to him, and starts to mix a vodka Sprite. Not my fave, but it will do. The music is loud, so we have to shout to hear each other, though he shouts louder than necessary. "I'm really glad that dog decided to let you go out tonight!"

"Cheers!" We clink glasses.

"Yeah, I was surprised you texted back. I thought you didn't have fun on the boat. But then I figured you just like to swim." He picks up a napkin to rub at a water stain on the glass table-top. "You're different. You're not like them." He gestures to his lady friends. "You're . . . real. You know?"

That, even from him, is nice to hear. "Thanks," I say, and genuinely mean it.

"And you're hot, too. But you don't flaunt it. And you don't care what anyone thinks. I like that."

I instinctively smooth my skimpy dress. Actually, I do care what people think . . . sort of. My eyeliner job took seven Q-tips and ten minutes, and I might lose a pinkie toe at night's end, but the heels are staying on. Oh, well. I like being thought of as low maintenance.

"Isn't this place great?!" His tone has a sharp, unfamiliar edge. His energy seems almost manic. He reaches past me to scour another sticky spot on the far side of the table. Maybe he's a clean freak?

I lean back to create some room between us and take stock of my surroundings. The glitzy chandeliers are fun. They look odd, though, hanging next to the industrial-chic HVAC tubes. Oil portraits of sexy women with pouty, sultry expressions stare down at the crowd. Their silky dresses spill open, revealing ample décolletage. In one, a woman lies on her side next to an overturned martini glass. In another, a brunette with teased hair bites her lip. Martha would call it "bachelor art." Still, I shouldn't be so dismissive of the evening. It's a pleasant novelty, after a long drought, to be around someone happy to see me.

Kevin, now evidently satisfied with the appearance of the table, has started to make me a second drink. "Sprite or cranberry?" He yells so loud I feel I'm at the wrong end of a megaphone.

"Cranberry," I say back, lowering my voice in the hope that he'll follow my lead. Shakily, he pours the vodka. This drink is stiffer than the first.

The booze does its work; soon, I feel I'm dissolving into the night. The music loosens my spine. I feel my inhibitions begin to melt, along with my regrets, my second guesses . . .

Kevin stands. "Come on." He leads us confidently to the dance floor, apparently unconcerned with stepping on toes or knocking drinks in the crowded bar. He snakes an arm around my back and presses me close. I hadn't planned on anything this intimate with him, in public or in private, but I allow it. Trip wouldn't touch me, so what the hell.

Swiveling his hips, he bends his head low so that his lips touch my ear. "You're so fucking hot. Your eyes are like a super-model's. I could do you right now." When he inhales, he makes a hissing sound. Then he grabs my butt. Hard. *Ouch*. This is what I wanted, right? New experiences. He slaps my butt again, even harder this time. *Ouch*, but . . . okay?

He leans in to kiss me. I let him. The inside of his mouth is mealy and unctuous, like an overripe banana. I involuntarily pull back. I don't like it. *Maybe I could learn to like it?* He leans in again, but I maneuver past and drop my head against his chest. He's tall, so I end up pressing my ear awkwardly against his stomach. We don't fit well together like Trip and I did, but I hold tight, because it's all I have right now.

We join his group for more drinks, then dance again. And again, 'til the music stops. Harsh overhead light flickers on: closing time. "Let's go," Kevin says. He walks fast, cuffing my arm tightly. I have to trot to keep up, to keep from falling. We weave through hordes of twentysomethings, steadying themselves as they orient to the world outside the bars. The boys lean against street lanterns, smoking. The girls sink onto the King Street curb, relieved to be off their feet and sitting.

"Where are we going?"

Kevin turns back, his eyes wide. "Your house!" he yells in an almost-militant voice.

"No, Kevin," I say, struggling to find the right words. So much alcohol, so quickly. "You can't stay with me."

"Yeah, but look at this." He lets me go and swings his arm wide, gesturing to the parking lot. I follow his gaze, unsure of what he means for me to see. "The car, Simons. I can't drive. I've had too much to drink." He hands me his keys. "Just let me stay with you."

I hand them back. "You could get an Uber."

"I got you *bottle* service. I took you out on my *boat*. You can't just let me crash?"

Well, that's true. Maybe that does warrant a bed for a night. I'm not cruel.

He raises his large hands, his palms facing me. "See? No touching." He stumbles, regains his balance. "I won't touch you."

"Okay, fine." We walk in hurried silence to my apartment. I choose a zigzag route, vaguely hoping I'll lose him, but he manages to follow, moving with the singular focus of a zombie.

As we ascend the rickety stairs, I hear Bruno scratching against the door. Taking two steps at a time, I race to intercept Bruno in order to prevent him from scraping off more paint with his sharp claws; Kevin trails close at my heels. "Kevin, this is Bruno." The dog wriggles wildly in my arms.

"Hello, Bruno." He nods heavily, as though he has weights in the front and back of his head. Stumbling into my kitchen, he swipes his hand along the wall, locates the switch. The kitchen floods with light. "Roaches!" He stomps on the ground with his polished, glossy shoes. *Bam!* One roach finds refuge beneath the slanting oven. He finishes off the two dying ones—unable to escape, stuck on their backs—in a series of clomps, leaving my kitchen floor a mess of exoskeleton shrapnel and greasy, yellow innards.

Bam! Bam! The roaches are dead or gone, but he keeps going. "Kevin, stop! Just stop." If it hasn't happened already, this idiot is going to wake the neighbors.

I steer him toward the sofa. Fortunately, Kevin seems willing to lie down. "You can sleep here. I need to take Bruno out to pee." Kevin collapses his long body onto the couch, yawns sleepily. Thank goodness.

I grab the leash and hurry Bruno down the stairs. He pees for what seems like a full two minutes. I give him time to sniff around, in the hope that Kevin will be fast asleep by my return.

When I get back, he's not on the couch. "Kevin?"

"I'm in your bed!" he shouts through a pillow. "I can't fit on that couch. I'm too big. I'm a big boy."

Fuck. Seriously? I find him flat on his stomach, lying as straight as a pencil on the edge of the bed. His face is turned to the wall. There's still plenty of room for me to get a decent night's sleep. A night on my stiff sofa would wreck my workday tomorrow, which has already been decimated by a night of heavy drinking.

"Okay, fine, but we are not hooking up. You're only sleeping here because I don't want you to drive drunk. You got that?"

Wordlessly, he gives a thumbs-up.

A minute later, he looks to be out cold. I retreat to the bathroom to change my clothes; I wear a big T-shirt *and* a sports bra and shorts *and* underwear to bed. I lie on my stomach, as far away from him as possible, my arms tucked under my chest.

* * *

In my dream, I am in the desert, and it's sweltering. I am surfing on sand. My board bobs unevenly, like a car bumping down a country road. I am thirsty. I want to drink water. I want to be in water. On the horizon, I see a sapphire lake. I glide on my board down the dunes toward the water.

The sand gives way to a caked, lumpy mudflat. On this terrain, the bouncing gets rougher. I spread my feet wider to avoid getting bucked off and having my body scraped against the hard clay. I bounce and bounce and bounce and bounce . . .

And then I wake up.

I am *still* bouncing. What the hell? My bedsprings squeak rhythmically.

I turn to see Kevin above me, straddling me, on his knees. He is still wearing his shirt, but he's naked from the waist down. "Yeah . . ." I hear him whisper beneath a slapping noise. He is masturbating, and . . . *ouch!* He spanks me.

OH. MY. GOD.

When I wanted freedom, I didn't want some drunk asshole sexually assaulting me. Is this what the single life is like—shiny clothes and genitals? Give me back the white dresses and pearls. Give me brunches and tea sandwiches. Rescue me, Trip. Take me home. Call me Cinnamon.

But he's not here; I have to save myself. I grab on to the bed frame and, thankful for every push-up I've done to be a stronger surfer, use it to wrench my body from underneath him and scamper out of the bed.

"Wait," he pleads, "I'm close." Still on his knees, he rubs a slimy, erect penis.

"Get out! Get out right now!" I grab one of my toe-crushing stilettos. I hurl it at him; it pings off his chest.

Kevin, still masturbating, uses his free hand to swat it away. "Just wait . . ."

I throw the other shoe, this time aiming at his dick. He blocks it.

Bruno charges, barking hysterically. Kevin claps his hands to his ears. "Your fucking dog!" He flops onto his back, moonlight illuminating his pornographic silhouette.

"Get out! *Get out!* If you don't get out this instant, I am calling the cops."

Kevin rolls to the far side of the bed and slips on his pants. "What's wrong with you? Taylor said you were kinky. You're a fucking little-girl prude."

Taylor—the pee girl? Is that where he got this whole idea? "Maybe I am," I say, thankful for the little bit of class still left in me. I run to the hall, get my phone. "I'm dialing."

"All right," he says, with his hands lifted again. "Jesus, just give me a minute to put on my shoes."

"Get out," I say, pointing at the door. *"Now."*

The shithead actually sits down on my bed to put on his shoes, but at least he's putting them on. I wait for him to get up and leave my apartment. As soon as he's on the other side of the door, I slam it shut behind him and turn the lock.

"Cunt," he mumbles from the other side of the door.

I exhale, not realizing I'd been holding my breath for quite some time. I slide against the door, onto the floor, finally safe. Bruno circles me and moves closer to lick my face.

I consider calling the police. Should I? Was I really ever hurt? He didn't rape me, right? I think of Rachel Ronan. She sent Sonny's texts to our news station, and look what happened. Even though my show ran only the one photo of her and Sonny, images of her life dug up from her personal social media account parade across thousands of television screens: snapshots of her drinking beer, dancing in a scanty outfit. Last I heard, Ms. Ronan resigned from her job, moved back home to Connecticut.

I broke off an engagement. I've puked outside an independently owned bike store and flashed boob at a musician after we had sex. I don't want my indiscretions blasted across the TV sets of the Lowcountry.

"Come on, Bruno." We huddle together on the couch, where I finally fall asleep.

31.

The Invitation

My phone buzzes, but I'm too hot to move. My body has cooled after a cold shower, but my face is still Johns-Island-tomato-red. Naked in bed, I study patterns of light through the blinds. The room still smells of bleach. I washed my sheets four times after that monstrous asshole accosted me a couple of weeks ago, and they still feel dirty. Maybe I need to burn some sage. My phone buzzes again . . . and again . . . with insistence. I finally roll over and snatch it from the bedside table. It's Mom.

"Laudie had an episode."

My heart tightens. "Another stroke?"

"We're not sure. We just got a call a few minutes ago. Your father and I are headed there right now."

"Is she going to be okay?"

"Honey, we don't know."

"I'll be there soon."

I fling myself out of bed to get dressed. I gather my wet hair in a low ponytail. Where is that other damn ballet flat?

I squat and sift through a rubbery pile at the bottom of my closet, chucking aside old sneakers, a pair of Doc Martens, and my stilettos from that icky night. Underneath a flip-flop, I spy something that looks like a pillow for a Barbie Doll—it's a little plastic bag with white powder inside. I'm no druggie, but I'm no idiot, either. That fucking Kevin was high on cocaine, which might explain his obsessive cleaning of the table at the club but most certainly doesn't excuse him of being a predator. I open the bag over the toilet and watch the powder spread in the bowl.

* * *

Cascades of string music escape from Laudie's room. I recognize this thunderous storm of violins and cellos as a section of Vivaldi's *The Four Seasons*. The music is brisk, allegro, as though urging me to hurry up. Summer has vanished. Fall approaches. Skipping every other stair, I arrive breathless at her bedroom door, anticipating my family circling my grandmother, weeping. Instead, the mood is calm.

A bouquet of damask roses on Laudie's mirrored vanity perfumes the air. A green light on the stereo blinks steadily, which plays at a volume just below deafening. Mom sits next to Laudie's bed. Dad talks with Shaniece, but I can't hear a word over the music. He wears a navy suit and a burgundy tie printed with mallard ducks. He waves me over.

"How is she?"

"She's better now. She calmed down."

"Calmed down? Was it a stroke?"

"Shaniece is pretty sure your grandmother has a UTI; apparently they can make her act a little goofy. A nurse already called in the antibiotics. Weezy's going to pick them up on her way."

"And that will make her feel better?"

"We think so."

The knot in my stomach eases. "Where's Tito?"

"Tito's outside enjoying his coffee on the piazza."

While Shaniece adjusts Laudie's covers, Dad unexpectedly opens his arms to me, inviting me into a bear hug. I'm not sure if it's in celebration of Laudie's turn for the better or a peace offering. I fold into his body, which is still as strong as I remember from when I was a child, when I thought he was Superman— out of uniform, of course. My wet hair dampens his starched button-down, but he doesn't pull away. Instead, he kisses me on the head.

Mom joins us, rubs the side of my arm up and down, over and over. It's meant to be tender, but it feels more like she's trying to scrub me clean. She breaks the circle and gestures for me to take a seat beside Laudie. "Mother," she says, "Simons is here to see you."

Laudie struggles to locate me in what must be some sort of shadowy miasma, some existential murkiness. I pivot the chair sideways to put myself in her direct line of vision. "Hi, Laudie. I love you."

A tiny rustle escapes from her throat, a wisp of sound. Even if the music weren't blasting, it would be impossible to hear. I take a guess: "You love me, too." I pat her skeletal leg. "I know."

She shakes her head, pleads at me with her eyes. "Letter," she mumbles, or at least that's what I think she says. I only catch the last, indistinct syllable.

"Laudie, what letter?" I spin around to my parents, who are talking with Shaniece. "Can you turn the music down? She's trying to tell me something."

Mom and Dad watch me, their noses scrunched. Shaniece crosses the room to lower the volume. I mouth a thank-you and lean in close to Laudie's mouth, which trembles with effort. This time, though, she speaks clearly. "The letter."

It's also clear to see that she won't be able to say anything more, at least for now. Whatever message she's trying to send, I want her to feel I received it. "I'll get it," I say, but she doesn't hear me, or at least she doesn't acknowledge that she's heard me. Her eyes are closed. She has fallen back asleep.

"Mom, do you think she'll get better?"

"Shaniece says the drugs will help, honey, but you know she's not going to get better."

"I do. Of course. Do we know how long . . . ?"

"We don't know. It could be months. Could be weeks. This is part of the journey."

"It's just so sad."

"She had a good life."

"Mom, I think she wants to tell me something. It has to do with a letter."

"She's probably talking about these." Mom rummages through her pocketbook, hands me two heavy white cards. The first is Caroline's debutante party invitation. "I need your journalistic eye. I had some proofs made."

Mr. and Mrs. Edward Chisolm Smythe
Request the Pleasure of Your Company

For Cocktails
Honouring Their Daughter
Caroline Jenrette Smythe
On Saturday, the Thirtieth of November
At Eight O'Clock in the Evening
30 Atlantic Street
Charleston, South Carolina
Black Tie

The Favour of a Reply Is Requested

"I don't see any typos, but are you sure you don't want your name on it, Mom? What about Carry Ann and Ed Smythe? Or even Caroline Ann and Edward, if you want to go formal?"

"My name is on it."

"As Mrs. Edward Chisolm Smythe."

"Everyone knows it's me."

"Mom, you're a person, separate from Dad."

"Hmm." She plucks the invitation from my hand. In front of us, Laudie sleeps, her breathing a bit less tumultuous. "Look at the date." She taps her finger on the line that reads, *Saturday, the Thirtieth of November.* "I think we got the best date. You know how by the end of the season you just don't want to eat another mini crab cake . . ."

"Yeah," I manage, feeling a tad sacrilegious talking about hors d'oeuvres in front of a dying woman. Mom hands me the second card. I start to read:

The family of Claudia Pringle Middleton wishes to convey its sincere appreciation for your recent expression of sympathy . . .

Am I really proofreading a card for Mom to mail, thanking family friends for the casseroles, notes, and flowers they'll send after Laudie dies? Instead of fussing over fonts and paper stock at the stationery store, shouldn't we be burning incense and lighting votives? Are there not ceremonies and songs for sending dying people out of this world? Sure, *The Four Seasons* plays on the stereo, but it hardly constitutes a vigil. We've even outsourced all the hands-on dirty work—laundry, diapers, medications—to the hospice nurses.

We are mainly spectators, dutifully waiting for Laudie to die so we can get death's messiness out of the way and move on to what we do best: choosing between ecru or white paper stock, observing the two-week-turnaround correspondence rule. We're all too fucking polite to do the real, messy, difficult, authentic work of life . . . and death. What is the matter with us? I look at

Mom, hoping she's absorbing the full measure of incredulity on my face. She waves her hand dismissively. "Honey, we know it's going to happen. I just need to get these cards printed now so we'll have them when we need them."

"Isn't that a bit like putting the cart before the horse? She isn't even . . ." I struggle for the right words. "She's still *here*."

Mom smiles, pats Laudie on the head. "Oh, don't look so worried. Besides, she likes them. I already showed them to her."

Jesus H.

Shaniece takes Laudie's blood pressure. She lifts a limp arm with one hand and pumps her gadget with the other. "Her heart rate's strong."

"Thank you, Shaniece. Call me the minute anything changes," Mom says. She gathers her purse and cups my chin in her hands. "Okay, honey, your father and I are going to scoot. We've got to get ready for lunch with the Lachicottes at Battery Hall."

"Y'all are going out to lunch?"

Mom squares her jaw. Her eyes flash with anger. She crosses the room and motions for me to follow her. "Come with me." She leads me into the bathroom and shuts the door.

The wallpaper is patterned with miniature roses. Terry-cloth towels hang from the rack; they're folded so that Laudie's initials—CPM, embroidered in white—are displayed. The room is small; Mom and I stand together on a shaggy bath mat. "How dare you!" She works hard to keep from shouting. She points a finger toward the door; behind it Laudie lies in her bed. "My mother"—she pounds her chest—"*my* mother is in that bed right now because you took her to a ballet. I come here every day, for hours, Simons, to be by her side. Just because I don't work and I'm old-fashioned doesn't mean I don't have a life. Things still need to get done. And I still need to eat. Louisa has been asking me for weeks to go to lunch, and I've been putting it off to come here. And here you are, picking at me, at everything I do. I hadn't said one word to you about Laudie's last day—her real last day—but you seem to have forgotten. I didn't think I'd have to remind you why we are here now."

I bow my head, steel my body to help absorb the onslaught of my mother's fury. "But, Mom, it was Laudie's idea."

"If I were you, I'd be quiet. Just hush." Mom leaves the bathroom and shuts the door behind her, enclosing me in a roomful of Laudie's personal things—perfumes, lipsticks, soaps, hand lotions, a collection of brushes and combs—that she might still be enjoying now if I hadn't taken her to the ballet. Sure, she wouldn't be pirouetting to the grocery store, but she would have had more time on earth with us.

I run into Laudie's bedroom, which is dead silent except for her labored breathing. Everyone else is gone. Someone cut off the music before leaving. I crouch to the side of Laudie's bed, stroke her bony body. "Laudie, I'm so sorry." I hope she'll tell me it's all going to be okay, that it's not my fault, but Laudie doesn't say anything. It dawns on me that she doesn't have to. She made it very clear: I must find that letter.

32.

Imagine

On this moonless night, at this distance, the Edisto house glows like the last embers of a fire. When I get out of my car, the animals welcome me. A whip-poor-will calls, then an owl. Tree frogs trill, intoning spirits from another world.

Weezy had begged me to come; it's time again for our Monthly Monday, after all. I thought of cancelling—what if Laudie dies while I'm out here? Weezy reminded me that I'm only skipping one morning visit and that I could see her tomorrow afternoon, on my way home.

The antibiotics worked. Turns out Laudie did have a UTI. She got a little better, but we're pretty sure she had her last real meal nearly three weeks ago. She might have had her last taste of food—a bite of watermelon—on Thursday. When I visit, I sometimes read to her. *Harry Potter*, of course. Other times, I just sit, both awed and terrified by her raggedly inhales that seem as though they could splinter her ribs into shards. Shaniece reassures me that she's not in pain. She's transitioning, she says.

Lately, Laudie seems to exist more and more in the realm of the unconscious. I wish I could bring her out here—to Edisto and the wild—and let the animals of night call her home.

Inside the cabin, ambient music flows from the master bedroom. I pad down the hallway to find Weezy on the floor. A candle flickers on the dresser. "Hey," she mouths with a big, sleepy smile, patting a spot next to her on the carpet. She switches off the recording.

"What are you doing?"

"Guided meditation. It's supposed to help me get ready."

Weezy slides a stack of pamphlets my way; they're dominated by photos of wrinkly babies and their makeup-less mothers. She riffles through the leaflets as though through a deck of cards. "Here's the one that explains how baths are nearly as effective as an epidural. And this one talks about the importance of mood lighting. Candles apparently have a soothing effect and help relax the moms' muscles, which makes it easier to push out the baby."

"It's still going to hurt, though, right? Aren't you nervous?"

She rubs her belly, which is already as big as a beach ball and she still has two more months. "The only thing I'm worried about is going into labor early. I doubt it will happen. Francie was on time, and second children tend to cook longer, but Ashley has that duck-hunting trip a week before the due date."

"Seriously?"

"He and his college buddies have been planning it for more than a year."

"I do." Did Laudie? Is Tito her Prince Charming, in a way? A quiet static, heard only on the stillest of nights, hums in my ears. The night animals have gone silent. "I miss Laudie. She's not gone yet, but I miss her."

"Of course you do."

"And I still feel like it's my fault. At least I think Mom does."

"That's absolutely not true, and you know it. Mom is scared, but she definitely doesn't think it's your fault Laudie is dying. Mom's very emotional right now."

"It was Laudie's idea to go to the ballet. Not mine."

"We know that. Mom's just grieving. Give her some time."

"You should have seen Laudie that day, Weezy. She wore her Chanel suit and her best jewelry—the giant pearls and the gold jaguar pin. She was so determined."

"I know how stubborn she can be. Hold on to that image. I'm learning about the importance of images. Listen." Weezy rolls onto her side and turns the recording back on. Her phone screen reads *Methods for a Loving, Natural Birth.*

"Now repeat after me," intones a soothing female voice. "'I love my baby. My baby loves me. I love my baby. My baby loves me.' Okay, now, deep breath. *Goooood.* Now go back to your paradise. Remember what it looks like? Picture it in your imagination. Go there. When you feel your body begin to work, to move your child into this world, go there."

While it's hard to fathom how any woman in labor could simply will herself through the pain, it's impressive how much this woman's voice has altered my mental state in the short time I've listened. I imagine Laudie, in the wings of a theater, changing from her Chanel suit into the costume of the Atlanta troupe's prima ballerina. She laces up her pointe shoes and secures her headdress made of diamonds and feathers. She takes a centering breath and glides into a giant theater awash with brilliant lights and enthusiastic, clamorous applause.

33.

Swell

October: my favorite month. Most of the tourists have packed up and gone back to Ohio and New Jersey. The beaches have cleared, and so has the humidity. Temperatures hover in the high seventies. The water holds the summer's heat; it's a few degrees warmer than the air. This oceanic heat fuels the big storms, sending them churning across the Atlantic. When hurricanes spin off the coast, we get swells. Today, Folly Beach has serious waves.

I tuck my keys in my wheel well, grab my board, and head for the beach access. I tiptoe past a new puddle, now the fourth permanent one on this footpath, even without a king tide. An elevated boardwalk built to protect the fragile dunes rises at the end of the trail. At its crest, the ocean comes into view. The sea is wild, alive, thrashing. Gray walls of water rise tumultuously, fall in crescendos. Crowns of spray leap and scatter in high arcs before collapsing into the thunderous booms.

Pelicans twist nimbly in the open sky, hunting for fish pushed upward by the choppy waters. One spots a fish and readies itself for the attack. The bird cocks its wings and torpedoes down into the chop. *Splash*. It pops up from under the water with a silvery menhaden suspended in its beak. The bird's gular pouch, the stretchy flesh under the beak, balloons to swallow dinner whole.

I place my board on the sand to rub on a layer of wax.

A child, maybe five or six years old, runs past me to dump a bucket of water into a hole in the sand. He hurries back and forth, absorbed in his project. His plastic toys litter the beach: an orange shovel, purple castle mold, red sand sifter. A muscle-bound action figure rolls in the surf. On my way into the water, I pick it up.

"Mine!" he shrieks. The child has an ear-splitting scream, a cry sharper than a gull's.

"I'm not taking your toy. I'm putting it over here so it doesn't end up in the ocean." I lay the action figure in the dry sand.

"Mom!" he shrieks. A woman walks toward us, her lips flat as the horizon. Her shirt reads: "lib·tard: *noun* 1. A person so open minded their brains fall out."

Instead of explaining why sand and shells make fine, natural toys for kids—that the world doesn't need any more plastic—I grab my board and run off into the waves. No one wants to hear my speech about plastic. Plus, judging from her shirt, we probably wouldn't have had a productive conversation.

I hop on my board to paddle out into the deeper waters. A massive wave rolls toward me. I attempt a duck-dive, pushing the board beneath the steamroller of a wave, but I don't get deep enough to pop up safely on the other side.

The wave tosses me like a rag doll and chucks my board high into the air. The leash tugs at my leg, like a giant hand curling around my ankle, yanking me back to shore.

Once I regain my footing in the shallows, I pull on my leash to retrieve my board. I squint to measure the incoming set and plot my course back out to the ocean. My only option is to try harder.

Eventually I make it past the break. As my reward, a plush, slow-rolling wave rumbles my way. I point my board toward the shore and kick hard. I catch the wave and pop up to a wide stance. I steer my board up and down along the ever-changing wall of water. I'm flying.

My ride ends. I'm back in the shallows, exhausted. I can manage one, maybe two more rides. Panting, I survey the surf, looking for patterns. Waves come in sets, and if I can paddle out between a group of waves, I'll have a better chance of making it past the break.

I hear a loud screech and turn to see the kid from the beach. He's pretending to shoot the laughing gulls soaring overhead. He jumps up and down in the surf, unaware that the outgoing tide carries him closer to me.

I start to put distance between me and this airhorn, but then I spy a surfboard torpedoing right at him.

"Watch out!" I race toward the kid and pull him under the water, pinning him down until I feel the wave has passed and the wayward board is safely between us and the shore.

Seconds later, we emerge. He is stunned. I look to shore, where his mother flips through a magazine; she wasn't watching. Thank God. First I steal his toys, then I dunk him underwater. What would she think?

The boy wipes his eyes, coming to his senses. He starts to cry and runs to his mother. Not wanting to stick around to explain, I hurry back into the ocean.

"Are you okay? Is your son okay?" A guy about my age hurries toward me. He wears a worn rash guard and blue board shorts. His skin reminds me of the pink and tan mottling on whelks. His eyes are the exact shade of palmetto fronds. While this man is definitely sexy, I wonder if he's the type of surfer to claim part of the beach. I know one thing for sure: he's an idiot. Who surfs without a leash, especially during a swell? There are kids in the water. Shitty kids, but kids nonetheless.

He lopes to pick up his board, flipped upside down and buffeted by the surf, and jogs toward me. His forehead is crisscrossed with fine wrinkles from marathon-long days in the sun. He's cute. Very cute.

"We're fine. Just got to be careful out here, you know?"

"I'm so sorry. My leash snapped."

Oh. So, he's not a total bonehead. "He's not my kid," I say, maybe with a little too much force.

"That could have been a disaster. I don't know how to thank you."

A pickup game of tonsil hockey? "Don't worry about it."

"What's your name?"

"Simons."

"I'm Ben."

"Nice to meet you." I hold out my hand.

"That's a good handshake. Is this your usual spot?"

Hmm. Maybe this is his territory? Fine. It's mine, too. "Yes, it is."

In my periphery, the mother to the vuvuzela is waving her arms, trying to get my attention. I half expect her to scream at me, but instead she calls out, "We want to thank you!"

Ben turns to look at the mother, who has lifted her son to her hip.

"Looks like they want to talk to the hero."

I pick up my board. "I guess I've got to go."

"I'll keep an eye out for you."

"Ditto." And that's the thing about life and love. One random person, at some random time, can make the day better. Chances are, I'll never see him again. But it's intriguing to think that I might. I'll keep my eyes open.

34.

Called Back Home

A north wind slices across Charleston Harbor, rocking my car as it reaches the pinnacle of the Ravenel Bridge. Finally, some cool weather has arrived—hopefully for good. The marsh grass below has begun its steady transition from a spring green to a winter-wheat color. The Lowcountry summer water—hot, soupy, and teeming with marine life—has morphed into a cleaner, clearer version of itself. No pudding-thick thunderheads cover the city, no tropical storms whip up suddenly. Wispy cirrus clouds meander overhead; migratory birds head south.

Dead leaves skitter across the parking lot. Angela is uncharacteristically outdoors. She's on her phone, pacing under the oak tree. I pull into a parking spot closest to the employee entrance, giving her some space. Whatever the call is about, she came out here for privacy. To my surprise, she motions me over.

Joining her under the old tree, I'm grateful that at least one developer in this town chose a living work of art over yet another asphalt parking spot. "Well, how much would that cost? Okay. But you say you don't think it would help much?"

Damn. It's gotta be her dog. "Cooper?" I mouth. Angela nods and resumes pacing, crunching acorns underfoot.

It's almost time for the morning meeting. I tap my wrist to let Angela know. She cups her hand over the phone and asks, "Can you tell the team to start without me? You run the meeting." I tell her to take her time.

* * *

The newsroom is arctic cold. A thin film of condensation coats my keyboard. I pull my blanket around my shoulders, chewing a piece of candied ginger while scanning the news feeds.

My cell phone rings. "Hi, Mom."

"Honey, your grandmother died."

What? No! I was just with her this morning. She was as she had been for the last week—her breaths were labored, but she was pink-skinned, at least in her face. That's why I didn't tell her goodbye. I thought I had time to gather the courage. I feel sick. "Was anyone with her?"

"Tito was in the room. And Shaniece. She died peacefully, honey."

"Wow." It finally happened. For every action, there is an equal and opposite reaction, right? So why didn't the earth shake or a meteor fall on Charleston? How is everything around me exactly the same? A momentous transition just occurred, and here I am, hunkered down for another day at News 14. "How are you holding up, Mom?"

"I'm hanging in there."

"I'm so sorry, Mom." *Sorry I took her to the ballet*, are my unsaid words. *Sorry I took her away from you sooner.* "Is there anything I can do?"

"We're going to need help with the reception. I already put in an order with the caterers, so that's covered, thank goodness. Maybe you could help your father arrange the furniture."

Mom babbles on about what couch should be moved where, but I am wondering where Laudie is at this very moment. Still in that hospital bed? Or—*yikes*—in one of those body refrigerators?

Beep. Bop. *Beeeep.* "Simons? What on earth . . . ?" Mom is randomly mashing telephone buttons. "Can you hear me?"

"Yes!" I shout, a little too loudly. A couple of heads spin in my direction.

"So, can we count on you to pick up the liquor?"

I duck behind my computer monitor, cup my hand over my mouth. Personal calls are frowned upon. "Sure, what kind?"

"Honey, I just told you. Write it down this time. Gin, vermouth, sherry, vodka, and whiskey," she says exasperatedly. "And some tonic water. *Oh.* That's Jim Mackey. I've got to go."

The Mackeys are the undertakers for South of Broad residents and have been for generations. "Okay, bye, Mom. I love you," I say, but she's already hung up.

* * *

At my door are two large square envelopes. On both, my name is written in elegant calligraphy: *Miss Simons Parks Smythe.* In the bottom corner of each is also written: *By hand.* In Charleston, "by hand" is considered the more elegant way to send formal mail, when possible. My mother carries the invitations on her walks, slipping the cards into mail slots along the way. When Weezy debuted, I delivered most of the invitations. Mom even made me drive over the bridge to Mount Pleasant to drop some off, which was ridiculous, but she paid me, so I kept my mouth shut.

I study the first, slimmer envelope, running my fingers over the edge, which feels more like fabric than paper. Laudie would have done the same. She appreciated the details—watermarks, fonts, paper weight, and whatnot. It's an invitation to Caroline's debutante party at Mom and Dad's, the one Mom asked me to proofread at Laudie's.

The bulkier envelope is for the ball, a large and lavish event that will honor perhaps ten young ladies at once. They will be formally introduced to society. (In previous generations, when the sexes didn't commingle so freely, this was a momentous occasion, an opportunity for potential marital alliances to be made.) As with all formal society events, the paper stock is always white or ecru; the printing is always in black. For an extra touch, some invitations include a family coat of arms at the top. Elegant yet restrained script spells words the European way: "honour" and "favour"; the word "o'clock" written out. The heavy card is protected by a flimsy square of tissue and feels wet to the touch. And the invitees' names are handwritten, often in gorgeous, painstaking calligraphy.

Also inside: the dance card. It's a tiny booklet tethered to a silky white loop. The women wear it around their wrists during the formal dancing before dinner. A tiny pencil dangles from the rope to write the names of dancing partners on the dotted lines next to songs chosen probably a century ago for the evening: a waltz first, two foxtrots, and so on until the midnight dinner.

Years ago, at my debutante ball, Trip jokingly started to write his name next to every song. Laughing, I snatched the dance card from him before he could finish. Now, I wonder whose name will be written on the dotted line.

35.

The Wake Up

Downtown Charleston is a labyrinth of one-way streets. The maze forces drivers to venture blindly into intersections, execute tight turns. It drives the tourists—expecting logic in the traffic patterns—absolutely bonkers. I've always liked the capricious, unpredictable layout of my town. It forces me to tack like a sailboat through hidden alleys and narrow lanes: Bedons, Zig Zag, Stolls, Horlbeck, Philadelphia, Little Lamboll. I wend my way through the antebellum warren until I reach South Battery. My grandparents' oyster-shell driveway jostles the liquor bottles in the trunk.

Before heading inside, I make my usual detour to Laudie's garden. The herringbone brick pattern along the pool points toward the wall of greenery. I walk beneath the camellias and into white sunlight. When I enter her garden, I feel hollow, weak-kneed. Only now do I fully understand that my grandmother is gone.

Most everything in her garden is dead now, or at least dormant.

The dried, brittle lantana crunch beneath my feet. The bare stalks of hydrangeas make me think of the hands of scarecrows. The rosemary remains green, but the mint has shriveled.

The last of the zinnias look like something out of an old photograph. Time-faded. Sepia-toned. I grab my shears to cut the last of the good ones. Their tough old stems don't yield easily.

The remainder of the zinnias, the dead ones, need to be removed. When I pull them up from the ground, it's as easy as lifting a tissue from its box. I rake my hands through the soil, gathering the soft webs of tired roots and tossing them in the shade of the sago palm. Soon, the garden is nothing but a mound of freshly turned soil. I can't help but think it looks like a grave.

I return the shears to my hook in the potting shed and search for a rag to wipe my hands clean. A drawer houses her tools: shears, florist's tape, narrow-gauge wire. Also inside, rolled up neatly, is an opened zinnia packet containing around thirty seeds. An unfinished project. I rescroll the packet tightly, keep it safe in my fist.

I head back to the car and stash the seed pack in my purse. I lay the wilted zinnias over the box of booze and haul it up the back steps. I hip-check the kitchen door to let myself inside.

I had expected to come into a house somber with death, but instead the atmosphere is festive with party preparations. But why am I surprised? Partying is what Charleston does best, and always has for more than three hundred bourbon-soaked years.

Ashley runs past with a stack of silver platters. In the dining room, Louisa takes inventory of the vases. Dad's bent over a folding table, snapping open the legs. He looks up. "Let me help," he says. He takes the heavy box from me, placing it on the massive mahogany table where Laudie had served thousands of meals. It seems he's warming up to me, but by no means am I out of the doghouse yet. "Tell her about Dr. Legare," Dad says to Louisa. "Simons could put it in the news!"

Oh gosh, parents with news tips—never a good idea.

Lousia holds two vases out for me to choose. "You knew Dr. Legare, of course. The widower."

I guess so. There are so many Legares in this town. I nod and place the papery flowers in the crystal one, Laudie's favorite. "Thanks, Louisa."

"Well, just before he died, he told Mr. Mackey he wanted to be buried with his dog. And Mr. Mackey said, 'I'm sorry, but I can't put your dog to sleep,' and Dr. Legare said, 'Oh, no, Coon's been dead for years.' He told him he buried Coon in his garden, but that he amputated the dog's tail first. And of course this was easy for him to do, since he was a surgeon. He kept the tail in the back of his freezer for four years. Four years, can you believe it? He phoned Mr. Mackey right after he did it. Told him to fetch it when the time came and put it in his coffin."

"You forgot the best part!" Dad interjects. "When his housekeeper was cleaning out his refrigerator, she nearly put it in the garbage. Apparently, he had told her it was a corn dog and that he was saving it for a special occasion."

"Oh, that's right. And then Mr. Mackey had to go and pick it up. And, of course, his housekeeper was wondering what on earth the funeral director was doing in the freezer. Isn't that a trip?"

I wish she wouldn't say "trip," but no one seems to notice. Dad and Louisa laugh, sharing details of rummaging through frozen hamburger patties and ice cream bars.

The buzz inside the house dies when Mom enters the dining room; the kitchen door swings shut behind her. She looks nearly like she always does: neat, pulled-together. She wears a kelly green shirt, matching cardigan, and khaki trousers. But her hair is a touch out of place, and she had buttoned her sweater incorrectly—one side hangs a smidge lower than the other. Mom drops into one of the Queen Anne side chairs pushed up against the wainscotting. "Andy's plane just landed." Andy is Mom's younger brother. He lives in Dallas. No one born in Charleston can understand this.

I circle the dining table to sit beside Mom. The stuffing in the chairs is so worn down from the decades I may as well be sitting in a shallow bucket. "Are you doing okay, Mom?"

"About as well as I can."

"Is there anything I can do?"

Mom blows her nose. "Can you go upstairs and get some photographs of Mother? So people can see her in her glory days."

"Of course."

* * *

Upstairs, it's déjà vu. The bedroom looks as it always did, before Laudie entered hospice. Most noticeably, the curtains are open;

full sun enters, strafing, as it always did this time of day, the bureaus, highboy, pillows, paintings, and chairs. On her dresser, the pearls she wore to the ballet spill over a silver dish. Her matching, monogrammed silver hand mirror and hairbrush rest beside her jewelry box. The medicinal vials and ointments have been removed from the bedside table. Her nightgown and robe hang on a hook at the bathroom door. Everything is in its place, as though she might walk in at any moment to change for a session at the barre.

The hospital bed is gone. Unhooked, unplugged, removed. I'm glad. I never liked it. It was just a primer for a coffin, anyway. Good riddance. Her and Tito's marriage bed, which had been moved a few feet over to make room for the hospice bed, has been pushed back to its proper location at the room's center. The blanket is neatly folded at the foot, just as always. I set the zinnias on her nightstand.

Around the room, photos of Laudie depict her as a wife, mother, and grandmother, but I want Charlestonians to see the Laudie that no one truly knew. On the mantel is a black-and-white studio portrait of Laudie taken in her early twenties, always my favorite photo of her. I lift the photo, the silver frame tarnished, to stare at my grandmother as a young woman: a brave and hopeful maverick. Her closed lips suggest mystery and a hint of mirth—a knowing Mona Lisa smile. Those wide-set, challenging eyes seem to look right at me. "The letter," she says. I blink hard. Obviously, she isn't speaking to me through her photograph, but the command feels so immediate, so unambiguous, that she might as well be.

What letter? I wrack my brain, listening for footsteps of anyone who might come upstairs. Agreeable sounds—familiar voices, the clink of liquor bottles and crystal glasses being arranged on the bar—drift up from the first floor. Everyone is busy, occupied.

With the coast clear, I duck into Laudie's closet. Dozens of suits, dresses, and ball gowns—a collection curated over more than half a century—wait to be worn again. When I rake the hangers to the side, hunting for a box of papers or mementos, Laudie's scent—a mix of Shalimar and Oil of Olay—almost overpowers me.

The shoe boxes beneath her dresses hold her pumps, sandals, and her adored collection of Capezios. I rifle through all the boxes, finding nothing but tissue paper and more shoes. Larger round boxes on the upper shelf contain her hats. In the top corner, stacks of zippered plastic bags prevent moths from eating her sweaters. Belts on hooks dangle like snakes from trees in the far reaches of her closet. I search high and low. No letter.

I ransack her dresser, sift through bras, stockings, and silk slips. No letter here, either, but I take a moment to stroke the leather soles of her ballet slippers.

"Simons?" Mom calls from the top of the stairs. "What are you doing?"

I stash her shoes back inside the dresser drawer. "I'm looking for something."

Though I should be picking out photos, Mom appears more curious than mad. "For what?"

"Remember I told you Laudie said something about a letter?"

"I do, but, honey, her mind wasn't all there." Mom crosses the room to check herself in the mirror. "Will you look at that? My buttons are all wonky."

"Mom, I really think she wanted me to find some sort of document, or whatever it was."

"Oh, Simons, what on earth could she have possibly been hiding all these years?"

Mom needs to know the real Laudie. She should know about the rebellious girl who jumped from train trestles and trespassed to skinny-dip. She should know the young woman who danced in Atlanta clubs where the music set people on fire. Mom needs to know about Laudie's secret love affair with a handsome man because, in a way, it's part of her story, too.

When Mom knows Laudie, she'll understand that a hidden but very alive part of Laudie surfaced in a Chanel suit that fateful day I took her to the ballet, demanding I take her on her final adventure. If Mom knew the real Laudie, she might have taken her to *La Sylphide* herself. "Mom, there's a lot more to Laudie than you got to know and what Tito has told us all these years." I hand her the black-and-white studio photograph of Laudie. Mom studies it, clasps it to her chest. I pat the bed, signaling for her to join me. "Let me tell you a story."

36.

The Receiving

A sharp wind whips over the Ashley River and funnels down Wentworth Street, stirring ripples in a giant puddle created by the recent king tide. The water is rising. And still, the builders build. Cranes dominate the Charleston skyline like leviathans. Construction crews crawl over our city like ants as developers squeeze more and more buildings onto the remaining peninsula wetlands. Few citizens understand the impending catastrophe. They're the ones who read science. They're the ones who raise their houses, jacking the old homesteads ten feet or more into the air. They're the ones who know we'll soon have to bury our dead aboveground, like they do in New Orleans.

The Mackey building is on high ground. The oldest structures always are; it's the newer ones from the twentieth century and onward that are built on low land or filled-in marshes. That Charleston is the Lowcountry is a fact that was not wasted on eighteenth- and nineteenth-century builders; they knew to build on high ground.

Once a Victorian mansion, the Mackey Funeral Home looks like something out of an ominous fairy tale. Charleston, with its trove of Georgian architecture, has few Victorian buildings. After the defeat of the Civil War, hardly any Charlestonians had the wealth to build the sorts of newer houses that were fashionable in the rest of the country. The Mackey mansion is one exception.

With its busy, drip-castle turrets and garrets, the building looks spooky and fittingly funereal. Sometime after it was constructed, a porte cochere was added to one side. This is where the coffins are loaded into hearses. It's also where mourners gather to queue up for visitations. In Charleston, it is common for hundreds of people to pay their respects; it's the last social courtesy that one can extend to a loved one or a friend.

Crimson barberry shrubs, office-park favorites, line the main path. Holly bushes rim the roundabout. Affixed to the front double doors is a matching pair of colonial door knockers; they are shaped like urns. The right door is ajar. Stuffy air escapes through the crack. I push on the door.

The foyer is surprisingly small. A faded Bokhara rug muffles my footsteps. The windows, heavily swathed in gauzy fabric, deflect the rays of afternoon sun.

Around the corner, Mom and Dad stand with Mr. Mackey in the center of a bay-windowed parlor. The room appears frozen in the 1960s, no doubt the last time it was decorated. It is sparsely furnished—just two wing-backed chairs and a side table with an open guest book and ballpoint pen. Portraits of stern, humorless people from another era hang on the beige walls. Everything seems preserved in a thin layer of dust and eternity. "Hi."

"You sure look like your grandmama." Mr. Mackey speaks quietly. The Mackeys never speak much above a whisper; quiet must be encoded in their DNA.

Mom walks over to me, her face wet with tears. I realize I've never seen my mother cry; the sight of it unravels me. "I looked everywhere for that letter. I must have gone through every paper in that house."

"Oh, Mom," I speak into her hair. We hold each other tight. When I told her Laudie's story, I didn't hold back. I told Mom everything: the skinny-dipping, the dancing, her love affair with John, and even the pregnancy scare. At first she listened quietly, playing with the pilling on Laudie's blanket. Then she sat up straighter, looking around her mother's room as if seeing it for the first time. "Don't worry about the letter now," I say. "We'll find it."

A door creaks. More stuffy air enters the room.

"Jim, we're ready." Charles Mackey, Jim's brother, waits at the threshold.

"Okay." He turns to Mom. "Whenever you're ready, we can view your mother."

Wait a minute. An open casket? She looked so horrid in the last weeks before death. I look to my mom, half-expecting her to prevent this sacrilege, march past the Mackeys, and shut the coffin lid herself.

I'm wrong. Mom nods assent, quickly transforming to stoic, and a flash of pride for my mother rushes through me. She's a lady, through and through. She opens her embroidered clutch and extracts a handkerchief for me. "Just in case." I dab my eyes—already brimming—and with Dad we follow the Mackey brothers to a smaller room that's connected to the main parlor.

With its Pepto-Bismol pink wallpaper and dingy lighting, the viewing room looks fittingly depressing. At the far end is Laudie's coffin, its open lid a yawning mouth. It has brass handles and ivory-colored satin lining.

Eight plant stands—four on each side—flank the mahogany coffin; each holds a floral display. Some arrangements are tall and sculptural; others are loose and blowsy; a couple are low and horizontal. The flowers themselves differ wildly from one another: roses, irises, hydrangeas, bells of Ireland, lilies, tulips, baby's breath, stock, asters, and gladiolas.

Each bouquet has a crisp little gift envelope attached to it. It's generous and thoughtful of people to send flowers, but wouldn't she have enjoyed them more when she was alive? With that many flowers, she could have spent her last days in an enchanted greenhouse. I should have bought her flowers, stacked her bedroom floor-to-ceiling with them. Why didn't I think of that?

Dad escorts Mom to the coffin; I hang back and am soon joined by Uncle Andy. His ruddy complexion is somehow subdued by this pink light. "How was your flight?"

"Uneventful and on time. Doesn't get much better than that." He jingles some coins in his pockets.

Together we survey the room, which will soon be filled with friends and family. Jim Mackey pivots the floral arrangements so their best sides show. His brother sets out bottled water, plastic cups, a box of Kleenex. Uncle Andy gestures toward my wet handkerchief. "I see the waterworks have been turned on. You've been holding up okay?"

"I'm sad. I miss her."

He runs a hand over his oily face. "Me, too."

"I haven't looked yet. I didn't know we were having an open casket."

"It might make you feel better. That's why they do it."

Okay. I'll go. I can't *not* look. I approach, each footstep heavy—leaden—with reluctance. Bit by bit, Laudie comes into view, looking like a doll made to look like my grandmother. Perhaps we Episcopalians are a bit like the Egyptians, sending our dead into the afterlife dressed for a party.

There's a sensation in my chest, a pressure; it's here that my powerful emotions dwell. The most prominent is a throbbing sadness. I ache for the life Laudie could have led, for the story she could have told. Why can't we all have happy endings? How can life be so unfair?

A second energy stirs beneath my ribs, making me queasy with guilt. I didn't prepare Laudie for this journey in any way. It was Shaniece who used a blue sponge to moisten her dry mouth, not me. Shaniece cleaned Laudie's body when she couldn't. I wasn't holding her hand the moment Laudie gasped for her last breath; I was at the office, doing the news, for Chrissakes. Maybe if I had been by her side more, there would have been an opportunity, a moment of lucidity, where she would have told me about the letter. She died wanting me to know.

Laudie wears a lacy lilac dress—one that I've never seen before. How hard it must have been for Mom to choose her mother's last outfit. The grip at my core loosens at the sight of Laudie's Capezio dancing shoes. Mom selected those over a pair of conservative pumps, which I imagine wasn't an easy decision for her—displaying her proper Charleston mother in what some would consider theatrical costume shoes. But she did it, and a second burst of pride for my mother washes over me.

I stare at Laudie's midsection, which is as immobile as her Chippendale sideboard. Of course she wouldn't be breathing, but a visceral, primal part of me is confused; her chest should be moving up and down.

Folded on her stomach, her hands have taken on an eerie, greenish cast. The embalming fluid has dissolved her blue veins. Her bruises, so angry and vivid just the other day, have vanished. She wears the jaguar brooch, the pearl necklace, and the gold watch she wanted me to have. I can't help but notice it is still ticking.

Her fluffy blond hair has been washed and neatly set into waves. Would she have wanted a ballerina bun? Somehow, the mortician unclenched her jaw. She wears a shade of lipstick—rose-petal pink—I have never seen her wear, but it does suit her. Then she opens her crystal eyes and stares right through me. She speaks to me just like she did from the black-and-white photo: "The letter."

I'm going crazy.

"Honey," Mom whispers, "people are starting to arrive. We need to form a receiving line." I follow her out into the front parlor, where I locate Dad, Weezy, and Caroline. Tito is sitting in a chair near the door, ready to greet his friends. Andy stands next to him. My immediate family falls into line beside them. I stand between my sisters, all of us in demure, chaste funeral dresses.

I've stood in a receiving line twice before: at Weezy's "coming out" party and at my own. "Coming out" is the old-fashioned term for debuting. At the ball, all glamorized in our gowns, we debutantes had to remain in the receiving line for the first hour of the party. Hundreds of guests came through to greet us. Some shook our hands; others air-kissed us. They wanted to keep our expensive updos intact and knew better than to leave lipstick marks on our cheeks. Still, there were always a few gregarious men in the line who bear-hugged, inadvertently impressing their metal cuff links on our bare backs or ramming their jackets into our powdered faces.

It was through the ritual of the receiving line, and later, at the grand waltz, that we debutantes were formally introduced to society. We were exuberant, charming, extravagant in our gestures. And for the occasion, we dressed in the uniform of all Charleston debutantes before us. We wore white.

Today, we wear black. We greet our tribe, the same people who suited up and dressed up for the big balls and cocktail parties, but this time, we gather to say goodbye. This is my culture. It's what we do.

The room quickly swells with friends, neighbors, acquaintances, cousins, and colleagues. They move through the receiving line before moving on to view Laudie. Most quickly say they're sorry for our loss so as not to hold up the line, but some pause to ask about my work or touch Weezy's belly or tell Caroline how beautiful she is.

A bottleneck forms around Mom, giving me an opportunity to look out the window. A queue of mourners snakes past the porte cochere, down the walkway, and out to the street. About midway in the line stands a man the exact same build as Trip, wearing—like most of the men today—a black suit. When he turns, a narrow tomahawk face gazes toward the window. Not Trip, thank goodness. I wouldn't know what to think or say.

The guy must be a Sanders. Everyone in that family, even the heavyset ones, have narrow heads. Like Mom and all the other locals, I can identify Old Charleston family groups by their dominant features: the Huguets have Roman noses; the Taveaus walk with a goofy gait; the Vanderhorsts, with their enviable olive skin, never have to hide from the sun.

Three of Caroline's debutante friends shimmy toward us. I recognize one of them—Bennett. She reaches past me to get to Caroline. "Hope it's okay to jump in line," she says. I step back so I don't get trampled.

"Totally," Caroline says.

Bennett turns to me. "I'm really sorry for your loss. I heard she was a remarkable lady."

"Thanks," I say, wishing she would go away but unsure why I feel so strongly. She spins back to Caroline, whispers something in her ear. Caroline hurries her along, says something about meeting up later.

A hulking figure makes his way toward the receiving line.

It's unmistakably Sonny Boykin; he stands a foot taller than everyone else. When he gets close, he eclipses my view of the room. He speaks in a proper Old Charleston drawl, which owes something to Bostonese (in which the r's are dropped) and something to the mellifluous Gullah language (in which the spaces between words and syllables are elongated and exaggerated, as though filled with syrup). "Cooper" is "Coop-ah." "Water" is "Wat-ah." "Dog" is "dawg." It's the accent of my tribe, and it's dying as my generation marries outside of the tribe or moves away. "Your grandmama was a great woman."

The controversy around him has died; Ms. Ronan dropped the charges. We may never know what he did or didn't do. Still, I have my suspicions. As Martha once told me, a good ol' boy can never fail. The princes and heirs apparent of Charleston are always forgiven. He leans over slightly; his large hand presses, lingers momentarily on my spine. I will my body to be bigger and look him dead in the eyes. "You have no idea," I hear myself say.

If he is insulted, he doesn't show it. Once he gets through the receiving line, he's greeted warmly by the crowd. Most of them likely presume his innocence. Even if any of them harbored suspicions, they would still be cordial.

"Hi, friend."

I jump. It's Martha. She wears a chunky sweater and a maxi skirt. Her eyes are a little puffy, but in the way that suggests she's had a good night's sleep. She's gained weight; the bit of extra fat makes her look younger, her skin springier, more voluptuous, more even toned. "Thank you for coming."

"Of course I would come. How are you holding up?"

Shitty. "Fine."

"I'm sorry about your grandma."

"Thanks," I manage, still trying to figure out if I'm glad she's here or hugely annoyed. That week she toured with the band—when she had lied and told me she was visiting her grandmother—I babysat her dog. I picked up his shit practically with my bare hand. She might or might not be dating Harry.

"Coffee soon? I'll call you, okay? I miss you."

Do I miss her? I'm not so sure. "Sounds good." There's no time to say much more; the line's too long, and now I'm the bottleneck.

Mom's friends—BFFs since Crescent Academy—flutter past in a two-tone flock of black and pearl, all lean and plumed like wood storks. A few ancient widows, escorted by their caretakers, shuffle down the line. We say our hellos to neighbors and what seems like the entire membership of Battery Hall. We've probably spoken to two hundred people. My feet hurt. I'm hungry. I'm hangry. I'm tired.

Weezy is, too. Unceremoniously, she breaks from the line. She waddles out the room through the thinning crowd. Poor thing. She's due in a few weeks, for crying out loud. I don't know how she stood as long as she did; her boobs alone are the size of honeydew melons. I look at Caroline, who sneaks a peek at her phone. "It's after six," she mouths at me.

"Let's go," I say. Caroline and I follow Weezy, neither of us making eye contact with Mom for fear of a reprimand. We find Weezy in the front parlor collapsed in a wing-backed chair. Caroline and I squeeze into the other. Together we sit in silence, listening to chatter bubble and fade from the viewing room.

I think of Louisa's story about Dr. Legare and his dog's tail. Maybe he wanted something authentic and unaltered alongside his body. Maybe Laudie would, too.

I slide my hand into my purse, run my fingers along the opened packet of zinnia seeds. What if I were to put some seeds in with Laudie so she won't have to take this journey alone? I could put a little life inside that coffin. And maybe a thousand years from now an earthquake will crack the very core of Charleston, split open her coffin, and release her zinnias back into the earth, where they would grow and flourish. It could happen. It's not likely, but it could.

I wait for the viewing room to empty. Andy leads the pack, pushing Tito in the wheelchair he has started to use on occasion. Mom follows with the last of the stragglers. "I'm going to see her one last time," I tell my sisters, moving fast so they don't come with me.

Alone in the strange room, I take one last look at my grandmother. She's somehow lost dimension. She looks flat, like a painting of herself. *Still life with Laudie.* Her body is not her; she is somewhere else, and for that I am glad.

The packet feels wrinkled and worn but full of potential. I sift the weightless seeds through my fingers, sprinkling some on either side of her hips, which still, after all these decades, form an arresting feminine arc. "I love you," I whisper, "and I promise to be brave."

37.

Cold Front

A cold front blew in. The lower temperatures jump-start the day, quickening all living things. Dogs sprint from porches to greet friend or stranger. Carriage horses whip their heads at stoplights, restless with extra energy. Locals walk at a brisker pace; they even talk a tad faster.

In anticipation of cooler weather, I drove to the beach in my wetsuit. Now, zipped up and sticky like a banana in its peel, I'm sweating.

Laudie's funeral isn't until this afternoon. It feels sacrilegious to surf the day she'll be buried. But what else am I supposed to do? The day stretches before me, and no other activity seems to come even close to the spiritual nature of the ceremony ahead.

Everything is in place for the reception. The furniture has been rearranged on the piazza to create additional space. The dining room chairs have been pushed to the walls. The

corkscrews are lined up on the bar, along with Laudie's sterling iced tea spoons for mixing drinks.

The windows have been Windexed and the silver shined
with polish. The hemstitched linen cocktail napkins have been
starched and pressed. Empty platters sit on the dining room
table; on top of each is a little note indicating to Mrs. Harley's servers exactly where to place what: "chicken salad sandwiches," "pickled shrimp," "mini quiche."

I plow into the ocean; this is not a day to inch in. The water
is warmer than the air, but not by much. My Goodwill wetsuit is
graded for much colder water, which is necessary, because like
most Lowcountry women whose natural element is heat, I chill
easily. The wetsuit will enable me to stay in the surf for thirty
minutes; any longer and I can't keep my core warm. The clock
is running, like Laudie's watch—which I'll soon wear. Mom
instructed Mr. Mackey to remove Laudie's jewelry before the
burial so she could give Laudie's favorites to Caroline, Weezy,
and me.

With my torso on the board, I kick and paddle against the
counterpush of the ocean; it's strong, but nothing like the hur-
ricane swell. Still, in these autumnal seas, maintaining homeostasis consumes huge amounts of energy.

I catch a few waves and take a moment to think of Laudie,
try to absorb the enormity of her death. A pale sun warms my
back. My hands are white from the cold. I open and close them,
hoping to generate enough warmth so that I can lift myself on
my final ride. My teeth start to chatter. My feet have stiffened.

"Hey! You, in the arctic gear." I turn to see Ben paddling toward me. He wears the same ratty rash guard. He has an easy smile—wide, generous, guileless. His longish curly hair doesn't fully hide his ears, which stick out, maybe the only part of him that isn't perfect. "Nice wetsuit."

I slide the board beneath me so that I'm in a seated position. I cycle my legs like eggbeaters to keep myself somewhat in place. "It is." I pull at the squishy fabric of my secondhand wetsuit. It makes a satisfying sucking sound as it forms an air bubble around my stomach.

He copies me, but his rash guard doesn't create the same sound effect. "How about a hot meal, on me? I still haven't thanked you properly."

A hot meal. Nachos. Grilled cheese, maybe. Or a tower of greasy fries. "I actually would really like to join you, but I can't. I have to get back to town."

"I'm glad you *actually* would." He winks. "Gotta get back to work?"

At 10:00 a.m. on a Wednesday, it's a legitimate question, but I don't want to tell Ben about Laudie and her funeral just four hours away. Then again, when's the last time I've been fully honest with anyone, including myself? What is there to lose? "I'm going to a funeral. My grandmother died." My face heats. My stomach flips. I miss her.

Ben doesn't say anything for a moment. He probably thinks I'm crazy for surfing on the day my grandmother will be buried. We stare at the ocean, bobbing up and down at different times like we're riding horses on a carousel. "I shouldn't have bothered you. You came out here to be alone."

"No. I mean I did, but . . ."

"I'm really sorry. I'll give you your space." Ben slips onto his stomach and skims across the ocean, past the second break.

38.

The Will of God

Per Mom's instructions, the family meets in the rectory. We wear various versions of the appropriate mourning outfit. For women, black—or a somber color like navy or aubergine—is preferred. Hemlines must be modest. In Charleston, it is considered incorrect for women to wear pants to a funeral. Loud colors, synthetic fabrics, and plunging décolletage are frowned on, too. Shoes should be closed-toed. Jewelry should be modest, and some old-school ladies still turn up in hats and gloves. The men wear dark suits, subdued ties, starched button-downs, lace-up shoes.

Mom stands near the door of the parish hall. The minister is speaking to her, but I can tell her attention is wandering. She stares at the program, tracing the text with one finger in the same way she ran her hand over Francie's fuzzy head when she was a newborn.

Dad chats with Andy near the window. Some male cousins—invited to serve as pallbearers—gather next to the mantel and wait to receive procession instructions from Mr. Mackey. Weezy has been offered the only chair in the room. She sits awkwardly, her feet splayed. Caroline massages her shoulders. I crouch next to Weezy, as far away as possible from some distant relatives from the Upstate. I can't make small talk right now.

"It's time," Reverend Montague announces.

The pallbearers go first. Dad and Andy push Tito in his wheelchair out the door. Mom follows, and the rest of the family gathers in a line behind her.

My eyes land on the black hearse parked in front of hulking columns at the church entrance. After Mr. Mackey opens its back door, the pallbearers silently maneuver the coffin over the curb and onto a roller. As we watch, the wind picks up and the temperature drops. We clasp our arms around our chests and follow the casket to the church.

St. Paul's is a giant sand-colored stucco church built in the early 1800s. The grand structure, with its sweeping arches braced by fluted columns, has always felt important. The vaulting space, the tall steeple, proclaim there is meaning to be found here, though I never could determine what it was, at least not anything that made sense; I felt alone among my family not to find it. Today is no different.

Two ushers open the secondary set of massive doors that lead into the church proper. Sunlight pierces the stained glass, scattering prismatic fragments of color around the church's high walls. Charleston's aristocracy turns to greet us. It's a handsome group. Some of Mom's friends wave their hands in restrained but affectionate hellos.

Everyone here has bathed, dressed, and made sure to arrive early; funerals are the one social engagement where punctuality is esteemed. In this moment, I'm grateful for the pageantry. Laudie deserves a proper formal send-off.

Andy wheels Tito down the aisle and parks the wheelchair beside the family pew. Dad unhooks the little latch to our pew, which is near the front. I sit at the end to make room for Mom and Caroline. Weezy and Ashley file into the pew behind us. Even though we have our own designated pew due to generations of our family having worshipped here, I can never get comfortable in it. The cushions scratch. My dress's tag itches, and the elastic around my waist is too tight. I am never sure when to sit, kneel, or stand. No one else seems to need to watch the crowd for cues as to when a prayer starts or hymn ends. The parishioners are attuned to some preordained protocol that I never wanted to memorize or decode.

The pews are unmarked, but just as with seats in a classroom, everyone knows who sits where and no one messes with the seating arrangement. There is so much order here, from the very architecture of the church to the repetitive form of the rituals. Perhaps most congregants, like my parents, find all that order comforting: same liturgy, same creed, same prayers, same pew, same church, same minister Sunday after Sunday and year after year. And according to some unwritten but very real Charleston hierarchy, the Pringle, Rutledge, and Middleton families sit in the pews in the front, the prime spots.

Some unfamiliar faces watch us from high in the balcony, which is generally where latecomers, newer members, or tourists sit. In the post–colonial era, the balcony was for Black people. In a house of God, where the brotherhood of man was preached, the enslaved congregants entered the church through the side door to find their segregated seats upstairs, where they tried to cool themselves in the summer heat with woven-rush fans. Eventually, Blacks left the white churches and built their own. Today, the most segregated hour in the South is 11:00 a.m. on a Sunday.

The audience today is all white except for Shaniece. She sits on the main floor, close to the aisle, near the front. She shares a pew with Louisa.

Laudie's service starts with flatulent blasts from the organ. Invisible hands fling open the doors of the narthex. Reverend Montague heads the procession, his hands wrapped tightly around a cross affixed to a long pole. We watch as he parades to the front. White-robed pairs of lower-ranked ministers trail him. All men. What do they think of the Timothy verses in the Bible? And Corinthians? And Proverbs? Do these men believe women should submit to their husbands? That they should keep quiet? Sure, these texts were written at a different time, but that doesn't make them okay today.

The stained-glass panels, as cheery as melted Jolly Ranchers, depict robed white men holding scrolls, robed white men extending a hand, robed white men worshiping a robed white man. It strikes me that with a haircut and some khakis, these men would look like the members of Battery Hall. The church feels like another club that exists to exclude. I shudder to think that this similarity isn't by coincidence but by design.

And then there's Mary. The lone female. How old was she when she got pregnant? Fifteen? Fourteen? Can a girl give consent at that age? Could she even say no to an almighty supreme being who wanted to impregnate her? Was she afraid? Was Ms. Ronan afraid?

In this house of God, beneath a giant, phallic steeple piercing the sky, I can't help but feel that misogyny is sanctified. I'm so over this religion; redemption be damned. I wait a moment for God to strike me dead with a thunderbolt for my blasphemy. Nothing happens. An idea occurs to me: a slogan. And then I wonder, where is that old button-making machine?

Reverend Montague slips past Laudie's coffin, steps up to the chancel. He gives a brief reading about death, life, and seasons for everything. Ecclesiastes. We sing a few hymns: "Onward Christian Soldiers" and "Amazing Grace." He delivers a eulogy, which is painfully generic. The theme: her commitment to family. One of Mom's cousins reads a few verses from the Book of John, and before I know it, I'm being elbowed by Caroline to hurry up.

Is that it? I glance over my shoulder: a few people tuck the hymnals away. One woman reapplies lipstick. Some check their phones.

Wait! What about her story? There's more to Laudie than her role as wife, mother, grandmother. What about tossing dolls into trees? What about her love of dancing, her dedication to ballet? Her consummate discipline? And he never mentioned that beautiful secret garden she tended for more than fifty years. Laudie had so many facets. Should I say something at the graveside?

The music changes tempo, and everyone stands. The pallbearers roll the casket down the aisle. Confused and numbed, my brain full of static, I follow my family out the church door. We wait at the stone steps as the men negotiate the casket around a sharp turn that leads to the churchyard. A stream of mourners gathers behind us, like reeds caught against a dock piling. Soon, we're surrounded. When the path ahead clears, we move with the crowd to the adjacent cemetery.

The Mackey funeral team has already dug a pit for the coffin. It's cavernous—eight feet deep at least. Two nylon ropes stretch over the hole, which is rimmed by a metal contraption, reminding me of a narrow bed frame. A bed for one. Communicating in a silent language, just nods and eye contact, the workers manage to lay her coffin on the straps so that it hovers above the hole. A dove perches on a crepe myrtle branch just above the gravesite. She preens and ruffles her feathers. I watch her, hoping for a sign, some magic from the universe.

Mr. Mackey beckons the family toward the dozen white chairs set up under a small canopy—our front-row seats. Weezy exhales audibly as she drops into the chair to my right. Caroline sits on the other side. As the sun slides behind the steeple and afternoon shadows advance over the churchyard, Caroline buttons her coat and Weezy rewraps her pashmina. We wait silently for the burial ceremony to begin.

In recognition of Tito's status as the paterfamilias, the minister asks if he is ready for the burial to begin. Tito nods. Reverend Montague pinches some soil, mixed with roots and clay, from the mound of dirt that's piled high behind him. "Ashes to ashes, dust to dust . . . ," he intones as he sprinkles dirt onto her coffin.

A gravedigger unlatches a hook, triggering the pulley system to lower the casket slowly, steadily, into the ground. Either the pulley system is mesmerizing, or I'm stupid with grief. When I hear a muted thud as it hits the pit's bottom, I wince, imagining Laudie's body being jostled.

The minister asks if any family members would like to put dirt on her grave. *Finally*: a way for us to be involved. I could probably shovel that whole pile myself.

Unsure of the protocol, I wait for a signal. Andy steps up first. He shovels a spadeful of dirt into the hole and passes the shovel to Dad. Dad rams the shovel into the pile and tosses a clump into the pit. I stare at him, willing him to hand the shovel to me, but he passes it to a cluster of second cousins, the pallbearers. My mother remains seated, as still as a museum bronze. I look to my sisters, who appear not even to consider the opportunity.

Is this ritual only for the men of our family? They don't love her like I do. They don't know her story. I may not know all of it, but I know more than they do. I want to rip the shovel from the male who wields it—some distant cousin twice-removed who barely knew Laudie. It's my job to cover her with the earth she loved. I am the one who should plant her like a seed.

But I don't. It would cause a scene. And people are here to

remember Laudie, not her rebellious, inappropriate grand-daughter.

After each male family member has taken a turn, the grave-diggers pick up their shovels and resume. Their bodies move in synch in an appealing, practiced rhythm. Scoop, *toss*. Scoop, *toss*. Scoop, *toss*. We watch them work while long shadows over-take the graveyard completely. The undertakers smooth the mound. The minister reads one more psalm. The mourning dove cries and flies away. Claudia has died. She is buried.

39.

Weekend Warrior

It's hard to work weekends, especially in these perfect late-fall days. Early November is for Edisto: for roasting oysters over a bonfire at night, watching the soupy fog curdle on the shoreline at sunrise, and kayaking in the tidal creeks at high noon. But I'm stuck at work.

The moment I walked into the newsroom today, I detected a change. Something's happened. There's an eerie stillness. It's always much quieter in here on the weekends, but this is a different sort of quiet.

"Simons."

An unfamiliar voice summons me from across the newsroom. I turn to see that the voice belongs to a man who looks like he could be Tweedle Dee and Tweedle Dum's older brother. He is widest at his middle. His body mass tapers upward at his pin-shaped head and downward at his little feet. Judging from his pallor, he probably hasn't been outdoors in years.

He motions for me to follow him into his office, which is a

corner room that I'd somehow never before been inside. Three of the walls are bare; the fourth has an interior window that overlooks a bit of the newsroom and all of Angela's desk, which is empty. No computer, no stash of pens, no highlighters, no stack of Post-it notes. Where are the photos of Cooper?

"I'm Don Pendergrass," he says gruffly, "your new boss. We're changing things up around here, Simons."

It's even more refrigerated here than in the newsroom. I rub the backs of my arms.

"I've watched your shows. You're the best writer we have."

"Oh, thank you—"

He cuts me off. "So why do you work the shit shifts?"

"I—"

"From now on, you're the six-o'clock producer. Monday through Friday."

Oh, wow. "Thank you." It's got to be a promotion, for sure.

"I know what you're thinking. It's not a promotion."

I blink hard, a bit stunned by his foretelling.

"It's not a promotion because I'm not paying you more. Just consider yourself lucky to have a job."

Well, *balls*. More stress but the same salary? Maybe I'd rather stick with the shit shift and work weekends.

"And no more namby-pamby save-the-turtles crap. The six o'clock is the crime and business show."

"Environmental stories *are* business stories. And crime stories, for that matter."

"Wrong. They are stories that just make people feel bad about themselves. People don't want to feel bad about themselves, or about the wreckage they're causing. They want to hear about how *other* people are bad. That's what pays the bills. We're running out of money. Did you know that?"

"No."

"Our reporters didn't know either. So much for being hard-hitting investigators." He reaches for a Big Gulp, sucks down a third of his soda, and bumps on his sternum as he suppresses a burp. "Who buys our ads?"

"Uh . . ."

"Car dealerships. Now even Granny's Used Cars won't buy our airtime. The dealerships are broke, too. We either need to figure out how to boost our ratings, or we need to figure out how to sell cars. And I don't know how to sell cars."

The AC has cycled on; an avalanche of cold air tumbles over my shoulders. What a waste of nonrenewable energy. My eyes land back on Angela's empty desk. "Do you mind if I ask where Angela is?"

"No, I don't mind. I fired her."

Oh. Oh no. Poor Angela. The newsroom was her entire universe, other than her dog. No friends. No family in town. Just old Cooper and his bandanas and Santa Claus outfits. Why did he fire her? She gave everything to her job.

"You're wondering why I fired her. I'll tell you why." His chair squeaks as he leans forward. "I had to trim the fat to keep this station alive. I'll be the acting news director until people stop shitting themselves and start buying cars again."

It's at this very moment that I realize I don't want to work here anymore. I can get a new job. Maybe not here in town, but somewhere daring, like New York. I'll start looking tonight. And the minute I get an offer, I'll resign. My shoulders relax. My body almost levitates I feel so light. What have I been doing here all this time? I never even liked it.

"What's that say on your jacket? That button thing."

After the funeral, I ransacked my house for my old button maker. I searched in the corners of my closet, under my sink, and in the cupboards next to the stove. I finally found it in a box I had planned on donating to Goodwill sometime around my move back to Charleston. It was one of those items that, when left alone long enough, was eventually forgotten. The last few nights, with steamy cups of tea and soy candles burning, I began to sketch again. I started with the slogan that came to me during Laudie's funeral. I pinned it to my jacket. "So OVER MALE GODS."

He looks at me as though I did just levitate. "You worship fairies or something?"

"Ha!" I laugh, actually enjoying myself for a moment. I'm on my way out of here. I have nothing to lose. Might as well have some fun. "Who doesn't? Tonight's a full moon. Kind of auspicious, don't you think? Maybe place that Big Gulp at the base of a tree, see if the fairies drink it."

Don considers this for a moment. "I'm a Republican."

I'm not exactly sure how his response makes sense, and as much fun as it is to say ridiculous things to this sweaty man, I'd rather get out of here and get on with my day. "Gotcha. I'm guessing I don't need to write today's shows."

"No. Meghan's on it." Through the glass window, I see her hunched over her keyboard. Her diminutive body seems to have shrunk now that she's been demoted. His phone buzzes. "Pendergrass, here."

I seize the moment to hustle out of the room to enjoy my first weekend free in half a year. As I weave through the windowless cube farm, it strikes me how much I don't ever want to come back.

* * *

On the way home, I blast my music, flipping through the dials and enjoying every song. Rap, country, gospel, metal. I want it all. And when I get to my apartment, I rummage through the old pile of CDs left over from the last tenant. I crank up the volume, kick off my shoes, and let loose. This time, it's my very own kitchen dance.

40.

Under Water

It's hard to sleep. The sheets trap too much heat, but when I kick them off, I get cold. Headlights from passing cars swipe the ceiling. I count them like sheep, toss, turn, try sleeping on my stomach. My phone buzzes. It's Weezy, and it's 12:34 a.m.

"Simons, I'm almost to your house."

"What? Why?"

"I'm having the baby. I need you to go with me."

"Oh my God. Is Ashley on that duck-hunting trip? Who has Francie?"

"She's with a neighbor . . ."

Silence. "Weezy? Weezy?" I check my phone to see if we've lost connection. "Weezy, are you having a contraction? Are you driving and having contractions?"

"Just go outside."

Shit. I am so not prepared for this. What do I bring? I flick on the overhead light and rifle through my possessions for what could possibly come in handy when bringing a baby into this world. I'll need my cell phone and charger for sure. In case running is involved, I grab my sneakers. I swipe my toothbrush from the silver julep cup by my sink and snatch a handful of panties. This could take a few days, right? I scoop my rumpled jeans from the floor and—with a kick—flip them into the air and onto the pile in my arms. I dash into the kitchen and grab a bottle of wine (for celebrating later) and a jar of peanut butter (the perfect food). I stuff everything in a reusable grocery bag and fly down the stairs.

Weezy's car is parked, its hazards flashing. She is waddling around the front of the car, her hand on the hood, making her way to the passenger side. The high beams illuminate her swollen silhouette, and I'm reminded of the opening credits to *Alfred Hitchcock Presents*. As I help Weezy into her seat, she all but falls in. "Where are your clothes?"

I'm still in my T-shirt and underpants. And my feet are bare and suddenly chilly. There's no time to get dressed. Who cares, anyway? "In my bag." I shut her door, run around the car, and sling my bag into the back seat.

I zip through the narrow one-way streets of downtown Charleston and roll onto the interstate. The highway is empty. I drive as carefully, as safely, as possible: my back straight, both hands on the wheel, speedometer precisely at the legal limit.

Weezy groans. Bracing herself, she grabs the door handle with one hand and presses against the dashboard with her other.

"Are you okay? What can I do?"

"I'm fine," she manages. "Just take the next exit."

The birthing center's parking lot is empty except for one car. A few lights are on in the building. A woman stands inside a glass door wearing a multicolored sweater and a red beanie. She loops a bulky scarf around her neck before walking outside to greet us.

"Hi, Louisa." She helps my sister from the car. "You must be the sister," she continues in her unhurried fashion. "I'm Vickie. Get her things and we'll go to the back bedroom. I already have the water running."

I dive into the darkness of the back seat, groping for our bags. "I forgot to tell you to bring your suit, Sims," Weezy yells.

Why would I need a bathing suit? What I need are pants. Still in the parking lot, I pull on my jeans, jam my feet into my sneakers, and catch up with my laboring sister and her midwife. We walk past the waiting room, lit by a lone Himalayan salt lamp, and down a long hall to the birthing suite.

The room looks like a stage set for a cheesy romance. A sleigh bed with crimson sheets dominates one side of the room. A massive hot tub occupies an alcove to my left. The midwife turns on a device that scatters aquamarine specks of confetti-size light across the ceiling. On a far wall, I spy clinical instruments, giving me a sense of relief that there is legit medical equipment in the vicinity. I set our bags near the door.

"Mmh . . . another one is coming." Weezy bends over the bed, her arms on the mattress, her hips up in the air. She digs her forehead into the bed and rocks her body back and forth.

"That's good, Louisa." Vickie rubs her lower back. "Breathe

through it." She wraps a blood pressure cuff around Weezy's arm and starts to pump.

"Ooh. They're getting stronger." Weezy stops swaying. She slides down to her knees on the hard floor and melts into a child's pose. "Ugh." I sit down to be with her. Her eyes are closed. She's somewhere else.

Vickie unwraps the cuff. "Blood pressure is good." She scribbles some notes on a clipboard. "Keep breathing. Just breathe through it."

Weezy's gasps intensify as her contraction climaxes. When the worst is over, she lifts her head, which is rimmed with perspiration. "Can you get my music, please? My phone's in the side pocket."

"Of course." I punch in her passcode, which is 123456, and shuffle through her playlists. "Is it 'Baby Time #2'?"

She manages a laugh. "That was for making this baby, but sure, you can play that."

A vision of a freckly, white-assed Ashley thrusting himself into my sister flashes through my brain. "Ew, no." I scroll a bit more, past "Methods for a Loving, Natural Birth," and land on "Tunes for Baby Boy." "I found it." I plug the device into the deck and press play. The first song is a country tune, probably Ashley's pick.

Vicky helps Weezy onto the bed. Weezy lies on her side, rubbing her belly in rhythmic, circular strokes. "Oof, here comes another one." She tucks herself into a ball. "Damn." She blows out a deep breath. "This hurts."

Her face is so scrunched her eyebrows touch. Her moans are otherworldly. "Owww. Oh my God, *OW!* Sims, this really hurts," she groans, a faraway expression on her face.

Another thirty seconds pass, and Weezy's breathing calms. "I'm going to need to check her cervix," Vickie says between scribbles on her clipboard. "Can you help her get undressed?"

I sit on the bed, coaxing Weezy's maternity pants over her hips. She lifts her arms, signaling for me to take off her shirt and bra. She's naked now, with dark nipples, a massive belly, and a thatch of pubic hair. She's the epitome of a fertility goddess, looking equally powerful and vulnerable.

The midwife tugs on a latex glove and then drives her hand inside my sister. Weezy winces, twists away. "Keep still, Louisa." She lifts her eyes to the ceiling, where confetti light swirls lazily. "You're six—almost seven—centimeters, Louisa. Good girl." She snaps the glove off and makes another note in the chart.

"Did you hear that? Almost seven centimeters," I say happily, though I have no idea what that means.

"I think I'm going to throw up."

Vickie slides a trash can next to the bed just as Weezy's body lurches. She vomits—over and over. The acidic, bile-soaked smell makes my stomach churn.

"Oh," she moans, rolling back into the fetal position. "Here comes another one."

Jesus. *Seriously?* This can't be normal. My poor sister.

"Just breathe through it, Louisa. You're getting closer with every contraction." Vickie takes the trash can from my hands and leaves the room, giving me a moment to plead my case.

I crawl onto the bed and rub her back. "Weezy, you don't have to do this. You're doing great, but there's still time to get you to a hospital." I don't want to scare her, but labor isn't supposed to be this excruciating, right? We need a doctor, not a jacuzzi and swirling lights.

"No," she says weakly. "I'm okay. I feel better now that I've thrown up."

"Seriously, Weezy! This is dangerous."

Weezy wraps a clammy hand around my arm. Her eyes glow with determination. "I'm going to do this."

I take a deep breath. "Okay, then. I'm here to help you."

Vickie returns with a new trash can, which she places beside the hot tub. "Are you ready to get in the water?"

Weezy nods, tries to stand. I hurry to help, ducking under her body. She leans into my support, her strength clearly ebbing. We lumber over to the bath. "Hold on." She stops to breathe through another contraction. I feel her body seize. Her stomach visibly tightens. "*Oh. Ah!*" She cries and dives forward, catching herself with her hands on the rim of the tub. I wait, helpless.

After a while, she nods to signal she's ready, but I can't figure out how we're going to get her in the giant hot tub. So that she doesn't bonk her head against the faucet, I straddle the bath—one foot out, one foot in. The water seeps into my sneaker, soaks my sock, and rides up the right pant leg of my jeans. Hoisting her up with all my strength, my arms shaking, I lift my other leg into the water and lower both of us into the tub. I settle us into a corner, hooking my arms beneath her armpits to keep her afloat.

"Uh . . . ," she moans. Her cries are becoming more guttural, more animalistic.

"Try kicking your legs, Louisa," Vickie offers, stirring a blue-gloved hand in the water. Weezy feebly starts to kick.

I don't think the hot water is working. Weezy doesn't look any less uncomfortable. She only seems more tired. And kicking? That's terrible advice. She's exhausted as it is.

I want Vickie to shut up. I want to haul Weezy away, leave this tub of misery, and get some proper medical treatment at a legitimate hospital. But here I am, wearing blue jeans in the water, keeping my sister from drowning while she's being tortured by this dangerous, screwball birth process.

Vickie runs the fetal heart probe monitor over Weezy's belly. I hear the strong swooshing of a heartbeat. "Baby sounds good."

Weezy manages a half-smile. She looks both gorgeous and nearly dead.

My arms start to tire. My back hurts, too. Sweat runs from behind my ears, down my neck. I check the wall clock; we've only been in this purgatory two-and-a-half hours.

Weezy's body starts to quiver. She shakes like she's being electrocuted. What the fuck . . . ? *Is* she being electrocuted? I look for a severed outlet, a smoking socket, or some indicator that my sister is indeed being shocked. I start to stand, ready to haul her out of this hellhole. "Weezy! *Weezy!*"

Vickie pushes a firm hand down on my shoulder, forcing me to remain seated in the tub. "Simons, sit down. You need to stay calm."

"What's happening to my sister?" I scream, hot tears coursing down my face.

"Simons, she's transitioning. It's a surge of hormones. Don't be scared. This is all a part of the natural process."

Natural processes. I hate them. In a less violent but more gruesome way, a natural process—the act of dying—overtook my grandmother, snatched her from this vibrant life and slowly dragged her to another world. And now here a new life begins, its initiation marked by howls, anguish, and blood.

The shuddering stops. My sister falls limp. Vickie plunges a fist up my sister's crotch. "I can feel his head, Louisa. Do you feel the urge to push?"

Weezy nods, passes out again.

I hold her—she's as limp as a sack of flour—and wait for the pain to rouse her from dreamless sleep. The Jacuzzi whirs. The clock ticks. From the small speakers, Michael Jackson croons about the man in the mirror. A trickle of water drips from the midwife's hand, which rests on the tub's rim. These are the sounds of waiting.

"Aye!" Weezy yelps, her voice spiraling higher and higher. "Ow, ow, ow. It burns. *It burns!*" She thrashes in the water like a harpooned fish. "Ah! Ah! Ah!" she howls in staccato bursts. Suddenly, she passes out again—as oblivious as a person in a coma of the next torturous contraction that will waken and wrack her any minute.

"How's she doing?" A slender woman in pink scrubs enters the room, another nurse midwife. Backup, I guess. A stethoscope hangs around her neck. She pulls various instruments and gauze from the cabinets and bangs the doors shut.

"I think she's gonna tear, if she hasn't already," Vickie tells her.

Tear? As in her vagina getting shredded?!

The nurse nods and pulls out a suture packet.

My sister comes to with a guttural groan. "Ow!" she cries, sucking air through her teeth.

"Here he comes, Louisa. He's almost there. Just a few more pushes. You are so close to meeting your baby boy."

Weezy steadies her gaze and summons a reserve hidden within her to birth her child. With an inhuman growl, she pushes. How is she so strong? How does any woman do this? How dare anyone beat or belittle a woman when this is what they do for the human race?

"That's it. One more. That's it."

She pushes again, releasing an earth-shattering roar. A plume of blood gushes from between her legs, making the water look biblical, as though it has turned into wine. Vickie bends over the rim, both hands in the tub this time. She lifts a wet, red body out of the water and places the squealing new life-form on Weezy's heaving, trembling chest. "I did it," Weezy whispers.

My nephew pinches his eyes shut and opens his mouth wide. He screams for his mother; she lays a hand on his wrinkly little body and kisses his head. Weezy looks up at me; I smile at her. In this moment, when we really see each other, we understand the enormity of the moment. We both start crying—true tears of joy. I hold her tight, so deeply grateful she is okay. It's over. He's here, and he's perfect. It's all going to be okay.

41.

Underground Again

While so many of the social rules that stratify the local gentry are nuanced and difficult to decode, there's one rule that is easy to follow: if a party starts after six o'clock, the men wear black tie. Tonight, at Caroline's debut cocktail party, the Charleston men will wear tuxes. The women will clasp on their finest jewelry. They'll dab on their special-occasion perfumes and suffer through a night of sore feet in their most expensive shoes. Mom's friends will wear dresses made of velvet or raw silk. The older ladies will stay warm on the ride over in their mink coats.

We'll drink top-shelf bourbon from crystal glasses and eat pickled shrimp with tiny silver forks.

It's the day of the party. I have strung lights between two palmetttos, weeded the window boxes, and pushed the porch furniture up against the walls and out of the way. Mom surveys the piazza, envisioning an imaginary crowd. "Should we put the bar inside?"

I tap my foot on the porch floor, which was constructed with a slight slant to keep rainwater from pooling. "It will be perfect right here."

"But Dan the Weatherman said it will get down to the low fifties."

"People will go out to the bar even if there's a blizzard."

"So true."

My phone buzzes. An unknown number. "Hello?"

"Oh, Simons, I'm so glad you picked up."

The voice sounds familiar but is hard to place. I take a few steps down the blue slate path for privacy, just in case. "Who is this?"

"It's Angela," she says.

Oh, poor Angela. I've been so caught up in my own life I haven't thought to reach out. "I'm so sorry I haven't called. And I'm sorry that asshole fired you. I don't know what he was thinking."

"I'm over it. I should have left years ago. I'm calling because I need your help."

"Anything. What is it?"

Her voice sails up to a high whine. "I had to put Cooper down."

"Oh no. I'm so sorry." I completely forgot. That should have been on my radar.

Mom calls from the piazza. "Honey, who is that?"

I signal to Mom that I need a minute. I walk farther into the garden—one that has been frozen in time. Except for removing the magnolia and adding the palmettos, the garden has

remained the same since I was a little girl. Its high, encompass-
ing brick wall shields us from the eyes of neighbors and nosy
tourists alike. Brick paths crisscross the rectangular lot, dividing
the garden into four boxwood-lined quadrants. A three-tiered
fountain, topped by a fluting Pan, splashes at the intersection.

My parents' garden is a vegetative extension of their person-
alities. It's organized, logical, and robust. Every plant in the
garden is indigenous to the Lowcountry; there are no tropicals
that might not survive the winter, no succulents likely to drown
in our frequent floods and thunderstorms. Everything in the
garden is—and forever will be—native to Charleston. I sit on
the Charleston Battery bench, which has been placed precisely
in the center of the back wall, feeling a bit like a cactus.

"Do you have a shovel?"

"A shovel?" *Sweet Jesus.* Is she trying to bury him?

"My shitty shovel broke, and I can't ask my neighbors because the HOA would go ballistic. And I can't leave him to buy
one because . . . well, I just can't leave him."

"I'll find one, Angela. I'll be right over."

I round the tiered fountain and follow the path that leads to
the back shed. Dad's shovel hangs neatly between a rake and a
broom. I carry it from the shed and trot past Mom, hoping to
avoid an inquiry.

"Simons, where are you going with that shovel?"

"Mom, I'm sorry, I've got to go help a friend."

"To what? Dig a hole?"

"Remember my boss, Angela?"

"The one who got fired?"

"Yeah. She needs help burying her dog."

"Oh, the poor thing. But can't someone else help, like a brother or something?"

"Mom, she doesn't have anybody. She's not from here."

Mom frowns while pondering that thought. "Okay, well, it sounds like you need to go. But before you do, I have something for you."

I follow her inside; Mom's house is poised for a party. Vacuum lines streak the entryway rug. A porcelain vase displays a cluster of camellias, Charleston's signature winter flowers. Unlit tea candles are arranged in threes here and there on the mahogany table in the dining room. A small note in the middle of a giant platter in the center reads, "Beef tenderloin." We pass through to the kitchen and around a case of Veuve Clicquot to the back stairs that lead directly to Mom and Dad's room.

Her rice bed—named for the carvings on the four posters that celebrated a long-ago cash crop—is neatly made. Her pillowcases are scalloped and monogrammed. Everything is in its place. Her dress for the night—a fitted burgundy number with a high neck and bell sleeves—is draped over the duvet. Her patent leather stilettos stand at the ready at the foot of her bed. Mom flicks on her dresser lamp and pulls open a drawer. She hands me a long box, velvety to the touch. "Open it."

Inside, Laudie's watch ticks away. Mom fastens it around my wrist. I give it a little shake to let it settle over my arm. "Did you know it was a gift from her mother?"

"I didn't know that," Mom says.

"She gave it to Laudie just before she went off to Atlanta so she'd call every Sunday at three."

"Maybe we should talk every Sunday at three. Now that you have that promotion and you don't have to work weekends."

"I'd like that, but it's not a promotion."

"Getting your weekends back sounds like a promotion to me."

"Yeah, it will be nice."

She turns to the drawer and digs out a tiny drawstring bag. "When I was going through Mother's jewelry, I also found this." She hands it to me; I pull it open. Inside is a key. "I didn't see any sort of safe around the house, so I asked your grandfather. He thinks it opens a lockbox."

"Like at a bank?"

"Yes. It could be nothing, but you got me thinking about that letter, and I thought maybe that's where we'll find it."

"Oh, wow, Mom."

"Now, don't get your hopes up. It could be nothing. And even if this key does open a safety deposit, it will take a long time to get the paperwork together to get it unlocked."

"Thanks for trying, Mom."

"I'm starting to want to find this letter as much as you do. I want to know more about my mother. I wish I had asked when I had the chance. I'm proud of you for even thinking of asking."

"Thanks, Mom."

"I'm also proud of you for being with Weezy. If I were there at that birth center, I would have dragged her to the hospital."

"Trust me, I thought about it."

"What was she thinking having a baby in a bathtub? And in North Charleston of all places?"

I laugh. "I know. *North* Charleston is on his birth certificate forever," I say in mock horror. For South of Broad residents like Mom, the zip code is just as important as the name.

Mom hoots. "I thought about that, too!"

I check the time, enjoying both the beauty and functionality of my new watch. "Mom, I've got to go. Angela is expecting me any minute."

Mom cocks her head to the side and looks at me like she's trying to see into my brain. "You don't have to do that, you know. You don't always have to tend to the sick and the dying."

"Or the laboring," I add. "I know."

"You're a lot like your grandmother. I imagine she might have done something like that, if she lived in a different time."

"I think she would have. Or maybe she did and we just don't know."

"Maybe." She smiles and runs a finger over the watch. "I thought it was foolish to go to the ballet, but I now see that in her way, and in your way, too, it was brave."

"Thanks, Mom."

"Now go on and help that poor woman."

* * *

The drive to Angela's is a slog through suburban blight, starting with the Waffle House, that grease trap of memories. Traffic crawls down the Savannah Highway Auto Mile. Concentrating the car dealerships along this suburban highway was a bad idea that only got worse as new, additional dealerships opened up, crippling the possibility of having a livable, walkable city. Car lots as big as football fields straddle both sides of the north–south six-lane road, making traffic appear as though it stretches sideways as well. Cars, cars, cars—sedans, SUVs, trucks, hybrids, convertibles—in every direction, as far as the eye can see. The only pedestrians for miles are the poor people who live in the nearby food deserts and who can't afford a car. To cross the highway, they hold tight to their babies and make mad, near-suicidal dashes across six lanes of harried traffic.

Angela's house is in a newer subdivision. Many homes here are unsold, unoccupied; some look unfinished. The landscaping could have been done in a single afternoon; it's neat but bland: mainly mounds of pine straw banked against the perimeters of the freshly painted houses. The new crepe myrtles barely reach my height, and the tops of the transplanted palmettos look bald with their chopped-off fronds.

Angela waits for me at the top of her driveway. She wears a gray shirt, pink shorts, and white sneakers. Her milky legs lend her a girl-like sweetness, but the shorter sleeves reveal an older body. Even with a good shovel, those office arms aren't strong enough to dig a pit for her dog.

I park the car and pull out the shovel. "You looked dressed for summer. Aren't you cold?"

Angela looks down as though to examine her outfit for the first time. "No. I'm hot."

I offer a hug; without hesitation, she leans in for an embrace.

The shovel scrapes noisily along the pavement when I drop it to wrap my arms around her. I'm not that tall, but I feel much larger than Angela in this moment. Without her job, without her dog, she's as tiny and fragile as a baby bird.

A blast of cold air whips through the spartan landscape, banging the back gate open. "I'm going to help you," I say, and lead her to the backyard.

A six-foot privacy fence encloses the yard. Yellow crabgrass grows underfoot. Wispy clouds filter a soft midday sun. A patio hugs the back door of the house. It's empty except for one table, one chair, and a large cardboard box. "He's in there," she says and then points to the corner of her lot at the small pile of overturned grass. "I started digging there."

So far, she's only dug enough to plant a tomato. I ram the shovel into the ground and stomp my foot on the spade. Scoop, *toss*. Scoop, *toss*. Scoop, *toss*.

Angela watches. The hole grows wider and deeper. I glance over at the cardboard box to eyeball the size of hole I need. I think back to how large the mound of dirt next to Laudie's gravesite was, how deep the cavity. I tighten my muscles to summon more strength. Scoop, *toss*. Scoop, *toss*. Scoop, *toss*.

My arms are getting fatigued. I'm losing energy; the dirt is getting heavier, too. It's saturated with groundwater. Have I reached the water table in just a couple of feet? Developers will put a house anywhere these days, but now is not the time to tell Angela she might have been swindled. Maybe another time I'll encourage her to buy good flood insurance. Scoop, *toss*.

There. Finally. It's big enough. "I think that's good, Angela."

She nods but doesn't move. Her eyes are fixated on the hole. A small puddle forms at the bottom. "Can you help me bring him over here?"

We drag the cardboard box from the brick patio and over the grass to the hole. Angela opens the flaps to look at Cooper, who is wrapped in a blue sheet. His golden fur appears freshly brushed. A red bandana adorns his neck. My eye catches a gnarled snout, teeth bared, reminding me of Laudie's twisted face in her last days on earth. "Grab the other side of the sheet, Angela. Okay. One . . . two . . . three." Together we heft Cooper out of the box and lower him into the grave. He's lighter than I expected. Just bones and fur.

Angela drops to her hands and knees to tuck the sheet around him like she's tucking a child into bed. She leans in, pulls the sheet back to pet him one last time. "Goodbye, Cooper. I love you." She folds the sheet over his head and stands up.

My heart aches for Angela. It actually hurts. I hand her the shovel. "Would you like to go first?"

Angela scoops a small heap of dirt from the pile and drops it onto the sheet. She scoops a couple of more times, each load smaller than the last, then hands the shovel back to me.

When I wrap my hands around the shaft, I feel blisters. I hold tight, drive the spade into the pile through the burning sensation in my palms, and get to work. Scoop, *toss*. Scoop, *toss*. Scoop, *toss*. I find a rhythm and don't stop until a small mound forms over Cooper's simple grave.

"Thank you," Angela says. "Really."

"Of course," I reply. "Anyone would do it."

"No, they wouldn't." She walks to the patio, drags the lone chair across the lawn, places it next to the gravesite.

"Angela, I'm going to leave News 14."

"To write about the plights of monarch butterflies and homeless polar bears, I hope."

"Ha. Pretty much. I actually have three interview calls lined up for jobs in New York."

She lowers herself to the lawn chair. "I sent a letter of recommendation for you."

"Where? The station? You're the one who got me the Monday-to-Friday shift?"

She laughs mirthlessly. "News 14 won't even accept my emails. They all bounce back. I was just asking if I could come get my lunch bag that I left in the break-room fridge. No, I wrote to an old colleague back in D.C. who works for the Environmental Defense Fund now. He said a communications director is stepping down and that he'll send me an email as soon as the position is posted."

"Wow. Thanks. D.C. wasn't really on my radar."

"It should be. There are a lot of good NGOs there. I think you'd like it."

"I'll check it out. Thanks. What will you do?"

The sun disappears behind a thick haze. Angela crosses her bare legs. "I think I'll just sit here awhile."

"I mean for a job . . ."

"I don't know. I am going to use this time to think. I have a lot of thinking to do."

"Are you going to be okay?"

"I'll be okay." She shifts her attention to the mound. "I just need some time alone with him."

I place my hands lightly on her shoulders. "Okay." As I close her gate, I take one last look at Angela. She's slumped over with her chin in her hands, her elbows on her thighs, staring at the little mound of dirt.

* * *

The messiness of death seems incongruent with the antiseptic layout of this suburban development. I am ready to leave this cookie-cutter place, but I'm not ready to go home. I need to shed the heaviness. I need to lighten up. I need the ocean. I take the Folly Road exit and drive to the beach.

A gray ocean boils beneath low-hanging clouds. Sky disappears into water; water disappears into sky. No beginning, no end, and everything cold. The beach is deserted save for a few die-hard surfers; fair-weather surfers like me have stored their boards for the winter. A wetsuit can only help so much. I tighten the strings on my hoodie and perch on a washed-up palmetto log.

A flock of Caspian terns poses on the sand. Their orange beaks and obsidian caps give them an air of self-importance. Some chirp and preen, but most stay immobile to conserve energy. All orient their bodies directly to the wind so when they're ready to take flight, they only need to hop up and pivot to catch the airstream.

Beyond the break, a pod of dolphins feeds. In organized succession, they pop their rostrums just above the water to take a quick sip of air. Above them, a pelican hunts for fish. Past the shore, a Coast Guard cutter slices through the rocky whitecaps.

A few surfers search for waves. One rides the whitewash all the way to the beach, likely his final ride of the day. When he reaches the shallows, he picks up his board and trots to shore . . . right to my feet.

"Simons?"

It's Ben, with the evergreen eyes. In a Pavlovian response to seeing him, my stomach growls. I also realize I must look ridiculous with just my eyes and nose poking out of my hoodie. I release the strings from my sweatshirt to pull the hood off my head. "How did you know it was me?"

"I didn't. I just thought I'd take a chance." He lays the board upside-down in the sand and sits next to me on the log. Coils of steam rise from the shoulders of his wetsuit. "So, I take it you're not surfing today."

"No. I just needed to be here."

"Still thinking about your grandmother? It's a lot to process."

Laudie. I pick up a whelk shard, doodle in the sand to try not to think about her so much. "I just buried a dog."

"Your dog died?"

"It wasn't my dog. It was a friend's. Actually, she's not my friend. She was my boss. Her shovel broke."

"Oh. You've had a lot going on. I should leave you alone. I'm sorry I keep interrupting your alone time." He stands to leave.

"No! Please stay."

"Are you sure?"

"Sure I'm sure."

"Okay." He sits down again, this time a little closer. "So you dug a grave?"

"Mm-hmm." I show him my hands. He takes them in his and examines the blisters. He runs a finger over my palm. A timid afternoon sun—as pale as corn silk—peeks through the mist, warming us for just a moment.

"Oh," he says, with a tone of wariness. He peers closer into my hand. "Hmm . . . just what I thought."

"Thought what? Are my blisters going to get infected?"

He leans forward and dips his head into my line of vision, forcing me to make eye contact. An energy zings through me, waking me up like a cocktail of caffeine and sunrays.

He traces a line across my palm. "It says here that everything will be okay." He flips my other hand over and smiles. "And here it says you're going to get a pho with me. Have you been to Chico Feo? It's on the island."

I have. From that funky little shack off the main drag, beach-goers order goat curry and pork tacos. The seating, a mishmash of chairs and benches, is outdoors beneath a sprawling oak. A giant bowl of noodles would be a lot more filling than Mrs. Harley's tea sandwiches. I'd love to go to Chico Feo, but I need to get home to dress in time. "I can't today."

"Oh."

"No, really. I really want to. I just have to get back soon. My parents are hosting a party for my sister."

"It's her birthday?"

"It's just a party." I leave out the detail that it's a debutante party. Too loaded.

"Cool."

I crunch up a dead sand dollar in my hand, waiting for him to try for another day. He doesn't. Perhaps I'm not worth the effort. That bright yellow feeling swirling through me just moments ago starts to fade. Maybe he's just some hot surfer playboy who gets bored easily. Dinner sounds tempting, but not the exhausting dating game. I dread being sidelined again by an ass-slapping bozo or ghosting musician. But I have to try, right? What's life without trying? Ben could be a playboy, but he could also be a nice guy. "How about next week?"

"I'll be out of town for work."

I wait for him to suggest a later date, but he doesn't. That's fine, I tell myself. This is still a good moment. I'm young and healthy. The ocean is breathtaking. The caffeine and sunrays are mine to keep, not his to take away.

Ben stands and brings his board to his side. He takes a bow and tips an imaginary hat. "Simons . . ." He trots away, but before returning to the ocean, he stops to drag a toe in the sand. In big sweeping movements, he draws lines, circles, and maybe a figure eight. I can't tell from where I'm seated; it's hard to decipher. I wait until after he jogs back into the ocean to find out what it says, but I don't wait too long; a wave could wash it away. When I read his scribble in the sand, I commit it to memory.

42.

Underdressed

It's never been a great shower, but right now the darn thing is barely a trickle. "*Come on!*" I yell into the nozzle. I dip my head back into the puny stream. The suds seem never-ending. My blisters sting from the soapsuds. I've got twenty minutes to rinse this shampoo out of my hair and get dressed for the party.

As soon as I feel I've gotten most of the soap out, I hop out of the shower and towel off. I gather my hair into a low bun and steal a minute to swipe on some mascara. As I brush my teeth, my engagement ring winks at me from the medicine cabinet. I close it shut. Trip and I are supposed to have our talk in about a month; I'm not ready for the finality of returning his ring, but it seems like that moment would be the right time. I yank a black cocktail dress from the hanger, step into my sling-backs, and clasp Laudie's watch around my wrist.

What finishing touch do I need? What would make Mom happy? I sift through a silver bowlful of sophomoric jewelry: a necklace with a roller-skate pendant, chunky rings with Jolly Rancher stones, a neon green cuff. My hand lands on the latest button I made. It reads: "VAGINA! VAGINA! VAGINA!"

Tee-hee. Why is that so fun? I pin the button to the inside of my coat, where no one can see it. There are times and places to make statements. I'm not ready to wear my button on the outside of my coat, but I am still considering that throw pillow for my couch.

With pearls, my plain outfit might be deemed passable. I drop to my hands and knees and search for the necklace Trip gave me what now seems an eternity ago. Lifting the dust ruffle and looking beneath my bed, I peer into the shadows. At the foot of a bedpost lies Trip's necklace, coiled in a forlorn heap. I extract a dust bunny from the chain and clasp it around my neck.

* * *

I scamper down the cracked sidewalks of Atlantic Street, careful not to catch a toe on broken slate or a wayward oak root. Mom's house glows festively in the winter night. All the lights are on, even in my old bedroom. A topiary props open the door that opens onto the piazza. I bound up the two stone steps and see that Mom decided to put the bar in the garden—an even better idea than on the piazza.

I arrive promptly at 6:00. Punctuality is usually not a South of Broad virtue. In fact, other than for a funeral, it is considered rude to be on time; every native knows you must come at least ten or fifteen minutes late in order for the hosts to find the corkscrews and check the linens in the powder room. So, there's a little extra time to help Mom.

Her Waterford chandelier—recently painstakingly disassembled, dusted, washed, and reassembled—sparkles in the foyer, splashing light on the staircase I raced up and down as a little girl. In the formal drawing room, to my right, a gas fire burns in the hearth. A charcuterie and cheese tray sits on the low mahogany coffee table; the Brie and Camembert sweat.

In the dining room, two servers who are dressed head-to-toe in black fiddle with last-minute preparations. One garnishes silver trays and Delft platters with snipped sprays of dendrobium orchids. The other lights tea candles, which flicker in little beds of holly on the table and sideboard. Mrs. Harley's food awaits: ham biscuits, pickled shrimp, blanched asparagus, Hollandaise sauce, sliced tenderloin, horseradish sauce, stacks of miniature rye, wheat, and pumpernickel bread. The endive chicken salad boats line a narrow silver tray. Crab dip bubbles in a chafing dish.

Mom, in her demurely shimmery merlot dress, tucks away a stack of mail in the kitchen. "Oh, good, you're here. Honey, I need you to help pour the champagne. The bartenders have their hands full right now."

"Sure." I throw my coat and purse on a kitchen chair.

"Simons, is your hair wet?"

"I ran out of time."

"What are we going to do with you?"

"I'm sorry, Mom."

Mom draws a slow breath. "It's okay. That's not important. How's Angela?"

"She'll be all right."

"Good." Mom places ten champagne flutes on the tray.

I pour the champagne. The stems rattle as I carry the tray back through the dining room and into the front hall. Our first guests are elderly. Charleston's golden-agers drive to the party location early to claim the closest parking spots. They wait in the car until their watches confirm it's a polite ten or so minutes after the hour.

A couple of Laudie's bridge friends hobble over the threshold. Mom leads them into the drawing room, where they settle in the Queen Anne chairs. Tuckered by the effort of getting up the porch and into the house, they gratefully accept the champagne.

Weezy and Ashley arrive next. Ever since Vance was born, I've been surprised to see Weezy standing up on her own, alive even. I can't forget, or even compute, the violence her body underwent that night—the tearing of her innards, the blood, the passing out. It seems amazing that she survived. And yet here she is, practically scintillating.

Her magenta dress tugs only slightly at her postpartum belly; she hardly looks like she gave birth just two weeks ago. She's wearing heels. She darkened her eyebrows; they give her face an elegant, mature look. She should have her photograph taken tonight. Ashley stands next to her. Neatly shaven, he looks even more boyish than usual in a tuxedo.

"Here she comes!" Mom clasps her hands together, her eyes wide to take in the vision of her youngest daughter. Caroline appears at the top of the stairs: she's the epitome of perfection. Her white dress is simple but striking. Cut slimly, it hugs her body and shows off her knockout figure. A thick braid drapes around her swanlike neck.

Her friend Bennett follows. She wears a turquoise dress that appears to be 1950s-inspired. It cinches tightly at her small waist; the A-line cut of her skirt dramatizes her curves. As she follows Caroline down the steps, the fabric rises and falls like a diaphanous jellyfish in the mildest of waters.

Caroline lifts two champagne glasses from my tray and hands one to her friend. "Is Mom paying you?"

"What?"

Caroline gestures at me vaguely. "You look like a waiter."

Bennett attempts to hide a smirk behind her champagne glass.

I stare at my sister.

"Oh, come on, Sims, your hair's slicked back and you're in all black . . ."

I glance at my simple dress. Okay, *fine*, so I am dressed like a server, but it's still a bitchy thing to say.

"Caroline." Mom narrows her eyes. "What has gotten into you? Your sister came here this morning to help with the party. She climbed the ladder to string the lights. She swept the porch. You should be thanking her."

"I'm sorry."

Mom's too annoyed to listen. She shoos Caroline and Bennett

to the drawing room. "Go say hello to Mrs. Ravenel and Mrs. Rutledge." They sail out, an armada of two, high heels clicking.

Weezy hugs me sideways, nearly making me drop the tray of remaining champagne flutes. "You look beautiful, Simons. You really do."

I study Weezy as she takes a drink. I still can't figure out how she holds any positive memories of that ghastly night. She describes it as "loving" and "beautiful" and "healing." I was there. It wasn't any of those things. It was gruesome. Painful. Nightmarish. A disco-balled violent bloodbath choreographed to the King of Pop.

It does seem Ashley has an idea of what went down that night. With jolly pats on the back, he thanks me for "subbing in," but I detect relief.

Weezy has always been kind to me, but she's been especially complimentary since Vance's birth. Any time I mention my new news director, Don Pendergrass, she's quick to suggest I should consider midwifery. No. Not a chance. But I will leave my job and probably Charleston, too; I'm just not ready to tell her that yet. Two of the three New York organizations asked me for a second interview—both video conference calls. I scheduled those for next week. I also heard back from Angela's connection in D.C.; I have a call with him on Tuesday.

A bevy of Mom's friends and their husbands appears at the door. The ladies pluck the remaining flutes from my tray. When Mom announces the bourbon's outside in the garden, the men head for the bar. I exchange hellos and retreat to fill up more glasses.

From the quiet of the kitchen, I listen to the party unfold. Our house is welcoming. The food is plentiful and delicious. Our friends are mostly happy. The women look beautiful. The men are handsome. We are educated, healthy, and prosperous.

It's a lovely scene, and it hardly looks any different than it did four years ago, when I was making my debut. I find comfort in knowing this is how it will always be in this house, in our little cosmos, for years, even decades and generations, to come. So maybe there's not a musician, a rebel, or a tattoo under this roof, but there is a strong sense of community.

Still, I can't shake the feeling that I don't fit into the mold, that I'm a non-native species in this garden of Eden. I don't know where I belong, but it's not here, at least for now. My hand instinctively tugs at my necklace.

43.

I Spy

A lanky teen guards the entrance of Battery Hall. He wears the workers' winter uniform: pressed khakis and a zipped-up parka in Battery Hall green. He's scrolling on his phone, preoccupied. He looks up just as my bike tires meet the bumpy brick driveway. "Excuse me!" His job, mainly, is to keep tourists and nonmembers out.

I pretend not to hear him. He won't do anything to alert the rest of the staff. For better or for worse, I look like I belong. I look like the daughter of a member. My entry ticket was printed on my genes. Why people don't understand white privilege, I'll never get.

Technically, guests must be escorted by a member, but the rule is rarely enforced. And if Dad knew my plan, he'd go ballistic. He's a fair man and is well-intentioned in his own, limited way. The problem is that he, like most club members, has a blind spot. They can't see the harm a place like Battery Hall does. While they see their club as an innocuous gathering place for like-minded people, Battery Hall preserves and champions a status quo that keeps guys like him on top.

Without Dad, I feel like an interloper; it's hard to imagine that not all wives and daughters feel this way. They are welcome as guests, putting their tabs on their husbands' or fathers' member numbers. I've asked Mom if that practice somehow makes her feel patronized or infantilized. She tells me she likes lunching here. It's away from the tourist mob scene. There's always a place to park. They take reservations, and she always gets to see someone she knows. What's not to like?

"But doesn't it bother you that you can never be a member? Because you are a woman?"

"Oh, honey." She swatted the idea away with the jangle of her gold bracelets. "Why would I want to be a member with all these stuffy old men?"

Feeling like a spy, I enter the foyer. On the far wall, each looking larger than I'd remembered, loom the portraits of past presidents. Now, all twenty-six pairs of eyes glare at me.

"Are you waiting for the rest of your party?" asks the hostess. Her eyes survey my legs.

I'm wearing pants. While pants are not expressly forbidden by the club, skirts are preferred. "I'm just going to use the restroom."

The phone rings, and she turns her attention to the reservation book.

In the ladies' room, a woman pumps soap from a silver dispenser. I don't recognize her, but Old Charleston is a small crowd, and I don't want to risk getting spotted. With my face averted, I dart into a stall.

44.

Overdressed

Tonight is the culmination of a year of dress shopping, ladies' brunches, boozy cocktail parties, elegant invitations, and old-fashioned and fancy debutante gifts like Tiffany pens and monogramed silver bells. At eight o'clock this evening, we'll go to the final ball for Caroline and the other debutantes.

When I debuted, with Trip at my side, I spent the year in a per-fumed cloud of southern elegance and warmth. I clinked glasses with my mother's pals and waltzed with Tito's less ancient chess partners. I feasted on crab cakes and caviar and drank as much champagne as I wanted. How lucky was I to have been born into a tribe that, whatever its shortcomings, celebrates its young women for the better part of a year? And with such pomp. I felt like a princess. I imagine Caroline feels the same way.

For the grand ball, Mom insisted that I have my hair pro-fessionally styled. After showing up with wet hair at Mom and Dad's cocktail party for Caroline last month, I don't have a case against it. I've been sitting in a sticky-hot vinyl chair for an hour. My hair has been blown, rolled, teased, and sprayed into a starchy mat.

The stylist is weaving my hair into a complicated series of knots reminiscent of nineties prom hair. *Ouch.* He rams another bobby pin into my scalp. The hair around my ears is pulled back so tight it gives me a facelift. My hair has been teased and jacked up into a fourth dimension, leaving my poor scalp pounding after all the yanking. *Ouch.*

The stylist jams another bobby pin next to my ear. I can smell his breath, which isn't unpleasant; he's been sucking on a peppermint the whole time. He steps back to admire his rococo creation, rolls the candy in his mouth, douses me in another cloud of hairspray, and looks to Mom for approval. They exchange triumphant smiles.

"Now, aren't you glad you came?" Mom wears her usual winter uniform: slim pants and ankle boots. But today, with typical forethought, she's traded her regular turtleneck for a buttoned blouse and zippered jacket, the better not to mess up her hair when she changes out of her clothes and into her ball gown.

"It looks really . . ." I search my image in the mirror, trying to find the right word. "Impressive." At least I won't be confused for a server tonight. "Thank you so much."

He whips the black cape off my neck with a flourish. "Have fun, sweetie."

Mom and I check on Caroline's progress. She sits in the premier seat of the salon, facing the window. Passersby turn to catch a glimpse of this live-action primp session. Caroline's stylist is still hard at work, flitting and darting around my little sister like a bee pollinating goldenrod.

"I have something special for you, Caroline." Reverently, Mom pulls a drawstring sack from her purse and hands it to Caroline, who opens the satin satchel. Inside is the antique pearl necklace I know well: the string of the highest-quality, opalescent, freshwater pearls. I, of course, have Laudie's watch, and I plan to wear it tonight. "Laudie wanted you to have this, especially for tonight."

Caroline dips her head so that Mom can place the necklace around her slender neck. "It's gorgeous, Mom." Caroline twists her head, admiring her reflection at different angles. "The pearls are ginormous!"

Mom and Caroline study their nearly twin images in the mirror. Both smile serenely, and I'm struck by how much they not only look alike but are alike. Both are happy in a natural, uncomplicated way. Serenely they follow the cultural path laid out for them generations ago: one of cotillions, Battery Hall lunches, pearls, debutante balls, ladies' teas, white weddings. They're happy. I'm glad they're happy.

45.

Waltzing Away

Bump ba da bum bump . . . *bump bump!*

Clay knocks briskly at my door. I told him we could meet at the ball, but he insisted on picking me up. At first I protested; it seemed ridiculous to go through this quasi–dating ritual since he's officially a relative. Now, however, I'm glad to have a proper gentleman caller. Is a man walking a woman to a car really that old-fashioned and chauvinistic? Or is it just considerate?

Clay flashes a gummy smile. Vestiges of braces stain his front teeth. He proffers a corsage composed of miniature yellow roses and baby's breath; it matches his boutonniere. Maybe his mother never informed him that corsages are a tad puerile for white-tie affairs. I'm already wearing Laudie's gold watch on my left wrist, the proper wrist for a corsage, if a corsage were proper. It took me the better part of five minutes to clasp the watch over my kid leather glove, so I extend my right arm. He puts on the corsage. "You ready?"

"Let's do this."

In the distance of the inky winter night, his truck looms like the eighth wonder of the world. It's massive—a tank with wheels the size of hot tubs. A small thrill leaps through my body. This is not the kind of vehicle to announce your arrival at a ball. But I've got a prom-date corsage and prom hair to match, so fuck it, let's have fun.

Clay extends a hand to help me up the truck's running board. We thunder down Meeting Street, Clay revving the engine at every red light. A few tourists stop to gawk at his truck. Clay doesn't acknowledge the attention, but I detect a smirk of pride. He hooks a left onto Chalmers, a cobblestone street paved with the ballast from eighteenth-century trading ships. We bounce up and down in our seats until he rumbles into a parking place. The engine shudders to a stop.

Clay links our arms, and together we cross Meeting Street to Hibernian Hall. The giant 1840 Greek Revival building has an elegantly straightforward structure. Its facade is a square with a triangle on top; six massive columns support the weighty pediment. The building is imposing and classical, like something out of Athens or Rome. No windows face the street. Colossal wooden doors guard the entrance, opening only on special occasions, and only to those who are invited.

Inside, our heels click audibly on the checkerboard marble floor. A towering arrangement of white roses dominates a table in the great hall's center. A pair of identical staircases—one on the left, one on the right—sweep in sinuous arcs from the black-and-white floor to the entrance of the second-story main hall. I crane my neck to admire the impressive rotunda soaring overhead; its tiers make me feel as though I've crawled inside a hollow wedding cake.

Clay drops off our winter coats at the coat check. We ascend the left staircase, the one with fewer people. I lift the hem of my navy dress—the hush-hush gift from Mom—to avoid tripping.

We join the guests in the receiving line. It's a march of penguins. Men wear formal black tails, white ties, no exceptions. They do, however, find ways to sneak in personal flair via their choice of cuff links. The men of Battery Hall will wear theirs stamped with "BH." Clay's are in the shape of mallard ducks.

Both men and women are required to wear gloves. Men's gloves are wrist-length. The women's gloves extend past the elbow, necessitating sleeveless dresses. (Women can wear any dress as long as it's formal, floor-length, and sleeveless.) These kid-leather gloves are increasingly harder to find and often must be purchased in Italy. When Louisa Lachicotte traveled to Rome the summer before Weezy debuted, Mom had her pick up four pairs.

The gloves have slits at the wrist; the openings allow a woman to free her hands without entirely removing her gloves—helpful when using the loo, for example. Kid leather, I note, is not all that durable; with use, and a few champagne spills, mine have stiffened and yellowed at the fingertips.

So have Mrs. Prioleau's, the ball's grand matron. Her wrinkly bosoms cascade over her dazzling, sequined neckline. Bedecked in her diamond necklace, multiple bracelets, a brooch, and sapphire earrings, she looks like she emptied her jewelry box for the occasion. She stands at the head of the receiving line, gloved arms outstretched, trilling welcomes to all the guests.

The nine debutantes, all in white ball gowns—which are essentially wedding dresses—stand in an alphabetical row to Mrs. Prioleau's right. Caroline is seventh in line. She chose the dress with the mermaid cut. Her aquamarine eyes shimmer like Laudie's swimming pool. She gestures to Laudie's pearl necklace, as if to signal to me that she's here with us tonight.

My sister is hands down the prettiest of the debutantes, but Bennett is a close second. I watch Bennett shake her head with laughter, flipping her glossy mane over her bare shoulders like a Kentucky Derby thoroughbred.

I'm jealous—not of her, but of her hairdo. What a relief it would be to remove these torturous bobby pins. Maybe I can do it after the Grand March.

The line moves quickly. Clay and I say our hellos to the hostess. I give Caroline a big squeeze, careful not to touch her hair or leave any red marks on her back. I say a polite hello to her friend. Clay high-fives and fist-pumps his way through the receiving line.

In homage to our ancestors, the evening's schedule is the same as it's been for 173 years. The ball starts at 8:00. Guests greet the debutantes, enjoy cocktails, and dance the foxtrot, waltz, and maybe even a tango. The receiving line ends at 9:00 so that the debutantes have some time to enjoy the formal portion of the evening before dinner.

There are rules for this first half of the night. Perhaps due to secrecy and discretion—but also due to decorum—photography is banned. Frankly, I like this rule; I don't like interrupting a conversation to huddle with a group for a photo. Selfies be damned.

Another rule: men are forbidden to spin their partners before dinner. At my debut, unaware of this embargo, Trip and I twirled and spun as we had many times that year in his apartment kitchen. A few days after the ball, a letter arrived at Mom's, politely reminding the Smythes of the committee's expectations of the evening. Mom had handed me the letter with a tiny shake of her head. "Simons, honey. It's not too much to ask."

Just before 10:00 p.m., the grand marshal and grand matron lead the whole assembly in the Grand March. As the band plays, the several hundred guests parade in couples to the seated dinner held in the downstairs hall. There, the debutantes and their dates will feast at a long table in the room's center. Each debutante has two escorts—usually one is a boyfriend and the other a brother or cousin.

The rest of us will dine at the round tables. We'll be seated male-female-male-female. Or as Mom always says, no matter if speaking of octogenarians, "Boy, girl, boy, girl." I'll likely be placed between Clay and Dad or Clay and Ashley.

At once, the waiters will serve our dinners—probably filet mignon, mashed potatoes, and asparagus. They'll top off our glasses so frequently it's impossible to tally how many drinks we've had for the night. Dinner will likely conclude with a choice of strawberry sorbet or crème brûlée. And coffee. And more champagne.

After dinner, we will return upstairs for the informal dancing. The men will unbutton their tails; some women will switch from heels to flats. Having spent the first part of the evening playing waltzes, the band will let loose with songs by James Brown, Aretha Franklin, and Earth, Wind & Fire. We'll dance the Lindy Hop—the dance we adored in cotillion, the one I danced with Trip—and we'll all twirl as much as we want. It's a grand time.

Clay and I enter the stately ballroom. Massive windows stretch from floor to ceiling. Three golden chandeliers, each hung from the center of an ornate plaster medallion, cast a warm, honey-colored glow. Tall monochromatic flower arrangements—masses of white roses, white orchids, white lilies, and white peonies—anchor the room, dividing it into six sections: two oversize bars and four food tables. On one table, clusters of grapes tumble from a huge sweetgrass basket. Wedges of Brie and chunks of Gruyère spill out of a horn-shaped cornucopia. Another table is laden with seafood: mounds of cold peeled shrimp, oysters on the half shell, and slabs of smoked salmon.

Onstage at the far end of the ballroom, the band plays a waltz. The drummer sweeps a metal brush on the snare, hits the drum head. It's a swirling noise, then a flat one—like the swoosh of a dress and the tap of a shoe—and establishes the rhythm for the first dances of the evening. The musicians wear matching tuxes with white stripes running along their lapels. The stage is decorated with garlands of magnolia leaves and ivy.

In this space of beauty and abundance—a room stocked with oysters, silver, friendship, silk, shared histories, and champagne—everyone stands taller, smiles bigger, and laughs harder. Although I came here with reservations, I can't help but feel enchanted.

For an instant, a ping of regret stops me in my tracks. If I were to marry Trip, I'd attend these dazzling affairs multiple times a year. Single women stop getting invitations after a while; it's just the way it is. My chest tightens. My dress feels two sizes too small. But then I think, Francie will probably debut, albeit twenty years down the road. I'll at least get invited to her ball. Plus, I can't spend my night thinking about what I will miss instead of enjoying it in the moment. *Ridiculous.*

I take a step forward, into the night. "Let's get a drink." Clay follows me to the bar. He gestures for me to get ahead of him in line. "You have to order for me."

"Seriously?" Clay tosses his head back. "That's hilarious."

While almost two centuries have passed since the founding of the ball, and many of today's debutantes become doctors and lawyers, formality is rooted in the traditional values that inspired these balls in the first place. The whole point was, after all, to find a husband for a daughter. Requiring the sons of Charleston to fetch drinks ensured at least some sort of interaction with the debutantes. Not to mention that it was considered unladylike for a female to approach a bar. Nowadays Caroline and other debutantes find their partners like anyone else—through a friend or online. The ball today is mainly an excuse to party.

I watch Clay cluster among the other men at the bar. I vaguely recognize most people here, but one man looks particularly familiar. He's in his fifties with thick blond hair brushed back into a modern pompadour. It's the state planning director who approved the Wildcat Acres project. When he reaches to get his highball from the bartender, I strain to see his cuff links. Sure enough, a "BH" winks back at me. God, Charleston is small.

"My lady," Clay says in a British accent as he hands me a pinot grigio. We park our drinks on a tall cocktail table and watch a handsome couple in their sixties foxtrot. They move as one unit. They probably have been dancing together for decades.

"Clay. Looking sharp." It's Ashley.

Beside him, Weezy looks even more svelte than she did at Caroline's cocktail party. She wears an emerald-green velvet dress. Her breasts, plump with milk, spill over the neckline. She looks fabulous. She moves away from the brothers, close to me. "Hey, Sims. I think your dance card goes on your right arm."

"I couldn't fit it over this," I whisper back. I show Weezy my corsage.

"Aw. That's sweet. But you look like you're going to prom."

"That's what I was thinking." I say with a laugh.

Ashley joins us. "Is your dance card full?"

I hold out my arm; the miniature booklet dangles from my wrist. Ashley pencils in his name for the next song, another fox-trot, then guides my arm over to Clay, who scribbles down his name for the following dance number—a waltz.

Weezy points to a pin on her dress. It's the gold jaguar with the ruby eyes. The cat's back is encrusted with emeralds.

And Caroline is wearing her pearls. And I have her watch. It almost feels like she's here. In a way. "I feel like Laudie is with us," I say.

Weezy squeezes my hand in agreement. "What was in the envelope?"

"What envelope?"

"The one in the safety deposit box. I thought she deeded you her car or something. She always liked you best."

The letter. "Where is it?"

"Mom didn't tell you? She's been looking for you." Weezy stands on her toes to scan the ballroom but soon gives up. There must be three hundred people here by now. "She told me Tito pretty much forced his way into the bank today to get the lockbox open."

"On a Saturday?"

"You know Tito . . ."

"Ready?" Ashley whisks me to the dance floor.

My brain lags behind, hovering over the cocktail table, wondering what on earth the letter could say. Is it a love letter from John, imploring her to return to Atlanta? Could it just be the title to her car? What is it?

It's hard to concentrate on dancing, but the muscle memory drilled deep during my years of cotillion tells me what to do. We fall into position: my left hand rests on Ashley's right shoulder; he holds my right hand in his left. He steps forward with his left, I step backward with my right; it's the standard for the start of this and every formal dance. Women move backward. *Step, touch, side, close. Step, touch, side, close.* Ashley steers us through clusters of guests, around the flower arrangements, and into a fleeting pocket of space on the dance floor.

And that's when our eyes meet. My mouth goes dry, and my stomach recoils at the invisible blow my ex-fiancé delivers by just being at the ball. It's Trip, standing alone on the sidelines. His jacket is buttoned shut; he's lost weight. A beard coarsens his jawline. I had always thought he might look handsome in a beard. His broad shoulders look strong beneath his fine tailcoat. He's handsome, well-mannered, and on his way to being rich. He's a twenty-point buck, a royal flush. I can't help that I'm programmed to be attracted to him. He's a catch. When our eyes meet, he coolly raises his highball in a toast.

I'm at Ashley's mercy. He's steering us closer and closer into Trip's orbit, totally unaware that he's dancing me nearly into the arms of the man I was supposed to marry . . . might still marry?

We're also closer to the hall entrance, where I observe Mrs. Prioleau dismiss the debutantes, freeing them from the receiving line. The string of debutantes breaks like a snapped pearl necklace. The nine young women whirl into the crowd. Just before I'm spun away, my eye tracks Bennett as she floats toward Trip and plants a kiss on his cheek. *What?*

Ashley leads me back to the middle of the dance floor. He remains on beat, but I've completely lost my footing. I step on his shoe and bump into two different couples. I'm more of a Ping-Pong ball than a lady at a ball.

In a zippy flourish, the song ends, and Ashley escorts me back to the table. We've stopped moving, but the room spins. I focus on Weezy, partly to see if she saw Trip, too, but mostly to slow the commotion in my brain. I need to focus on something external, find a spotting point like a pirouetting ballerina does.

"Weezy?" Ashley extends a gloved hand to his wife and bows like a courtier.

"Honored," she says, cupping her gloved hand in his. They head to the dance floor.

Shit, don't leave me, Weezy!

Clay downs his drink, playfully straightens his bow tie. "I guess I'm up."

"Mind if we sit this one out?" I can barely say the words. I thought I had moved on. But seeing Trip here, looking so handsome, the object of another woman's affection, guts me. And totally overwhelms me.

"Sure thing." Clay shakes the ice in his glass. "I need to refuel, anyway."

I dart around the flower arrangements and slink between the food tables, keeping my eyes down to avoid conversation and escape the ballroom as quickly as I can.

The ladies' room is luxurious and spacious. Two debutantes primp in front of an immense mirror, which is wreathed in a gilded frame of carved acanthus leaves. A pair of antique chairs painted gold are positioned along the back wall. They look like thrones.

I'd like to sit in one of the chairs to think a minute. Take some deep breaths. Maybe have a good cry to clear the confusion from my brain. But I don't want to decompress out in the open. I check the stalls; both are occupied. I walk up to the mirrored vanity above the sink and silently interrogate my reflection. A dolled up version of me glares back. *Why is Trip here? Is he dating Bennett?*

My hands grow hot in the gloves. My sequins may as well be little solar panels on Mercury. The bobby pins on my scalp feel molten. But why am I melting over a man I left cold? *Pull yourself together, Simons. Make a plan.*

My thoughts begin to gel, starting with the most mundane. First plan of action: remove torturous bobby pins. I take off my corsage and unbutton my gloves to free my hands. One by one, I lay the bobby pins on the sink's rim. My hair springs wildly from my head in exaggerated curls, like a clown's hair. With the pain gone, the next clear step appears in my mind's eye: get the letter.

The door swings open. Winter air from the checkerboard-floored foyer creeps into the bathroom, curls around my ankles. In the mirror, I see Bennett. She freezes. "Oh," she starts. The door behind her swings shut, enclosing us in the room together. The two primping debutantes have left, but four pretty shoes can still be seen from beneath the stalls. "I guess Caroline didn't tell you."

Turning, I survey her from toe to head. Her dress is hemmed exactly an inch above the floor, to make it look like she floats. She actually does appear to hover. Her skin is perfect, like poured, molded plastic. When our eyes meet, she lifts her chin slightly.

I'm not sure what to say to the person who could very well be dating my ex-husband-to-be. It occurs to me that I don't have to say anything. I walk past her and out the door.

Caroline must have been grabbing the outside handle just as I open the door; she nearly falls on top of me. She's wide-eyed and apparently speechless.

"How come you never told me?" I say, and walk past her before she has a chance to answer. Maybe I don't want to know the answer.

In the ballroom, the grand matron crosses the stage. With a gloved finger, she taps three times on the microphone, clears her throat. "Ladies and gentlemen, please find your partner for the Grand March to dinner."

Shit. One thing you don't do at a ball is abandon your date. In fact, this rule is so ironclad that it isn't even expressly stated in the rulebook. Guests march in pairs. Heterosexual pairs, it goes without saying. Heterosexual Caucasian cisgender Protestant pairs. I hurry back to the bathroom to find Caroline and her friend huddled in discussion. I place my hand on my sister's shoulder. "Caroline, can you tell Clay I've got to leave?"

She looks back apologetically. "I'm sorry, Simons. I didn't say anything about Bennett dating Trip because I didn't know if it was going to go anywhere. I didn't want you to get hurt."

So that's how Trip knew Laudie was in the hospital—through

Bennett. Caroline told her, but what does it matter? "I just need to leave."

She grabs my arm, tears forming in the corners of her eyes. "Really! I've been caught between a friend and a sister."

"That shouldn't be a tough decision." I shake my arm free and hurry downstairs. I've got to move fast if I want to make a clean escape. I run down the curved staircase, one hand on the rail, the other holding up the hem of my dress. The coat-check attendant exchanges the ticket stub for my coat just as the grand matron's husband peers over the railing to corral straggling guests.

"Simons, wait!" Trip races down the stairs. He reaches the first white tile of the checkerboard floor and stops mid-step. "Just wait."

I thought I could avoid him. I thought if I hurried from the ball, I could run away from any feelings for him. How do exes ever become friends? How can they chitchat idly when once, long ago, their legs were intertwined, twisted in the bedsheets? "What are you doing here, Trip?"

"I was invited."

"But you knew I'd be here. You knew my family would be here."

"You're related to half of Charleston. Have you placed an embargo on the whole city?"

"It's just hard for me to see you with someone. I wasn't expecting that."

"You really threw me for a loop, Simons. You're the one who said we were single. What am I supposed to do? Wait for you?"

Is that what I wanted all along? For him to wait? "I'm so sorry, Trip."

"Sorry about what? Which part? Let's have it out, right now. Let's get your little talk over with." His words are harsh. He's hurt, I know.

I place my hands on his shirt, the pleated bib warmed by his heart. "I'm sorry about everything. I'm sorry I hurt you. I'm sorry I let you go. I'm sorry I wrecked our relationship."

"What are you saying, Simons? What do you want? Do you even know?"

What do I want? To be carried up the stairs to the dance floor, join him in line for the Grand March, where the guests parade—for themselves, by the way—to dinner? No. I don't want to do that. Not tonight. Maybe not ever. I have other plans.

Trip pries my hands from his chest. "Well, you need to figure that out. If you want me back, you take everything. All of me. Sometimes I think you're too afraid to be out on your own. You need to figure out if I'm what you want. I used to wish I were, but now I'm not so sure." And just like that, he's finished. Ascending the stairs, head down, he's unaware that Bennett waits for him on the balcony. "And, Simons"—he turns, asks in afterthought—"what did you do to your hair?"

My hair. Does he really care about my hair? I have a sudden impulse to throw my head down and back, making my hair bigger, wilder.

That's exactly what I do.

46.

Resurrection

On the other side of the heavy doors the night is chilly and starry, a night painted by Van Gogh. Propelled by a force beyond my control, I run. I run down Meeting toward Broad Street. I run over blue-slate sidewalks and beneath rattling palmettos. I run past the storefronts, law firms, antiques shops, and art galleries, my path illumined by old-fashioned street lanterns.

I keep running down the oyster-shell driveway and make it to the entrance of the formal garden, where I stop. My plan was to retrieve the spare house key I nailed in Laudie's potting shed, but the kitchen light is on. I walk up the back staircase. The door is unlocked. Tito sits at the kitchen table. An electric space heater is positioned at his slippered feet. He doesn't sit at the head—his usual spot. Instead, he sits in Laudie's chair. He's in his pajamas, wrapped in a plaid bathrobe, wearing his reading glasses. He holds a piece of paper.

"Tito?" I fold my coat, lay it on the counter, and join him at the table.

He turns to me, surprised but not startled. "Why are you all dressed up?"

"I was at Caroline's debutante ball."

His rheumy eyes search my face. "I'd forgotten it was tonight. That's some hairdo."

"Thanks."

"Your mother said this was meant for you. I imagine you don't blame me for peeking."

The piece of paper, faded and obviously folded and refolded many times, has the look of a cherished heirloom, a beloved artifact.

On this day, the 14th of November, 1953

　　Miss Claudia Parks Pringle, in accordance with the faculty of the Atlanta Civic Ballet, has been accepted to dance for the troupe in the year of 1954.

Laudie was good enough. She made the cut. She turned the opportunity down.

"I lived with her for sixty-six years and she never told me."

I examine the document. I can see my fingers through the nearly transparent paper. "Maybe she kept it a secret because she wanted a part of her life that was just hers. For her, alone."

Tito considers the thought. "How about a glass of sherry?"

I find the sherry in an old crystal decanter on the dining room bar cart, select two glasses, wipe off the dust. I pour sparingly. Tito hardly drinks anymore.

"What was Laudie like back then? Before Atlanta."

"Those were our courting days," he begins. "She always wanted to go dancing, so I took her—mostly to the Folly Beach Pier." Tito's wet eyes gleam. "She was determined to dance every song, and I just didn't want to. And she particularly didn't like waiting to be asked to dance. She would just tap a boy on the shoulder, and he would do as she said."

"But she was so pretty. Wouldn't the boys line up to dance with her?"

Tito laughs. "They were scared of her, I think. Didn't quite know how to handle her." He chuckles. "And my mother didn't approve of Claudia. She said she was too hot-blooded."

"Why? What did she do?"

"Oh, she was stubborn."

"But how?"

"She had her opinions. Didn't stay quiet like the other girls. But she got quiet after Atlanta." He takes a small sip. "She learned."

I search his face for signs of remorse or insight, but his expression remains neutral. Tito will almost certainly never understand his immense privilege as a white male raised in a cradle of wealth and power. He reached that pinnacle when he was elected president of Battery Hall. He'll likely die oblivious of the struggles of others.

Images from Laudie's stories flash into my mind: the simple freedom of going to the theater whenever she wanted. Of walking into a club, arm in arm with her lover and dance partner, all eyes on them. Of practicing her ballet at her windowsill, her dream very much within her reach.

"Maybe she didn't want you to know what she gave up to be with you. That she could have been a prima ballerina instead of a housewife."

"I hadn't thought of it that way." It's hard to tell if it's emotion or old age causing a tear to roll from his eye. We sit in the kitchen's stillness. My grandfather, the widower, stares at his knotted hands, as scaly and blotchy as the trunk of a crepe myrtle. "I fussed at her. I shouldn't have fussed at her so much."

I stand and place my hands on his bony, coat-hanger shoulders. I kiss his bald, speckled head. "It was a different time."

He makes a little steeple of his index fingers. "I could have been less critical."

"She forgives you. I'm sure she does."

47.

Over Easy

By now, the march is over. The gentlemen are seating the ladies—pulling out their chairs and helping them to scoot closer to the dining table. Courtly and old-fashioned. The ladies have partially removed their gloves, the better to hold a fork; they have tucked their bejeweled evening bags under the table or hung them on a chairback. Some have surreptitiously reapplied lipstick or perfume. Men and women alike hydrate with ice water served in sterling goblets. They pass warm bread baskets and ramekins of butter, already waiting on the table, to the left. Always pass to the left, Mom had taught us. They are doing what generations of Charlestonians do best: eating, drinking, and being merry.

When I decided to dash out of a debutante ball, I may have thrown away my chances for eating raw oysters in ball gowns for a while, but I didn't give up food and company entirely. Certainly not. I'm ravenous, and I refuse to go home to sniff containers of Tupperware to determine what leftovers are safe to eat alone on my couch. The night is still young, and so am I.

I head down the back brick steps. My heels sink into the oyster-shell driveway as I make my way to the street. Salty wind from the harbor cools my face, still overheated from Tito's kitchen. I pull my phone from my purse and dial the number I committed to memory weeks ago that day on the beach.

"Hello?"

"Hi, Ben? This is Simons."

"Oh, hey, Simons. I was wondering when you were going to call."

"I thought tonight would be a good night," I say, letting my mouth widen into a huge smile.

"What's up?"

"I'm calling to see if you'd like to get something to eat, like, right now?" I bite my lower lip in anticipation of his answer.

Silence on the other end of the line. Then, a muffled conversation. I feel my bravery waver, restrengthen. I'm not afraid of no. If I want a life of adventure, I've got to take risks, like calling numbers drawn in sand. I let the thrill of the moment, this electric space between yes and no, ignite me to my core.

"Hey, sorry about that. I had to pay for parking. I just flew back from a work trip and have only had about eight pretzels for dinner. So, yeah, I'm super hungry. You live downtown, right? I can pick you up in fifteen minutes."

I do a little dance in the driveway, because what the hell. "Fantastic." I tell him how to get to my apartment and brace for a mad dash. I need to move quickly so there's time to run home and change out of my glitzy evening wear.

I run up King Street, past Lamboll, Tradd, Broad, and Queen. I take a shortcut through the Unitarian Church cemetery, where a meandering brick path leads me around marble crosses and tilting gravestones. I run down the middle of Archdale Street, hook a quick left onto Beaufain, and keep pace past Memminger Auditorium.

At Coming Street, I hit the home stretch. My breath is steady, like a metronome. I'm inhaling and exhaling to the beat of my stride. I pass the College of Charleston library, cross Calhoun Street, and enter the residential area where the streets narrow, the gardens shrink, and the houses are closer together. One by one, the houses fly past me; each door I pass is a tangible mark in my progress to a new and exciting future. The freedom in each step makes me feel as though I could fly.

When I turn left onto my street, I slow to a trot. Half a block down, a figure stands beneath the streetlamp just outside my apartment. *Ben*. While I might not be able to pick his face out from a crowd, I recognize the way he carries his body. It's the same on land as it is in water: loose and self-assured. He stands with his legs slightly apart, one hand in his pocket, the other behind his back. I slow to a walk to join him in the pool of lamplight. He wears a blue fleece embroidered with what I imagine is his company's logo. His brown hair is messy, a little dirty, even.

"You beat me," I say in between breaths. I'm hot. I take off my coat.

"Wow. You look like a princess."

"Oh, gosh," I kick at my gown.

"I'm flattered you got so dressed up."

I laugh and pat at my poofy hair; I can tell it's ballooned since leaving the ball. "Long story . . ."

"Well, I can't wait to hear it. Where do you want to go?"

"I don't know. It's almost eleven."

"Let's go somewhere we can talk."

"I'd like that."

He raises his eyebrows, appraising me. "What would you say if I took you to the Waffle House?"

"I would say great."

"Will you keep on your Cinderella costume?"

"Sure."

* * *

The Waffle House is brightly lit—the silver paneling along the kitchen galley doubles the light. Red stools dot the brown bar; the brick patterned linoleum floor was recently mopped. Jimmy Buffett croons from the jukebox. A cook cracks an egg; it hisses when it hits the griddle. Another employee stacks plates on a shelf along the back wall.

The restaurant is warm. We remove our coats. Ben gestures to a booth. I slide in; he takes the opposite side. "I didn't know you had curly hair."

Beneath the fluorescent glow, I notice his lashes are blond at the tips and he has a fleck of brown in his left eye. "I don't.

It was pinned up all day and I just took the pins out. It's pretty straight."

The server plunks down two menus on the table. "Coffee?"

"Just water, thanks."

"Orange juice, please." I scan the menu: a collage of brightly colored offerings: toasty brown pancakes topped with a golden mound of melting butter, fried eggs with googly-eyed yellow yolks, pink circles of ham. I switch positions to get comfortable in my dress and accidentally kick his leg. The touch turns my brain to fuzz, making it hard to figure out what I want to eat. "I'll have eggs over easy, please."

The server takes a quick look at my dress, but her face reveals nothing. She probably has seen it all. "Toast?"

"Yes, please."

She turns her attention to Ben. "And you?"

"The waffles. Thanks."

Ben places his arms on the table, his palms up. I once read that men unconsciously display the undersides of their arms to show a possible love interest that they've got a softer side. I'm not sure if I believe that, but I can read his evergreen eyes. He likes me.

The drinks arrive. We raise our glasses. "Cheers," we say together.

"So, you just got back from a work trip? What were you doing?"

"I'm an engineer. Our firm mostly does government contracts, so I fly to D.C. a lot. Maybe once a month."

Since I last saw Angela, when we buried Cooper, one of the

New York environmental organizations has moved me onto the third round: another video call. After a couple of talks with Angela's connection in D.C., I have been invited to interview in person. I leave next week. And now I can't help but imagine Ben visiting me in D.C. Maybe he will, maybe he won't, but aren't possibilities what make life interesting?

"What about you?"

"I'm a news producer, but I'm leaving my job soon."

"To be a princess?"

I laugh. "To work for an environmental organization."

"Which one? The Coastal Conservation League?"

"Maybe one day. No. I'm going to leave Charleston for a bit." Before letting him know about D.C., I want to gauge his reaction. He frowns. Good.

"Where are you going?"

"I'm looking at jobs in New York and D.C."

"D.C. Definitely D.C. Then I can take you to the Waffle House at least once a month."

"Perfect."

He reaches across the table, I put my hand in his, and although it may look inconsequential, and although we are in public in the bright glare of the Waffle House, it feels like the most intimate thing I've done in years.

The waitress arrives with two hot, greasy plates. We dig in, big mouthfuls and big smiles. My toast, crisp and buttery, catches the runny yolk. The Minute Maid juice tastes like candy. My plate is clean by the time she returns. I want more. "May I have an order of the pecan waffles, please?"

"Sure, hon."

They arrive steaming and smelling of brown butter. The syrup dispenser leaves my hands sticky. Every tactile sensation—my gummy hands, the curve of the booth on my back, the flatness of the silverware, the fullness of my stomach—feels like a small gift. They are.

When the waitress puts the bill on our table, I take it.

"No way. Please let me do it." Ben looks concerned, scared even. "Seriously. I like taking you out."

"I'm glad you do. But at least tonight, I want to pay. It just feels right."

"Then I'm going to leave the tip." While I'm trying to make some sort of statement about my independence from him, or anyone at the moment, he's trying to be a gentleman. I get it.

"I'm tipping, too. You can leave extra."

He leaves a ten on the table before helping me into my coat. "What's this?" He gestures to the button I pinned to my coat's inner lining. Oh God, it's the one that reads: "Vagina! Vagina! Vagina!"

Even if I had anything clever to say, I can't seem to make my mouth move.

He laughs. "I think they're exciting, too."

I feel my cheeks blush.

"Come on, let me take you home."

We walk to his car. The wind from the harbor, just down the road, blows my disheveled hair even wilder. Beneath the street-light, I can see his breath.

At this point on a date, most ladies wait for the guy to make the first move, to take ownership of the situation, and reveal, at least in the moment, what the next step in the evening will be.

Well, if I'm writing my own stories these days, I need to make the first move. No, I won't shove him against the car, thrust my hand down his pants, and squeeze his balls. This is different. Romantic, hopefully. I stand on my toes and place my arms over his shoulders.

"Oh." He appears genuinely surprised. "You seem to be a woman who knows what she wants." He locks his arms around my back.

"I'm working on that." I run my hand against his warm neck, through his soft hair. He tightens his hold on me, sending blood rushing through my every artery, vein, and capillary. I lean into him, and feel a strong pull bringing me even closer. It reminds me of the time I played with magnets as a kid. If I got them close enough, they'd come together on their own. My lips tingle. My tongue softens. I close my eyes, and we kiss.

He pulls away for a moment. "You're a good kisser."

I bring him close again. "I know."

48.

Cold Brew

Martha waits in the courtyard of the coffee shop. She's at our favorite table, under a tree. I suggest we move closer to the fountain, into the sun. It's freezing out here by Charleston standards, not even fifty degrees.

She nods and gathers her things: sunglasses, orange Bic, a soft pack of cigarettes. She seems to have completely forgotten about Bruno, who, still leashed to the table, scrapes his nails against the concrete. He's balding like Tito: pink patches of exposed skin dot his snout and ears.

Martha doesn't budge. "I'm going to get your dog." I walk across the patio, slowing for the little ground finches who subsist off muffin crumbs. Bruno jumps to his hind legs to greet me, his neck straining against the leash. When I rub his back, chunks of gummy fur stick to my palms. He smells like an aging bachelor: moldy laundry and tobacco smoke. One eye drips clear mucus. I unfasten him. "Come here, buddy."

Martha's hands tremble as she lights a cigarette, and I wonder if she hasn't already had a few cups of coffee. When she exhales, two dirty plumes tunnel down her nostrils. Brown roots sully her once-raven hair. When she crosses her legs, I spot a rip in her skirt. She looks as bad as Bruno. I consider delaying the breakup.

"I've missed you, Simons." She takes a big gulp of coffee. How she hasn't burned a hole in her mouth is beyond me. Even with a generous splash of oat milk, mine's too hot to sip.

"I miss you, too, Martha." *The good parts of you*, I think.

"Yeah, but it's more than that for me. I miss my old life. It was simpler. You have a simple life. You know?"

Simple? I try not to feel insulted. She is not wearing her standard huge sunglasses, but it's still hard for me to read those opaque eyes.

"Look, can we just go back to the way things were?"

"The way things were when?"

"Can we just move on and forget about the whole Harry thing?"

"I don't know what—"

She wraps her hands around the chair rails, squares her body with mine. "Jesus, Simons, you don't have to pretend you don't know. Be real for once. You're mad at me because I was fucking Harry."

I'm not shocked. I don't know what to feel at the moment, but I definitely don't feel shocked. I had my suspicions.

"I never even really liked him," she adds.

I rub my temples, trying to make sense of her calculations. "So, you knew I liked Harry. You didn't even like him, and you slept with him anyway?" Saying goodbye is going to be a whole lot easier than I thought.

"It just happened. We were on tour. When you share a tent . . ."

"No. It didn't just happen. That night, when you brought Harry to my apartment, I think you got jealous."

"You're crazy." Her face is wreathed in the coffee's rising steam.

"Maybe you felt like we were in some sort of competition."

"Seriously, Simons. Shut up."

"We couldn't survive a love triangle."

"I wouldn't call it that."

What genuine friendship can be unraveled by a man? I see more clearly than ever that Martha and I are terrible for each other.

"Oh shit. Don't cry, Simons." She rolls her eyes.

"I'm not crying," I say plainly. I can speak plainly because it all feels so simple: it's time for me to move on, to be intentional about my relationships, like Weezy said. I need to invest in people who are honest with themselves and who care about me, and to let others go. "I'm over Harry," I tell her. "I don't care about him anymore."

What I do care about is Laudie's past, the passion for ballet that she traded for security. I care that she gave adventure a chance and that she guarded a secret that powered her through a lifetime of compromises, concessions, and criticism. I care about my family. I care about the people of Charleston: the independent store owners, the people excluded from Battery

Hall, the women who aren't believed. I care about our great city, slowly sinking, and the floodwaters and king tides and the disappearing land. But I don't care about Harry. I care for Martha; I want her to be okay. But it's time for me to let her go.

"Oh, good," she says, relieved.

I stand. "Goodbye, Martha."

"You've got to go to work?"

"I don't work weekends anymore . . . ," I start to explain, but realize she never paid attention to my schedule in the first place. "Martha, I care about you. I wish you well. But I can't do this anymore."

She scrunches her face, looking at me like I've gone out of focus. "What are you talking about? Do what?"

"I think we need some time apart. I think it might be best for both of us."

She laughs mirthlessly. "Simian, are you breaking up with me?"

"Yeah. I am. At least for now."

Martha leans back in her seat. She studies me for a long time, tapping a finger on her lips. "I respect that." She smooths her hair to the side, revealing the beautiful curve of her jaw. My knockout ex-friend. "Do we get to have makeup coffees?"

"Ha. We'll see."

"Where are you going?"

"To D.C. For an interview."

"D.C.? Why?"

"I've just got to get out of here. See what's out there." I bend down to say goodbye to Bruno, perhaps for forever. He lunges at me, ready to smother my face with frantic licks. The poor guy. I want him to smell better, look healthier, and not have a chronically leaking eyeball. I dig in my purse and pull out the gold-and-pearl necklace that's been zipped into a side compartment for weeks now. I fasten it around the dog's neck, which is about the same circumference as mine. It's a ridiculous look for a ridiculous animal, so it somehow works. I press his head firmly in my hands and hope to confer my well wishes onto the little beast.

I have a goodbye gift for Martha, too. I take a button out of my purse and place it on the table in front of her. It reads: "CURIOSITY DOESN'T KILL EVERY CAT."

* * *

Rounding the corner, I head north toward my apartment and into the heady scent of burning wood—someone at the end of the block is tending a fragrant oak fire. A handsome couple crosses the street toward a row of old, sherbet-painted single houses. I see the elegant steeple of St. Sebastian's in the distance. Overhead, a solitary gull cries, flying east toward the ocean. I live in an achingly beautiful city.

But if I want to protect it, to keep it from sinking, I must leave. Instead of writing the local stories about miscreant politicians or arts festivals, I need to help change the narrative. Sprawl must come to a full stop. We need to rethink our car culture. With multimodal transportation for everyone, we could turn parking spaces into bike lanes. We need to build more densely, more vertically. And the citizens must use all their creative energy to find a solution to save our sinking city. Instead of erecting a massive seawall, cutting off our access to the element that makes our home so special, we must find a way to work with the rising water, and in a way that's fair to all communities. And that's just for starters.

49.

Leaving on a Jet Plane

The sound of knocking floats up my stairs. "Coming!" I yell. Ben's here. He insisted on driving me to the airport.

I'm hunkered over my laptop, moments from sending an email to the anonymous-tip line at work, the one Jasmine reads religiously. This could be her big story. The subject reads: "Battery Hall—Charleston's Hidden Power Network." I write that the Coastal Company owner and lead developer for Wildcat Acres are members, and so is the state planning director who approved the lucrative deal. I list the names of other powerful members—they are city council members and heads of banks. They dominate boardrooms and hold seats in the legislature. I put Judge Sonny Boykin's name at the top of the list. How are women supposed to break these glass ceilings when the roof really resides in an all male-club? How can their stories be heard fairly when the lead characters controlling the narrative are almost always male?

I attach a shaky image of the wall of portraits and finish the email with perhaps the most damning and distressing images of all—the watercolors from the ladies' bathroom: the white-washed scenes of enslaved people on plantations.

The minute Jasmine sees the email, she'll make some calls and ask for interviews, and because it's the weekend, she's the anchor who will break the story. She's the smartest, most tenacious newsperson I know and is my best shot at getting this story national attention.

By the time the story gains traction, I'll be in a high-rise somewhere near the Washington Mall. I won't be around to be quizzed if I know anyone at Battery Hall. The story must be about the issue, not the source. It must be about power, racism, sexism, exclusivity; not about a father-daughter family drama.

When I return, if I find the story hasn't gotten enough coverage, I can pick up the torch as a lame-duck producer. I'm on my way out of the station; I could run as many packages on this topic as I want. If the story does have legs, I can monitor it closely, help steer where it goes. We could invite organizations across the Lowcountry to speak with the club members. We'll hold them accountable. And I bet there are club members who are ready for change. Together, we can find a way to bring Charleston to a more just and equitable future. The story will be told.

I click "submit."

I stash my computer in my carry-on, double check for my ID, and grab my phone. There's a text from Angela. It's a picture of a Labrador puppy with big, dopey eyes and golden fur. "**Pee**

Dee wishes you luck in DC!" My heart warms. She got herself a dog. Of course she named it after another river in South Carolina, but I haven't yet met any dogs named Pee Dee. I like it.

"Precious! Thanks so much. Fingers crossed!"

I zip up my phone. I'm wearing boots and my thickest sweater. My wool coat is folded over the top of my rollaway suitcase, which bounces down the steps behind me.

On the other side of the street door, in the airy light of a perfect winter afternoon, stands Ben. He thrusts a fistful of flowers in my direction, clears his throat. "I found them while I was waiting for you." He gestures with his other hand to the patch of green on the right-of-way, just beyond the shade of the crepe myrtle. He brings them to his nose. "They don't smell like anything, though."

I take the bundle in my hand and count five petite zinnias, three magenta and two tangerine. All are missing at least a couple of petals; the ones that remain have browned at the edges. They're vestiges of a long-gone vibrant summer season, but zinnias nonetheless. How could I have missed them?

"Thank you." I kiss him. "They're perfect."

He smiles bashfully, scratches at the nape of his neck.

I check my watch—Laudie's watch. We still have time. "Can you wait a minute while I put these in water?"

"You think they'll last until you get back?"

"I just have a thing for zinnias." I hurry back up the stairs to the kitchen. Winter light streams through the ancient windowpanes, illuminating the lip of my couch, the corner of my bookshelf, and the old-but-scrubbed-clean linoleum in the kitchen, which has been bug-free since the first chill of the year.

I line the flowers on my counter, cut the stems at an angle, and carefully lower the zinnias into a delicate porcelain vase. I place his bouquet on my coffee table. From this vantage point, the mantel frames the bouquet; the cherubs smile at it from either side. I pause to admire the scene—zinnias at the center—and think of Laudie.

Acknowledgments

Mary Alice Monroe, I am deeply appreciative of your generosity and wisdom. When you read my manuscript the first time, you told me to give Laudie a story. When you read it a second time, you circled moments of tension and wrote, "hit this hard." And when you read it a third time, you wrote a beautiful and heart-felt endorsement. You also showed me the power of the tribe. From the bottom of my heart, thank you.

To the other women of the tribe. Nathalie Dupree—the Grandest Damest in all the Landest! We miss you in Charleston. To the nuclear-powered Marjory Wentworth, thanks for cheering me on. Thank you, Sandra King Conroy, for the exquisite blurb and for being possibly the sweetest person on the planet. Patti Callahan Henry, I met you the evening you spoke on *Becoming Mrs. Lewis*. We sat at Mary Alice's dining room table, and while we were supposed to be celebrating you, you asked me, "How can I help?" When you got a call from a certain special someone at HarperCollins looking for a new southern voice, you, Mary Alice, and Signe said, "Gervais."

Ah, Signe Pike. I'm a total fangirl (*blush*). Thank you for opening up your home and your heart to me and my family, and especially for nudging me to think of my study as a sacred space. You bring magic to my life.

And to the rest of my ladies in the Mango Club—Melissa Falcon Field, the day we met, you offered to review my manuscript. *Who does that?!* And Meagan Gentry—thank you for coaching me on the legal parts of the book. You're a badass attorney and I'm so excited for you to make the transition into the writing world.

Lauren Sanford, thank you so much for sharing your art expertise and for introducing me to the Kit-cat Club. And to the eternally cool Jessica Murnane—thank you for your support and interest in my career transition. One day, we'll have that lunch date. (And, by the way, I'm now up to Two Parts Plant.)

Ann Close—thank you for sharing your lifelong knowledge of publishing. You are an exceptional coffee date. Thank you, Kate Bullard Adams, for not holding back. Will Breard, Maggie David, Carolyn Matalene, Jennifer Wallace, and Aunt Susan Gaillard—thank you for reading earlier drafts—I hope you'll be pleased with the way this book turned out.

Thank you, Sarah Mae Ilderton. You were right, that's how he would have done it. And to Beth Gavin for getting us all together; you're the glue. Thank you, Katie Crouch, for being so kind as to share your literary contacts. I also want to thank my dear friend (and national treasure), Samar Ali. Samartime, you've been inspiring me since 1999.

Thank you to my whip-smart agent, Kristyn Keene Benton—you're a next-level connector. I look forward to working on many more projects with you. Plus, I just like chatting on the phone and hearing Charlotte coo in the background, so let's do that, too. Thanks also to Cat Shook. You had me at "Waffle House."

I want to take a moment to thank Anne Rivers Siddons, an elegant and graceful southern lady who was possessed of a masterful storytelling mind. I miss dinners at her home, where, in her big red-rimmed glasses, she served us hearty soups, her Maine Koon cats rubbing against our legs.

And Patricia P. McArver—my guardian angel. You went out of retirement *again* to take over The Citadel Public Speaking Lab so I could pursue my dream. Thank you for your leadership and friendship. I love you!

Momunit. Babs. Babulous. Barbarella. Glama. Barbara G. S. Hagerty. Mom. You've read this book at *least* six times and you still pick up after the first ring to answer my questions about everything from syntax to formal evening wear. Thank you for always believing in me. Every child should be so lucky.

To my siblings. Hart, you reminded me, "leap, and the net will appear." It did. More than your advice, it's your example of living that gave me the courage to jump. And Curry, the marketing mastermind, I'm so grateful for a confidante who says what she thinks. Sorry about the bugs. To Richard, thanks for helping me keep the creative juices flowing by letting me collaborate with you on your songs. Let's get that tattoo.

And to my dad, Richard Hagerty, who showed us that you can earn a living in the day, be a serious artist at night, and start a band in retirement. Rock on, Dad.

I'm so grateful to Dottie Benton Frank. She wrote stories about the Lowcountry that captured her reader's hearts and imaginations. She also hooked her editor, Carrie Feron, on stories about the South, which, in a way, sent her searching for me.

Carrie, there are many writers who search their entire lives for an editor like you. I won the literary lottery. Thank you for your guidance, for showing me how to think of my story in a new way. Thank you also for your patience—I realize many of my ideas for book titles and covers were outlandish. Even when you end up saying no, you consider the thought, and that means a lot to me. You also laugh at my jokes, perhaps the greatest gift of all. Keep sending texts of zinnias and Dash and your life up North. And be sure to book that trip to Charleston because I adore you and want to give you a giant, in-person (not virtual) hug.

To the business savvy bibliophiles at HarperCollins—Liate Stehlik, Jennifer Hart, Ryan Shepard, Emily Fisher, and Brittani Hilles—I'm thrilled to be on your team. Thank you, Asanté Simons, for fielding *all* of my questions. I need lots of specific direction, as you know. To Andrea Monagle, the copyediting whiz. You healed Simons's toe (otherwise, as you pointed out, she *should* have gone to see a doctor). And even seventh generation locals don't know it's called "White Point Garden."

Thanks to the locally owned businesses in Charleston that fueled my writing: to The Works and CPY—all those chaturangas boosted my energy and the wheels have helped me revert the hunch in my back from years of bending over a keyboard. And cheers to the neighborhood coffee slingers, Harbinger and Huriyali (Jade, here's your shout-out :o)

Finally, I want to thank my little family. To Sofia, at five, my bright, curious, critical thinker—your love of books will take you far. And Miro, my charming, witty three-year-old who already thinks out-of-the-box: may you always do things your own way. And my husband, Anthony—top chef, bass player, bearded mustachian, beer brewer, superman composter, sailboat racer— you make every day easy and fun. I love you.

And lastly, I want to thank my grandmother, Aggie Street: the flower gardener who inspired this novel. I miss you. I love you, and I hope I made you proud. Every spring, I plant zinnias.

Meet the Author

About the book

Insights,
Interviews
& More...

Meet Gervais Hagerty

Gayle Brooker

GERVAIS HAGERTY grew up in Charleston, South Carolina. After reporting and producing the news for both radio and television, she taught communications at The Citadel. When not writing, she works on local environmental and transportation issues. She lives in Charleston with her husband and two daughters. *In Polite Company* is her first novel. ∿

Reading Group Guide

1. When Simons presses her father about his membership in an all-male club, he tells her that it's very normal for the sexes to separate. What is your opinion of single-sex organizations?

2. As Simons debated calling off the wedding, she considered the financial stability Trip would provide as a husband. Should money be a factor in determining lifelong partnerships? What about parental approval?

3. While Simons doesn't invite Kevin into her apartment, she does allow him in. She wakes up to find him sexually assaulting her. She runs from him and kicks him out. If you were Simons, would you have called the police? Pressed charges? Why or why not?

4. All cultures have both positive and negative aspects. What do you love about your culture? What could be improved? How could you help make those improvements?

5. Why do people join clubs? What is it about belonging that is rooted so deeply at our core?

6. As people mature, friendships change. What do you think of the relationship between Martha and Simons? In what ways have you ▶

experienced friendships that have changed?

7. Months after the breakup, Simons was hoping to run into Trip when she was dolled up for a night out. Instead, he discovers her barefoot, rooting through a trash can. Even when we break off a relationship, why would we still want to be desirable to our former companion?

8. Laudie was shaped by the times she lived in. How does your current culture shape who you are? Are there some aspects of your character that wouldn't change, no matter the era or circumstance you were born into? If so, which ones?

9. From statues in public parks to paintings in a private club's bathroom, art is being viewed with fresh eyes. What should be the standard for removing public art? Should the standards be different for a private setting? How?

10. Upon meeting her new boss, Simons realizes she never actually enjoyed her job as a news producer at the local TV station. Is your current job fulfilling? What would it take for you to make a radical change? Would you leave your hometown, family, and friends for a better job? ∾

Discover great authors, exclusive offers, and more at hc.com.